THE
BOOK of LIES

THE

BOOK OF LIES

MARY HORLOCK

HARPER ● PERENNIAL

NEW YORK ● LONDON ● TORONTO ● SYDNEY ● NEW DELHI ● AUCKLAND

HARPER ● PERENNIAL

FIRST U.S. EDITION

Designed by Claire Naylon Vaccaro

Library of Congress Cataloging-in-Publication Data

Horlock, Mary.
The book of lies : a novel / Mary Horlock.—First U.S. edition.
p. cm.
ISBN 978–0–06–206509–4 (pbk.)
1. Life change events—Fiction. 2. Friendship in adolescence—Fiction. 3. Family secrets—Fiction. 4. Truthfulness and falsehood—Fiction 5. Guernsey (Channel Islands)—Fiction. 6. Channel Islands—History—German occupation, 1940–1945—Fiction. 7. Diary fiction. I. Title.

PR6108.O73B66 2011
823'.92—dc22

2010046608

11 12 13 14 15   OV/RRD   10 9 8 7 6 5 4 3 2 1

to
for
because of
Darian

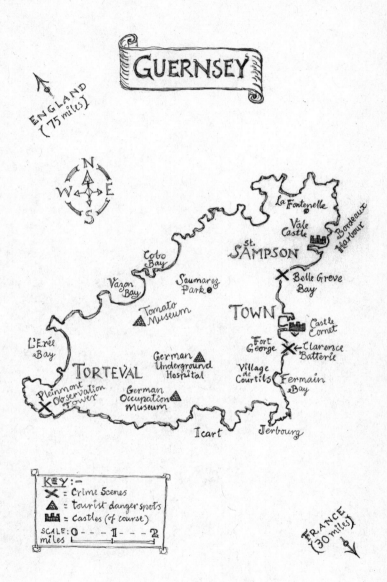

GUERNSEY

ENGLAND
(75 miles)

N
W — E
S

La Fontenelle

Vale
Castle

Bordeaux
Harbour

St.
SAMPSON

Cobo
Bay

Belle Greve
Bay

Vazon
Bay

Saumarez
Park

TOWN

Tomato
Museum

Castle
Cornet

L'Eréé
Bay

Fort
George

Clarence
Batterie

TORTEVAL

German
Underground
Hospital

Village
de
Courtils

Fermain
Bay

Pleinmont
Observation
Tower

German
Occupation
Museum

Icart

Jerbourg

KEY:-
✗ = Crime scenes
▲ = tourist danger spots
🏰 = Castles (of course)
SCALE: 0 - - - 1 - - - 2
miles

FRANCE
(30 miles)

THE
BOOK OF LIES

my name is Catherine Rozier, please don't call me Cathy. If you do I'll jump. Don't think I'm bluffing. It's a 3000-foot drop and even though I'm fat, I'm not fat enough to bounce. I'll dive headfirst into ye ancient Guernsey granite out-crops and then my mashed-up body will be washed out to sea. Of course, if I get the tides wrong I'll be stranded on the rocks with seagulls eating my eyes. I know for a fact they'll eat anything.

Killing myself wouldn't be too clever, but then nei-ther was killing Nicolette. It's been a fortnight since they found her body and for the most part I am glad she's gone. But I also can't believe she's dead, and I should do because I did it. Yes. That's right. I killed Nicolette on these very cliffs and I'm frankly amazed that no one has guessed. When her body was dragged out of the water, the verdict was she'd fallen. Ha-ha. (Only I'm not laugh-ing.) Why hasn't anyone worked it out? The Germans were right, the people on this island are a bunch of half-wits. When they landed here in the summer of 1940 they must've thought they'd won the War already. They called Guernsey A SMALL PARADISE. *Excusez-moi*, but since when did a few manky palm trees make a paradise?

And when everyone finds out what I've done there'll be no more pretending what this island is. If you want me, come and find me. Assume I'll be skipping along Clarence Batterie, stretching out my· hands towards St. Peter Port, preparing to take the plunge. If this counts as my last will and testament I hereby bequeath my unspent book tokens from last year's prize-giving to my mother. I'd also like to make it clear that although my disappearance from this miserable rock coincides with Christmas, it has nothing to do with her New-Recipe Mexican Turkey.

Obviously she'll be upset. I was supposed to be the first in the family to go to university.

But at least I made front-page news (kind of, sort of, almost). Nic's death was all over the *Guernsey Evening Press** for four days on the trot, and they even used one of the photos I took of her—the one in Candie Gardens where she's leaning back against a tree with her hair spread out across her shoulder. Did I mention she was beautiful? She got a full page because of how she looked. When you saw her perfect face, it was hard to imagine that she was ever such a bitch. But she was. My so-called best friend was a Liar and a Traitor who deserved everything she got. I won't go into the details of how I know

---

* "Schoolgirl Killed in Cliff Fall at Clarence Batterie," *Guernsey Evening Press*, 3 December 1985.

this, but I won the Inter-Island Junior Mastermind so, trust me, I'm rarely wrong.

Nicolette Louise Prevost had to die.

I now realise we should never have been friends, but some things are destined, as per Shakespeare and his tragedies. When she found me that night, on these very cliffs, I knew she was planning something deadly lethal. Do not think for a minute I am a violent person. Just because I like watching mindless violence on television doesn't mean I want to go round cutting throats (or that I know how to). I was scared and I panicked—do you blame me? It was pitch-black, and the rain beat down so hard I could barely open my eyes. When she came at me out of the darkness it was like my worst-ever nightmare. I screamed but the wind just took my voice away, and there was no one there to help me, which is how she always liked it. We fought, we kicked. She grabbed my hair but I grabbed hers, too, because I'm not stupid. It was like *Friday the 13th* (*Part 1* or *2*). If only I could've ripped her head off and had fake blood spurt everywhere.

But, of course, it never happens like that. All I did was push her. Honest. That was all it took. One big push and she was gone. Gone. I still can't believe it. She vanished into blackness, and the churning sea swallowed her. How cool was that?

And fair enough that a part of me is glad. It's how it should be. I was doing the world (or Guernsey) a favour. Bullies should be punished, right? They are like the Nazis, picking on poor, isolated people and pulling them to bits. What I did was not an Abomination (excellent word). I should even feel a teensy bit happy and proud. So why do I feel cheated? Nic's gone and left me with this guilt, and I know I should go, too. Then somebody else on this stinking rock can feel guilty in my place.

But don't think I'm going quietly. First I'll write this down so that everybody knows. It's such a good story I could turn it into a book, and perhaps it won't look so bad once I see it there in black-and-white. After all, being a murderer isn't such a big deal for this little island. This is Guernsey, please remember, where there are plenty of secrets no one's ever meant to talk about. If you're British you'll know how us Guernsey people have been accused of all sorts. Usually we blame the Germans. Me? I blame Dad.*

The trouble started with him dying and no, I didn't kill him, although I admit I thought about it. Dad was the expert on Guernsey's Guilty Past—he had boxes full to bursting on that very subject. He was the one who first told me that History has a bad habit of repeating, and he had a bad habit of always being right. Mum was never interested, though, which was/is a bit of a problem.

Mum doesn't care much for real-life events and says the newspapers are just too depressing. She prefers her

---

* Emile Philippe Rozier (1938–84), late of Sans Soucis, Village de Courtils, St. Peter Port; Guernsey's most famous/only local/modern historian and the founder/editor of The Patois Press and author of its many historical guides to Guernsey and the other, less important Channel Islands.

crime and murders bought by the yard from the Town Church jumble. It's funny, because she's a total prude and won't even swear but she'll plough through any amount of blood and gore as long as it's not real.

I'd love to pretend that none of this is real for her sake, at least. Poor Mum. How do I even begin to tell her what I did and why? If Dad were still here he'd know what to do. He'd start by saying that you have to go way back. Perhaps if Mum had done that sooner she would've seen what was ahead. If I'm writing this for anyone I suppose I'm writing it for her. She knows what happened to Dad, and what happened to Dad is definitely connected to what happened to Nic. It's amazing, really, how everything connects. But what would you expect on this tiny island? We all know each other, or worse, we are related.

We talk about getting away and seeing the world, but we never do. We stay here making the same mistakes, over and over. I'm a murderer and it's not just my fault. I can blame the Germans, and I can blame my parents, and I can blame my parents' parents. Don't you see? Once you know your History, it does explain everything.

It turns out I was a murderer before I was even born.

12TH DECEMBER 1965

TAPE: 1 (A SIDE)

"The testimony of Charles André Rozier"

[Transcribed by Emile Philippe Rozier]

Faut le faire pour le register: This is the testimony of Charles André Rozier, a useless wretch now often thought a half-wit, the eldest son of Hubert Ebenezer Wilfred Rozier and Arlette Anne-Marie of Les Landes. Back when people talked to me, they only called me Charlie. I was born the year of Our Lord 1928, when this island of Guernsey was still that small and perfect paradise. Would that we could go back to that time, would that I was never born at all!

But I was born and I did live, and this miserable life is all I cling to. The rest was taken from me by one I counted as a friend. He was just a kid, like me, when he stole everything I valued. I call him many things. Murderer. Traitor. You can call him Ray Le Poidevoin. As solid a name as Guernsey granite, but common for this island. Let's hope he meets a common end.

Eh me, Emile, I want the wrongs righted but you won't read my story in the *Press*, and I don't want it printed there, neither. They say I am the guilty one, only out for revenge, but they have been lying since the War began and don't think it's over yet. Only today I was on them cliffs by Clarence Batterie, knee-deep in pink campion and squinting at the sun, but every view was framed by German concrete. It is an abomination what has happened to this island! And as I stood there I imagined Ray was aside of me, watching the black clouds of death rise up from the horizon. It was just like in that summer of 1940, a hot summer that chilled me to the bone. I looked down into the crystal, twinkling sea and near surrendered to it. I felt my knees buckle and the ground slip away, but you know what stopped me? It was old Ray pulling me back like he did that once before. Emile, it is a curse on me! I am *ever* in his clutches.

Why is it we find this little rock so hard to leave? If only I were again on the streets of St. Peter Port, the kid that I once was, holding tight to our mother's hand. I remember how we pushed our way through the chaos of weeping and shouting. It felt like the whole island was on the move and if ever there was a right time to go, it was then. The

Germans were too close for comfort. Everyone knew what they was doing to France—we heard the guns loud and clear—so I was to be packed off to England with my classmates. But as I stood with my teachers on the quay I didn't feel scared. Words like *war* and *death* didn't mean too much to me, and England meant the ends of the earth, a million miles away.

Reckon there must've been something evil in me even then, since that day was the first time I'd ever felt special. Before, I was just *p'tit* Charlie with too-pale skin and twiggy legs who got poked and teased and laughed at, but as we marched up the gangplank I felt something stirring deep inside. I've spent a long time trying to explain what it was that made me do it, and I cannot find a simple, single reason. Perhaps it was the fear and mayhem, perhaps it was the heat, or perhaps it was a bit of island madness. As that bright sun beat down I felt my cheeks burn up, and then I started screaming.

"I shan't go. You can't make me! You put me back!"

Back then I had a pair of lungs, me, and I could shout myself inside out. I was lashing out with my elbows and kicking like a donkey. *Quel tripos!* The boat was already moving as I lunged for the side and started going over, and I would've ended up in the water had it not been for Ray. He was right at the edge of the pier, holding on to the railings, leaning over to me. All I saw was a big, brown hand and then I felt this grip so tight it cut off all the blood. I was safe, or so I thought, as Ray Le Poidevoin reeled me in.

"What the Hell do you think you're doing?" someone asked.

"He's going to stay and kill some Jerries!"

I laughed although I didn't know why, and I
clambered with my new friend up onto the harbour
wall. Someone tried to grab my shirt. Did I hear
my mother shout? I turned to watch the boat move
off and the sea open up. Then I turned back to
St. Peter Port, to the crowds that thronged forward. Nobody could touch me and I thought I was so
clever: this was history in the making and I would
help to make it. Did I realise then what a dark and
damnable history it would be? No, but I should have
had an inkling when Ray pointed upwards, into the
rich blue, cloudless sky.

"Look!"

I lifted my head and nearly toppled backwards
from the effort.

There were German planes circling high overhead, and they looked like little silver fish. The
world itself was turning upside-down and would
never be righted.

"Now, *man amie.*" Ray whistled. "Now the party's
starting!"

13TH DECEMBER 1985, 5:30 A.M.

[MY BEDROOM, 2ND FLOOR, SANS SOUCIS,
VILLAGE DE COURTILS, ST. PETER PORT,
GUERNSEY,* THE CHANNEL ISLANDS, THE WORLD]

'm not a party person. I've never liked crowds of people: all that pushing and shoving and possible sweat. But if I'm faithful to the facts, that's where my story starts. Saturday, 25 November 1984 to be precise. The day Nicolette had that stupid party. I should never have been invited, and everyone was morbidified that I was.

And by everyone I mean my classmates at Les Moulins College for Cretins, the only all-girls' school on the island. They mostly hate me for no good reason. Just because I sit at the front of the classroom and get all the questions right and hand my homework in early. And they call me Cabbage because of it. Teenage girls are *très* mega horrible, and Nic was exactly like that but prettier. She'd been moved from the Grammar School, hav-

---

* To be more exact: Guernsey is part of the Bailiwick of Guernsey, which is part of the Channel Islands, which is only vaguely part of the United Kingdom and does not want to be part of Europe, and on maps of the World we don't even exist, so the World can bugger off.

ing been put down a year on account of her dyslexia. For some people (me) this would've been embarrassing, but my classmates took one look at her long blonde hair and big green eyes and turned dyslexic, too.

It was pathetic how they fought to be her friend, scrambling to sit near her and jostling to get her attention. No better than boys now I think of it. I didn't join in because I never do, and maybe that impressed her. I was also busy with my Festung Guernsey* timeline, which secured me an A+ in our Living History project. There was a bit of a fuss over it, actually, because I'd included quotes from local people who'd had to work for the Nazis, and some of my classmates didn't like seeing their surnames underlined in luminous green. Nic thought it was hilariously funny, though.

But that wasn't why she invited me to her party. The truth is, she was the new girl in class and she invited everyone.

Even Vicky. Vicky Senner lives down the road from me and our mums have been friends forever. She's called Stig because she's dark and hairy and is a champion builder of dens. Before Nic came along, she was the closest thing I had to a best friend, and we agreed to go to the party together.

I was (I'll admit) excited, and I was curious to see inside Nic's house. She lived on Fort George, one of

* Aka Fortress Guernsey, so-named by the Nazis after they occupied the island in 1940. *Festung* denotes (excellent word) the vast amounts of building work ordered by Hitler to fortify/destroy Guernsey's natural beauty (see E. P. Rozier, *The Concrete Truth*, The Patois Press, 1970).

those modern fancy housing estates* Dad used to call a TRAVESTY, and as per ever he was right. Les Paradis looked exactly like Nic's birthday cake—all sickly-rich and cream-coloured. It had chandeliers in every room and gold-plated knobs on the banisters.

Therese Prevost, Nic's mother, gave me the full guided tour.

Therese is very important to this story although I'm sure she'd rather not be. She's extremely beautiful, like an older and more French-polished version of Nic. You could easily make the joke that they were sisters, except that Therese had done all the fussing older women do: she'd had her hair multicoloured at Josef's in Town Church Square and her lips tattooed a dried-blood red. And she always wore heels—this explains why she walked so slowly. I sometimes thought she floated across a room, and she had this way of holding her hands out to each side like she was waiting for her tan to dry.

The first time we talked properly was at the party. I was hiding in the kitchen, chatting away merrily to absolutely no one, and Therese wafted in. When she realised I was alone she smiled politely.

"Is everything OK?" she asked.

I made a joke about how I had lots of imaginary friends who were all very funny and not remotely dangerous.

"Ah." She nodded. "I'm always talking to myself as

---

* Guernsey has a lot of these modern estates now, and the houses are very elaborate because they are funded by Swiss bankers whose vast/immoral earnings fiddle the local tax laws. Not that there are any tax laws, and not that the bankers are Swiss.

well. I say you get a better class of conversation that way. People frown on it but I find it therapeutic."

I spread my hands flat on her Italian maybe-marble worktop and told her she had excellent good taste. That's when she showed me around the house. I was especially impressed by the automatic blinds in the conservatory and the impulse jets in the shower. There were also mirrors everywhere, which reminded me of the house of Victor Hugo, the famous/tortured writer.* He'd lined his walls with mirrors so as to spy on his family and send them all mad. This was after he was thrown out of Jersey for smoking cannabis and kidnapping street children.

Therese was definitely riveted when I told her all of this, and I'm sure she would've liked to hear more if Nic hadn't interrupted.

"Sounds like a fucking perv to me," she said, leaning against the doorframe.

I remember how she smiled as I spun round to face her. She could say the meanest things and still look so angelic.

Of course I told Nic she was very wrong, and that Victor Hugo was an artist-genius type, and therefore eccentric/not appreciated until dead.

After an awkward silence (which I'm used to), there came the screams from the sitting room. I hoped some-

---

* Victor Hugo (1802–85) is the most famous person to have ever lived in Guernsey (apart from Oliver Reed, who is an excellent drunkard and actor). He (Victor Hugo, not Oliver Reed) lived at Hauteville House in St. Peter Port, which is now a museum, which is never open (see E. P. Rozier, *Victor Hugo's House–An Inventory*, The Patois Press, 1978).

one had been mutilated, but they were only playing Twister. We found Vicky crushing Shelley Newman, who had straddled Isabelle Gaudion, whose skirt had somehow vanished. And they thought I had problems.

Nicolette looked at me, rolled her eyes, and nodded to the stairs. She didn't look back as I followed her up to her bedroom, she didn't even turn round once we were inside—she just went and stood by the window with the light surrounding her. Then she raised up her arms to pull her hair off her shoulders and spun back, flashing all of her midriff. That was one of her little moves. She always wore short tops that gaped and therefore showed her skin.

"Sit down."

I plonked myself on the deluxe-goose-feather-down-duvet-you-can't-even-buy-in-Creasey's and watched Nic crouch in front of me. She was rummaging under the bed for something.

"Your mum's nice," I said, trying not to look down her bra.

"She's a dumb whore."

I'd only ever heard of whores in the Bible and Jackie Collins, so I got a bit excited.

Then Nic stood up and I saw the bottle—whisky. It had been hidden in a sock. She unscrewed the top and took a long gulp, and then offered it to me.

"Thanks." I pretended to examine the label. "Whisky is my favourite tipple."

She laughed. "Do you always talk like an old man?"

People are generally impressed by my use of the English language, so I was annoyed and drank quickly and half choked. It's funny because now I can drink a small bottle of it a day, and often do. Well, that's not funny. Anyway, as I coughed up my guts Nic sank onto her bed and twirled strands of hair around a finger.

"Pathetic party, isn't it? Next we'll be pinning the tail on the donkey. I'd rather slit my own throat." I felt her eyes turn onto me. "You're a funny one: always on your own, acting like you know better . . . how come you weren't joining in downstairs?"

I focused on the glossiness of her lips.

"Because I do know better and I don't like games."

She nodded. "Mum thought it was something else. She thinks you're sad because your dad died."

I stared at Nic's lovely oval face. I scanned her chin with its tiny dimple, the glossy lips, the outlined eyes.

"I don't feel sad at all." I took another swig of whisky. "Besides, my dad always said we carry the dead with us, so in theory he's right here."

Nic blinked. "If you're trying to freak me out it won't work."

I handed the bottle back to her.

"Who taught you to do your makeup?"

"Taught myself."

I must've felt brave on account of the whisky.

"Teach me."

Nic pulled a shiny red bag off her dresser and made me sit up straight. We were suddenly very close, facing each other. She sucked her bottom lip.

"Where to start?"

I stared into her eyes, probably (definitely) hypnotised. I remember how her bangles clinked against me, I remember the smell of her perfume (she called it Anus Anus but actually it smelled like lilies). She had different coloured creams and powders and pencils and she used a bit of all of them. It was strange, letting her prod at my cheeks and pull back my eyelids, but it made me feel dead special.

Then Isabelle burst in and ruined it.

"There you are! What are you doing? *Oh-my-God! Oh-my-God!*"

(Isabelle was very keen on her amateur dramatics.)

She grabbed the whisky and threw herself on the floor, giggling.

Vicky was standing behind her.

"A private party, is it?"

NB: A lot of Guernsey people end their sentences with "eh?" or "is it?," which I think sounds common-as-mud. Dad said it demonstrated the fact that we are more French than English.* It is also possibly a sign that Vicky/French people are simple-minded.

"Come on in." Nic was smudging blusher on my cheek. "I've finished. You look great, Cat. Much better."

No one had ever called me Cat before and I liked it a lot, but Nic was so close it was like she was going to kiss me and I thought she had to be teasing me. There'd been some rumours, you see. Aside from associating me with a leafy vegetable I was also sometimes called G.A.Y. A few months earlier I'd been in the hockey pavilion having

---

* The French only ever shrug and say *n'est-ce pas?* They also add on an extra *me* and *te* just for effect and sadly Guernsey people do the same (e.g., "Where are you going, you?" or "I've got three heads, me"). It's just embarrassing.

a lively chat *toute seule* and two girls in the fourth year had caught me. They'd claimed I was rifling through their gym gear when I was only sitting on it. Very upsetting, it was. Especially since I didn't ever think about sex, unlike every other girl in my class. They might've gone round pinging each others' trainer bras and pretending to smoke their tampons but I wasn't bothered with any of that.

Nic wouldn't let anyone else near the whisky but she made me drink a lot. I gulped back as much as I could, and was feeling queasy by the time she stood up.

"OK, I'm not playing nanny to you lot anymore. I'm off to have some *real* fun."

Real fun meant having sex with someone called Simon, who was 17 and worked at Fruit Export and drove a lime-green Ford Capri. They did it at Jerbourg Point and Pleinmont and Le Gouffre and he was very good with his tongue but his willy had a kink in it. (I have no idea what that means.)

Nic asked us to name our best sex positions. Isabelle suggested doggy-paddle and Vicky collapsed under the weight of her own giggles. I felt I had to say something.

"If you're going to do it out-of-doors, don't go on the cliffs near me. They found evidence of a mass grave left over from the German Occupation."

Isabelle rolled her eyes and muttered, "Here we go," so I swore on Dad's (more recently) dead body and made everyone embarrassed.

Par le chemin, although I have sometimes made things up, this is rock-solid-Guernsey-granite truth. They were found five years ago, and were believed to date back to the 1940s. Dad said it was obvious they were the bodies of poor foreign slave workers* who'd been brought over by the Nazis to build their secret bunkers and possible gas chambers but the Guernsey Tourist Board hushed it up because it was in big trouble.† Of course, Dad hypervented as per THE SHOCKING WHITEWASH and wrote a trillion letters to the newspapers on this very subject, but his letters were never published, which made him hypervent more. (I had a theory that all this hyperventing killed him, but that's just one of a few.)

Nic liked my little story of shameful lies and death and licked her Boots 17 Cherry Pie–coated lips.

"Where do you go with your boyfriend then?"

Vicky said I'd never had much luck with lads since I'd always so closely resembled one. (Ha. Ha.)

My supposed-to-be best friend then explained how, on our last outing to Beau Sejour Leisure Complex, I'd been stuck in the turnstiles until someone had given me a push, saying: "There you go, young man."

My hair was Evidently (good word) too short back then. I hate my hair. It's very fine and strawlike.

Nic chuckled. "Some people go for pale and interesting. That's what you are: pale and interesting."

She winked at me then, and it felt warm and light, like in photosynthesis.

---

* Between 1941 and 1944 about 16,000 foreign slave workers were brought over to the islands to build new defences. A lot were starved, beaten, and worked to death. Dad had tracked down some survivors and recorded interviews with islanders telling him what they'd seen. It was properly gory and I can't believe people let it happen. (But they did.)

† "The Costa Brava Costa Nothing" according to the *Guernsey Evening Press*. (Tourism is in a slump due to cheaper flights to/cheaper cocktails in places of guaranteed sunshine.)

That was all it took, really: the drink, the smile, the wink. I was different and Nicolette liked different.

Maybe she sensed the cosmic and magnetic connection between us.

Maybe she guessed I was ocean-full of deep-sea depths.

Or maybe she wanted someone fat and frumpy to make her feel better than she already was.

The plain fact is, I didn't care—it felt better than the Yellow Sash of Excellence, which I'd already worn three terms on the trot—so I decided not to think too much about it. Nic was like the sister I'd never had but always wanted.

And remember: two sisters, like two brothers, can be completely different.

13TH DECEMBER 1965

TAPE: 1 (A SIDE)

"The testimony of
C. A. Rozier"

[Transcribed by E. P. Rozier]

P'tit Emile, man buoan fraire. You are my dear and only brother, but how can two brothers be so different, eh? You got the good stuff: the brains, the looks, our mother's love, whilst I, *bian sûr*, was poisoned. Nothing is equal between us or ever will be, but I should find some comfort in the fact we do not look alike. 1940 wasn't a good year for a little blond boy. They'd started to call me Fritz and would frogmarch around me. I have our mother's delicate build and colouring, whereas you, Emile, you are more like our father with your steely eyes and wave of coal-black hair. Would that I had your dark and too-good looks! That might've saved me some of my troubles.

I wanted a brother badly, me, and when you came along I was so proud. Had there been less years between us we could've been *copains*, things might've turned out different. But you were still a baby when the War broke out and I had no time for playing nursemaid. I was puffing out my pigeon chest and thinking big. I wanted Ray for my brother.

A damned stupid idea, if ever there was one. Ray Le Poidevoin was two years older and already a strutting cock. Didn't I know that he was trouble? He was a born fighter, with beady eyes glinting at any opportunity. That day when he plucked me off the boat he'd been collecting all the stuff people had left behind. The wealthy had abandoned their big cars on the docks before running for the boats, the poorest had bundled up their belongings into sheets. No wonder Ray thought it was a party, it was his Christmases and birthdays all rolled into one.

"What's your name?" he asked of me.

I told him it was Charlie and he ruffled my hair.

"Well, Charlie, when the Hun come they'll think you're one of them. How comes you're so pale? You cannot be an island boy. Perhaps you are a spy."

I was so pent-up from the excitement I jumped to my feet, tears of fury in my eyes. But he easily held me back.

"At ease, soldier! I'm kidding."

Then he reached into his jacket and pulled out a hip flask.

"How old are you?"

I told him I was a month off thirteen and grabbed at it quickly, taking a greedy slug.

Mon Dju, I thought, this is how evil tastes!

Ray was laughing now. "We'll make a man of you yet. Are you ready to kill for your country?"

"I shall be ready," I squawked, still feeling the fire in my throat.

Ray crouched back down and I followed suit.

"You got a weapon?"

I shook my head and he narrowed his eyes like he was thinking deeply, then he dug into his jacket and pulled out a pocket knife. He'd flicked it open and was jabbing at the air.

"It might not look like much but the blade's sharp and could slit a man's throat. You know how to use it? You can have it. I've another."

He placed it in the palm of my hand and as I turned it over it twinkled like a jewel.

I thought that meant I was like him, Emile, I thought that meant I was in his gang. Happens I thought a lot of things that day which never quite proved true. As the sun sank into the horizon I was back to the little kid I'd ever been, too scared to go home and face the wrath of our mother. *Au yous,* back then she had a tongue as sharp as any knife. You know why we called her La Duchesse? She didn't just act like she was royalty but she made her word the law. The youngest out of seven children, she'd had to fight for everything. Now she was always fighting me.

I see her standing in the hallway with her hands on her hips, still wearing her fancy coat with lace about the collar. She'd waited two hours to give me a good lamming.

"Why do you test me so?" she asked, twisting my

ear this way and that. "Making a scene in front of our neighbours. As if I haven't got enough on my plate with a baby to look after and your father working all hours to keep the business going!"

Hé bian, the business. Our parents had decided to stay on the island to keep their livelihood. Our father had started his own printing firm, called The Patois Press. It was everything to him and I'm glad you mean to continue. You, Emile, and you alone, can prove it was worth all the trouble and pain. Back then, we only printed posters for the Odeon, local advertisements, and parish newsletters—nothing fancy like what you have planned. Pop was a quiet soul, wanting a quiet life. Arlette was the firecracker, always going off. Of course, she came from a lesser family so she had more to prove, and as for Pop, well, he was much changed from his time in France, fighting in that "war to end all wars." It must've cut him to the quick to see another coming.

Not a day passed when we didn't see German planes circling in the skies. We knew something bad was coming our way. Boatloads of refugees arrived from France, telling tales of the barbarous Hun. At every street corner I gobbled up gossip, making notes in my little pocket pad. And the stories I heard!

"They slice the arms off little kids for sport. They are man-eaters. They use women and babies as cannon fodder."

The French are a race prone to exaggeration, as I now know, and they never stopped stoking my fevered imaginings. If only I'd stayed in school and listened to my teachers, eh? But the schools were all closed down, so I was on the loose.

Hubert would shake his head at me, like he saw the bad things stewing in my brain.

"*Si nous pale du guiabye nous est saure d'l'y'vais les caurnes*" is what he said . . . "Speak of the devil and you shall see horns." He was always talking in patois to me. *Hé bian*, that language has been dying for longer than I've been living. I miss hearing it spoke and I miss hearing him speak it.

He'd make me sit with him in the office so as to keep me out of trouble. Of course, with half the island gone our business had gone with it. There were signs on every hedgerow saying "Why Go Mad? There's No Place Like Home," but by then we were going mad being stuck at home. Pop turned to his Bible and I hid my head in stupid comics, losing myself in cartoon adventures. What I knew of the War came from *Rover* or *Wizard*, and of course our father had no time for it. I caught him flicking through them once, mumbling to himself.

"It won't be like that," he said, his long arms hanging limply at his sides.

"So"—I placed myself squarely in front of him—"tell me what it will be like."

He shook his head. "There aren't words to describe the horror."

It wasn't the first time I'd asked him, nor the first time he'd refused.

"Who wants the truth, eh? What I've seen, Charlie, it won't make a good adventure story for little boys like you."

How it made my young blood boil! Now, though, I understand it all too well. If you have seen something so terrible why tell of it, since words give it fresh life and substance? Bury the past. Deny it as long as you can. The only trouble is, the more you deny something the more power it will have. Look what has happened with our Occupation: our States deputies want it tidied into a tourist guide and treated like a day trip, but there are dead and rotting bodies buried in the tunnels and lying at the bottom of our cliffs. Can't you smell death? It is a travesty and it is a whitewash!

Vère dja, j'pourrais t'encaöntair d'pis maïr haôute jusqu'a bass iaôue . . . Emile, I am your big brother, I am your bad brother, and that's how I'll be remembered. I'll admit I did wrong and that I've got blood on my hands, but I'll not stand here alone. There are people on this island who have got away with murder. I've been shelled out enough times on this, but I'll not be silent no more. You write down what I tell you, word for word, and remember it's all true. Then I'll die easy.

You do it for me, Emile, let your pen be my revenge.

13TH DECEMBER 1985, 5 P.M.

[DAD'S STUDY]

know I shouldn't call this Dad's study anymore—
he's been dead a lot longer than Nic—but this is
still my favourite room. I do all my best thinking
in here, and I like to remember how it used to look.
There was a huge desk with paper stacked up all around
it, just like the walls of a fortress, and books and box
files were jammed onto every spare shelf, or scattered
all over the sofa. Dad said he had a system but I never
worked out what it was. (Not that I was allowed in here,
or could even make it through the door.)

Today it's clean and empty: Dad's books have gone,
plus all the files and shelves, and Mum's painted the
whole room white. She said Dad had let things get out
of hand, so what he called his LIFE'S BLOOD was actually mostly scrap paper. There's a lot more space and
light now, and you can even see the carpet, and that
definitely makes Mum happy. She's finally got her own
office. People were shocked by how quickly she sprang
into action, how she took over the business and turned it

around, but she needed a fresh start, and I suppose she had a lot to prove.

You see, when Dad was alive, our ye olde family business, The Patois* Press, wasn't much of a business at all. Dad's books never sold as brilliantly as we'd hoped, and we were always tripping over them. Even his magazine, *The Occupation Today*, which had real-life subscribers and contributors, was running at a loss. Without Mum's common sense we'd have definitely gone bankrupt. Dad couldn't accept the trouble we were in because he didn't care about money/my schooling. Mum said that he was so wrapped up in the past that he couldn't think about the future. She said you can't change History—the things that have already happened—but the future is wide open.

Now, Mum reckons what's ahead makes her happy and I should want her to be happy. Isn't that what all children want for their parents?

And yes, I do admire her, because she kept up appearances and pretended things were fine, when they really weren't. It was a bit like when the Germans invaded Guernsey: most islanders tried to ignore them and carry on like normal. This is called sangfroid, which sounds better in French, because in English it's cold blood. I wouldn't call Mum cold-blooded, but she is a pragmatist, and it's a shame Dad won't see how she's transformed

* Only ye olde people (and Dad) can speak Guernsey patois. It was spoken a lot during the German Occupation, because *most* Germans couldn't understand it. Now it's dying out, as per everything. It's Medieval Norman French mixed with Latin, Welsh, Scotch, and Brandy (kidding!). It sounds a lot like someone speaking French badly without their front teeth (see above ref. old people).

the business. A third of Guernsey's advertising flyers are now produced by The Patois Press, and we've (trumpets, please) just launched our first-ever Escape to Guernsey Calendar.

Mum, it turns out, is an excellent businesswoman.

Which is why she wasn't around much after Dad died, and why she never noticed when Nic started to come over. I'm not blaming her (really, I'm not), but because she was always working Nic and I could please ourselves. Nic really liked our house—I thought it was shabby compared to Les Paradis but she called it "real." She snooped in every room and Dad-filled cupboard and decided that this room, Dad's study, was the best place to sit. It was seven months and eleven days since he'd died and not much had changed. I thought she'd find it creepy but I remember her sinking onto some cushions on the floor and looking right at home. After that the study became our den, and nobody noticed the mess we made because it was a mess already.

At first Nic made me nervous. She was the expert in sex and boys and makeup, none of which I knew about. I usually hate it when someone knows more than me, but Nic had this way of talking. She was so honest and I felt like we could tell each other (almost) everything. She actually listened to me, as well. She couldn't believe it when I told her Mum and Dad had slept in different rooms, and that we weren't allowed a TV, and that Dad's fingers had turned black and died before he did. I remember feeling so proud when she lifted up her head, scanned the dusty shelves, and said: ". . . and I thought *my* parents were fucked."

I was the only girl in our class with a dead dad and it made me demi-exotic. Nic wasn't scared of death, like some people. Is that why she liked me? I don't know. I just don't know! She definitely liked Dad's study, though, and in between plucking off my eyebrows/trying to pierce my ears I told her grisly stories about the German Occupation.* They were much better than the brainless trash you read in *Jackie* or *Just Seventeen*.

But the one story I couldn't tell her was the one she most wanted to know. I had this huge pile of papers that I'd been carefully putting in order. I'd labelled it "The Whole Grim Truth" (very catchy, I know), because it was the story of Uncle Charlie, Dad's older brother, who got in trouble with the Germans and ended up being starved and tortured and driven mad. He only just survived the War and he was the reason Dad made himself an expert on said German Occupation.

Nic wanted to know what Charlie had done to get in so much trouble, but I decided not to tell her. I just said he chose the wrong friends, which I think was good and tactful.

Of course she was disappointed and wrinkled up her pretty nose.

"What? That's it?"

"Trust me," I replied, "that's enough."

* E.g., the one about the Underground Hospital as a gas chamber, or the one about Guernsey as a breeding ground for the Aryan race, or the testimonies of ex-prisoners from the Alderney Death Camps (see E. P. Rozier, *Guernsey Gas Chamber and Other Myths*, The Patois Press, 1968–69).

Then we stared at each other for ages, until she blinked and I won.

"You should have a drink." I pointed to the desk. "Third drawer down on the left."

She reached over and pulled at the drawer and a half-drunk bottle rolled towards her.

Whisky, of course. That was definitely one of my top-ten moments.

I'd never have dared drink Dad's whisky before, but now it felt better than perfect. Very soon Nic started doing impressions of people at school. She was very good and would've made a brilliant actress or model or TV presenter. After she'd done Mrs. Queripel with her manic-secret-nose-picking, she did Adèle Mauger and her dying-pig laugh, then she jumped up and grabbed a wad of papers.

"Well! Top marks again, Cathy, you bring History to life! Gosh, you put us all to shame. I'm rather overcome. I can't hold back any longer. Come here and give me a kiss."

She leaned in and puckered up and I had to burst out laughing. It was a pretty good impression of Mr. McCracken, our form teacher, who also taught History, which was (of course) my best subject.

"He thinks the sun shines out of your arse, *and* he's your next-door neighbour. Star-crossed lovers!"

I pointed out that Mr. McCracken lived three doors down at La Petite Maison, and that *star-crossed* meant "doomed."

"Still. He's obviously into you, the way he always

smiles at you and talks to you after class. I mean, what a *sleaze*. He's gagging for it."

I shrugged.

"And do you see him much out of school?"

"On the cliffs sometimes."

Nic fluttered her eyelashes and crossed her hands over her heart, "I bet he plans it! So it's like you and him and the wind and the waves?"

"No."

"Well, it should be! What are we doing here? Let's go and *find him*."

I'm glad to say we didn't find him that day. If we had, I'm sure Nic would've embarrassed me horribly. She could make me blush tomato-red, and teasing me about Mr. Mac became her favourite sport. So what if I played along. That's not a crime, is it? And I didn't take it seriously—it was just a silly game. If she was rude about him it annoyed me, but what could I do? I knew that our friendship wasn't equal. I suppose it was more like a marriage, where one person is always more in control. Nic was beautiful, so she could do and say whatever she wanted. I didn't think of myself as weak or under her thumb, I just thought I was happy. I'd always said and done everything right up until then but I hadn't felt alive.

Most people are not by nature good—they're just afraid of getting caught being bad. Even Mr. McCracken. Poor Mr. McCracken. Mrs. Perrot had told him to be firmer with his pupils, but he wasn't really built for it. He'd always say, "Please" and "Now, quiet . . . that's enough!"

and blush as badly as me. Maybe it didn't help that he had cheekbones like cliff edges and all that flicky hair. But what was he thinking, coming to work at an all-girls' school? Talk about asking for trouble.

Nic was trouble. She said I was his pet but it was never like that. I was polite and attentive to all of my teachers. Maybe I was more relaxed around Mr. Mac, but that was because I saw him all the time—in his garden and cleaning his car, and out on the cliffs with his camera. He was a mad-keen photographer and used to wander on the beach for hours, fiddling with his lenses.

Just to be clear, when I went out on the cliffs I didn't go because Nic suggested it, and I wasn't in search of Mr. Mac. No. Not at all. I just went to check the Moorings, like I did every week.

The Moorings are these slime-covered cement steps that wind down the side of Fermain Bay. If the tide is high enough you can dive off them into the sea, but at low tide you can walk straight onto the beach. Dad used to time his swims precisely so he could dive off them every day. Have I mentioned he was a champion swimmer? He wasn't bothered by the sub-zero temperatures.* He could execute a perfect dive off the top landing and he sometimes didn't surface for a full five minutes, and by then he was already halfway across the Bay. He'd power through the water like a propeller on a speedboat.

---

* The sea in Fermain is the coldest in Europe. This is the fault of the Gulf Stream but I do not know why.

Dad was so fit and healthy, much fitter than Mr. Mc-Cracken. Mr. McCracken definitely couldn't dive. He'd snap in two! That's probably why he was embarrassed when he found me clearing the stones on the beach. It was a wet and windy Sunday (a lot like today) and I was on my knees in soggy sand. I tried to explain how divers might cut themselves on any sharp rocks and that Dad had always done it, just to be sure. But Mr. Mac looked at me like I was a nudist.

"Well, maybe I'll find something else, like an unexploded land mine or an ammunition dump."

Mr. Mac inspected the sky (which was all sorts of grey).

"Now that would be something."

I nodded back and relaxed my grip on a smallish boulder. I wanted to ask after his wife, because I hadn't seen her in ages. Mrs. McCracken was an artist before she packed her bags and demanded a divorce. I think she designed school badges or something quite particular. She had thick, wiry hair and always wore skirts that skimmed around her ankles. Dad had called her a "hippy," which was a bad thing.

I stared out at the empty sea and wondered what to say, but before too long Mr. McCracken pepped up.

"Your father swam whatever the weather. I'd see him down here even on the wildest of days. I used to think he had webbed feet!"

When I was little Dad had let me perch on his feet while he did his sit-ups and I recall he did have very long toes. But he'd stopped doing those exercises a long time ago. He'd also stopped swimming although no one had noticed. I'd see him set off for the cliffs with his trunks rolled up in a towel and I should've wondered why, when he came back, his hair was still bone-dry.

Mr. McCracken asked after Mum and called her a Trouper, but I thought he said a Grouper, which is a fish. I replied that Mum didn't like water and hot climates. We stared at the steps and the seaweed and the rocks.

McCrackers looked slightly dazed.

"I love the sea here. I've been all over the world but there's no sea like here."

He had been to Australia and swum with dolphins and climbed Ayers Rock. He had also scaled the pyramids of Egypt.

I asked if it was true that all the people who had built the pyramids had been buried alive in them.

"No, that's a myth. But when the pharaoh died his family would kill themselves so that they could join him in the afterlife. All his belongings were buried with him, all his treasure, as well."

I then told Mr. Mac how the Germans had buried slave workers in the bunkers and tunnels by accident on purpose.* McCrackers said a lot of the stories about the German Occupation were exaggerated, so I offered to drop round spare copies of Dad's many books and pamphlets.

I don't want to bang on about it, but Dad really was

---

* There is at least one definite example of this, when 100 slave workers were caught in a rock fall in the tunnel they were digging by La Vallette, which is, by the way, just under Clarence Batterie. Nobody could get them out and so they were left for dead, but no one will admit it (see E. P. Rozier, *Bunker Baedeker*, The Patois Press, 1977, p. 34).

Guernsey's Most Famous or Notorious Modern Historian. He knew everything about the German Occupation. He was even an expert on the bunkers and fortifications, and there are a lot of them, too, because when the Germans came they were worried the British would want us back.* The Germans are not known for their architecture (I have seen pictures of Frankfurt) so you can imagine what carbuncles they created. Dad called them OUR CROWNING HORROR but was always campaigning for their upkeep.

Mr. Mac began to look Mc-worried.

"You must be lonely without your father."

I stroked my imaginary philosopher's beard. "But I was lonely when he was here. He was so strict: he never let me do anything. I mean, at least now he's gone I can go out and have some fun."

Mr. McCracken nodded gravely (no pun intended), then he said I was brave for putting on a face. "Your classmates won't understand what you've been through. Children—teenagers especially—can be cruel, and they've got short memories. I hope they don't expect you to bounce back and be normal."

I reminded Mr. Mac that I was never normal, and he laughed.

"Yes, Cathy, but even so."

"Don't worry," I replied, staring out to sea, "I know only too well how children can do and say terrible things without realising the consequences. They can

---

* Hitler clearly didn't have a clue.

cause terrible harm and possibly also death. Nobody understands death until it happens to them."

Mr. McCracken's eyes twitched and he asked me what I meant. So I explained how Dad's elder brother was my age when he betrayed his entire family to the Nazis, shot his father in the head, and was then sent to a concentration camp.

I was aware, as I was saying it, that I'd got the facts slightly muddled, but I didn't like to backtrack. Mr. Mac looked both puzzled and nervous, which seemed like a good combination, and I just wanted to leave it at that.

TAPE: 1 (B SIDE)

"The testimony of C. A. Rozier"

[Transcribed by E. P. Rozier]

(CHECK PATOIS WITH MRS. MAHY)

Emile, I killed your father. He was my father, too, but I never did deserve him. *J'ai bian d' la misère!* I'm sorry for what you have lost and how you have suffered as a consequence of my actions. A son needs a father to guide him, and you never knew yours. What damage I did! I was meant to help him with the business and that was the promise I had made. With the schools closed I swore I'd not be idle. I said I'd work alongside him, make him proud.

I may as well have shot him in the head, then and there.

Mon poure Hubert, how little we understood each other. Few would know by looking at this stick of a man that he'd been gassed and imprisoned by the

Boche once already. The only clue was in the hack-
ing cough, that terrible weakness in his lungs.
Tch! It is a curse on me, that I saw him as a weak-
ling whereas once he'd been a hero. A braver man
and a better soldier than I could ever be.

I'd never imagined those delicate fingers pulling a trigger and killing someone, and I didn't
even know he'd owned a gun until he'd given it up.
Earlier that month we'd been ordered to surrender
all our weapons to the local authorities. They'd
collected our rifles, machine guns, shotguns, and
air guns and dumped them in the sea. Make sense of
that! We were to be left completely defenceless. At
least La Duchesse had her wits about her. She took
our meagre savings out the bank and hid it in Pop's
strongbox under a floorboard of the spare room.

"Forget it is there," she told me. "Nobody will
lay their hands on what we have worked so hard
for."

Au yous, we were burying our secrets underground long before the Germans even came, and
others still were burying their heads. Our lily-
livered constabulary were saying, "The Germans
won't bother with us. We've got nothing to offer:
a small town, a few shops . . . what use are we to
them?" The only person who kept busy was Ray Le
Poidevoin. He had set himself up as a petty dicta-
tor with a makeshift army underneath. Not a bad
outfit, truth be told. Together they were taking
full advantage of everyone's indecision, clearing
out shops and abandoned houses, claiming livestock

and God knows what. I heard they'd had a good few
parties on those nights before the Hun took hold.
To me that didn't look too brave or soldierlike,
to go stealing other people's stuff. Ray said it
wasn't stealing, though, since shopkeepers wanted
rid of their stock before the Hun came.

You should've seen the scuffle outside Ogier's,
our one decent shoe shop, after some old stock had
been left out on the pavement. There was Ray right
in the middle of it, trying to match some ladies'
boots. When I found him squatting there I couldn't
help but smile.

"Don't think they'll fit you," I said. "And they'd
make a funny kind of weapon."

Ray was a big lad and could've cracked me like
an egg so I don't know why I had to taunt him.

"You make a lot of noise for a little man." He
straightened up. "Seeing as you know so much: how
long will the War last?"

I told him nobody knew that.

"Right, then." He pointed to my feet. "And how
much longer will the soles on those shoes last?"

I stared down at my battered sandals. *Le fishu
Ray*, he had a point.

"The enemy is advancing," he goes, "and they'll
take everything that's ours. Will you be fighting
your battles barefoot? Use your loaf, *man amie*,
and stop your gloating. We've got to think in the
long-term. We need to gather supplies for ourselves, and goods to barter with. This isn't a game
of conkers."

I felt about ten inches tall. "But I don't have anything the Jerries would want."

Ray pulled his shoulders back and played sergeant-major.

"Then look sharp and steal it."

It's hard to explain now the sway Ray had over me, but there was a lad with such confidence and swagger and I wanted some of it for myself. That wasn't a crime, was it? I left the thinning crowd and skulked off towards the harbour, brooding on his harangue. Ray was right, there was no two ways about it, I couldn't sit around and do nothing when these other lads were at it, and if I didn't own something, perhaps I should steal it. But what? All I'd managed before was an ice cream off the Vazon cart.

By now I'd drifted across the Esplanade and passed the Albert Memorial, then I didn't care to walk no more. I rested my elbows on the railings that overlooked our pretty harbour. It was a bright day with a warm breeze and I could feel the sun on my neck. I closed my eyes and remembered all the other summers I'd enjoyed on the island. And that's when it hit me. I opened my eyes and she was staring me in the face.

Her name was *Sarnia Chérie*, after the song—*"Sarnia, chière patrie, bijou d'la maïr"**—and she

* "Sarnia, dear Homeland, Gem of the sea, Island of Beauty my heart longs for Thee." The Guernsey anthem, composed by George Deighton in 1911.

was bobbing aside a jetty down the way. A fine little Dory sailboat belonging to my schoolmate, Horace Vaudin. Horace was now away in England, so it wasn't like he'd be needing her. Of course! I'd loved that little boat as if she was my own. We'd been out on her every weekend that previous summer, up and down the east coast and over to Herm and Sark. There's a photograph somewhere that shows me perched on her bow, grinning with all my crooked teeth. Reckon I'd just caught the biggest fish because I look so proud, squinting into the sunshine with Herm in the background. I had few talents, I wasn't quick or clever, but I could handle a boat well enough . . . and there she was, like she'd been waiting for me.

Mon Dju, I thought, it's not my boat but if I don't take it someone else will. I ran down to the jetty to check her over. What did I imagine, eh? That I'd hide her away like a nest egg, or use her for spy missions? Who knows what was in my donkey brain. Now, after all these years have passed, I'd happily sail anywhere to be free of these memories. Perhaps I should go to Australia and look up all those Guernsey folk who emigrated after the War. There's quite a number who uprooted themselves, Emile. You cannot blame them for wanting to wipe the slate clean and go where the past can't catch them up. But it's funny that they chose a land of convicts.

If you're interested, the last I heard Ray Le Poidevoin had settled in Adelaide. *Ray, man amie, j t rencontrai dêns l'enfer. J'sis arrêtaïr pour té!*

14TH DECEMBER 1985, 9 A.M.

Did I mention we had a boat? I've got a photo of her here. She was called *La Duchesse* and Dad built her from scratch in our front garden. It took two-ish years and destroyed all the rose bushes, which upset Mum *très* much. But Mum only had herself to blame because she was the one who suggested Dad take up a hobby. She said he worked too hard and needed an escape.

La Duchesse was very demanding, and we had to go out sailing most weekends, to Sark and Herm and even France. Mum didn't enjoy it like she was meant to, and I got terrible windburn. In spite/because of this, Dad started threatening to sail around the world. I know for a fact that he'd mapped out a route to Australia. A lot of Guernsey people settled there after the War, so I wondered if Dad was planning a new life without us. Then I had a dream that the boat was caught in a storm and hit a rock, and he was drowned. This made me quite afraid and not want to go sailing at all. I would've preferred roller-skating at Beau Sejour or playing Atari games with Vicky.

Now Mum's sold the boat to Kez Le Pelley and I sort of (almost) miss it. I miss being bored and getting shouted at, and having to pee in what is really just a bucket. I feel especially bad because I found this old photo in among Dad's files. It was obviously taken years ago, because it's black-and-white and very crumpled. It's of a boy, and he's grinning cheekily and sitting on a sailboat. He's got my fair hair and dimples, plus those God-awful crooked teeth. For the record, I look a lot like Uncle Charlie, which is (I think) important. It is also damning proof that I still look like a boy.

I took a lot of photos last year but now I've sort of stopped, and I'm not sure why that is. Oh well. Mum never really approved of it. She thought it was a ruse to impress Mr. McCracken. Of course if she'd done her research properly she'd have realised that it started after Dad died, when I couldn't find one good photo of him. It was all quite upsetting. I searched and searched and in the end I had to make do with one of the press photos from the unveiling of his (Un)Official Occupation Memorial. That was from May last year and it's obvious Dad's not well.

Dad was the most handsomest of men, I can't say it often enough. He had the face of an old-fashioned Hollywood star or Greek god, with a proud, jutting nose and masses of dark hair that swept back from his forehead like a wave. He had a few frown lines but they just made him look clever, and the grey hairs were I think quite flattering. But I've got no proof of this. That's why I started taking photos of our house, our neighbours, their pets, Mum gardening, Fermain, the Pepper Pot, Blue-bell Woods, etc. I was scared I'd miss something, plus I needed evidence. And that's why I took so many photos of Nic. I must've known she was another thing that wouldn't last.

There aren't many of the two of us together, although there's one from last autumn that I love. Nic's kicking up her legs like she's trying to do the can-can, and I'm falling backwards and laughing at the sky. My face is pink and round as the moon, and I'm hiding something under my blazer so I look deformed as well as fat. But anyone would look fat next to Nic. She had a tiny waist and the buttons on her shirt are mostly undone so you can almost see her belly button. Her hair's pulled over to the left and she's got gold hoop earrings in. She's the only person I knew who could make our uniform look cool. I still don't know how she did it.

The photo was taken in Town. Guernsey is so small it only has one town which is called Town (to avoid any confusion), but it's not much of a town, it's really just a High Street.* This High Street has the same shops it's always had, which includes a Boots the Chemist, Ogier's Shoe Shop, and Creasey's the (not-really) Department

---

* Note also the Village de Courtils, which has no shops but is called a Village on account of its postbox. Note also, the Priaulx family's house, which is called Vue du Lac, although there isn't even a pond, and Les Paradis, so-named on account of its two dwarf palm trees. Guernsey is so small people have to exaggerate.

Store. There was mass hysteria when Etam arrived. Kentucky Fried Chicken came but didn't stay.*

I know exactly why Nic and I are laughing in that photo. I'd just stolen a big bottle of Gordon's Gin off the shelves of Les Riches Food Stores. That's what's hidden under my blazer. I was feeling quite proud of myself before Nic snatched the camera from my pocket and demanded we take a picture.

But I shouldn't have worried since there's a good tradition of thieving on this island. After the evacuations in 1940 everyone stole from everyone else, and the police didn't know how to stop it so they didn't do anything at all. Then the Germans arrived and stole everything back for themselves. Then everyone decided to steal stuff from the Germans.

It is therefore no surprise that our local law enforcers still do nothing, preferring to sit on the Esplanade eating Mars bar toasties. And no wonder Les Riches just gives the booze away, lining it up at the till by the exit. It only took a minute for Nic to distract the cashier into frozen foods and I was reaching over and grabbing what I could. Talk about an electric buzz! Seconds later I was running down the street, my rubber soles slapping on the cobbles. I don't know why I thought I was being chased, but I only stopped when Nic was by my side.

"For a Lard Arse you can't half run," she laughed.

Then she grabbed my Instamatic out of my pocket.

"This is a historic moment—your first criminal act! Say: 'Screwdriver!'"

* "Kentucky Fried Cat!" ran the headline of the *Guernsey Evening Press*.

Perhaps I'm not that happy in the picture after all. I remember wondering if the photo was evidence. But there wasn't much time for thinking. Nic was running ahead as per always, and I was trying to catch up. A couple of cars beeped their horns as we zigzagged across the Esplanade. Nic flashed her knickers in reply. We skirted round the harbour and I looked down along the jetties to where our boat used to be moored.

Nic followed my eyes. "What you looking for?"

"Nothing," I replied, tripping over my feet.

We were halfway to the breakwater when Nic climbed over the railings and smiled back at me. I warned her she might fall. The wind was whipping up her hair so it looked like she was under water already.

"Hold my hand," she said, reaching out.

I took it and held on as tightly as I could, and she swung away and carried on walking, still on the wrong side of the railings with the water right under her feet. I used all my weight to keep her upright.

Nic was always doing things like that. Silly little things to catch everyone's eye. I don't know why she was such an attention seeker, but she hated me telling her off.

"What do you know? You've lived your whole life in your fucking bedroom," she'd say. "What's the point in playing it safe?!"

Maybe that's why people weren't surprised when she ended up dead. They also knew she'd been drinking. We both drank too much, but being with Nic was like being drunk already. It made everything blurry and therefore good.

I felt guilty after I stole that bottle of gin, but it's nothing compared to how I feel now. Nic's dead and I killed her, and who can I tell? Not Constable Priaulx, that's for sure. He came round here two days after they found Nic's lovely corpse. It was still blowing a gale outside and I was huddled close to the fire, hoping my polyester fleece would spontaneously combust. I was still in shock and I honestly thought he'd arrest me there and then, but he called it a Routine Enquiry. Of course, that's all anything ever is for Constable Piggy, since he's far more interested in eating than solving possible murders. He thinks that Guernsey is the safest place on the planet. He thinks Nic's death was an accident. I was all ready with my big confession. I was going to tell him the-truth-the-whole-truth-and-nothing-but-the-truth. But I never got the chance.

"We've heard the news and it's just awful," said Mum, ushering him into the sitting room. "The poor, poor parents, my heart goes out to them. Who would think that something like that could happen? I really don't know what to say, and there's probably not much we can tell you, since we only just found out ourselves."

Constable Priaulx rearranged his tummy folds and sank into our sofa.

"It's terrible, I know. I was wondering if Cathy had seen Nicolette on the Saturday."

"We both did." Mum wouldn't look at me. "Nicolette came here at about 5 P.M., she was keen for Cathy to go to the party over at Vicky's, but Cathy said she wasn't up to it. We've both been under the weather."

I sat there, waiting for the handcuffs, for Constable Priaulx to see the guilt all over my face.

"I've had a cold myself." He shook his head and sighed. "Who'd want to go out on such a wild night? There'll have to be an enquiry as to whether there should be barriers up around the cliff edge at the Batterie."

Mum shook her head.

"And nobody saw a thing?"

"No, no," sighed Constable Fathead. "After Dr. Senner closed the party down a group of them went to Bluebell Woods with what was left of the alcohol. Nicolette must've wandered off. It's unclear what she was up to."

I remembered how Nic ran at me from the shadows and tried to grab me round the neck.

Mum was saying, "I let Cathy walk on the cliffs all the time and I never think about the safety issues," and Constable Fattie ate his fourth biscuit and poured himself more tea.

"But it's different at night. You can't see in front of your own hand."

I wondered if they'd forgotten I was there.

"She could've jumped," I said quickly.

C.F.P. cleared his throat.

"What?"

"Surely not," Mum whispered. "*Not* Nicolette."

Constable Priaulx asked me for the names of the lads Nic hung around with but I pretended not to know. I stared at his Ormer* nose and wondered how many times it had been broken. He must've been called Lard Arse when he was a kid, or maybe something worse. I wanted to tell him that Nic had been a vicious bully. I wanted to show him the bruises on my arm. But then what?

Constable Priaulx may be Guernsey's Fattest Policeman™ but his brain is not pure lard. If I had told him that I'd been with Nic on the cliffs, he'd automatically assume the worst. I'd never get a chance to explain myself properly or tell my side of the story. It's not like I'm used to confessing to murder, and I was afraid I'd get muddled and mess it up. So instead I let Mum witter on.

"Cathy and Nicolette used to be a lot closer but they were very different. Just recently they'd drifted apart and I was relieved. I did find Nicolette a bit of a handful."

I stared at Mum but she'd lowered her eyes to the table in front of us. She was reaching for my photo album.

"That's not to say they weren't still friends. Just look at all these snaps."

Mum handed Constable Priaulx the album and he opened it casually, glancing at the pages.

"It looks like you two had some fun." He smiled.

Mum nodded. "They were inseparable."

I envy Mum her selective remembering. She's obviously deleted the unexplained cuts and bruises, the

* An Ormer is an intriguing mollusk-thingy unique to Guernsey's beaches. It tastes of nothing and is therefore pointless, but people still like to collect it, and can only do so at certain times of the year, which makes them call it a delicacy. (This is a good example of how Guernsey people have too much time on their hands.)

strange phone calls in the middle of the night, the missing homework, and the hours I spent locked in my bedroom.

"Of course, Nicolette was a wild one. I wonder if she wasn't already drunk when she called round here the other night. She was in such high spirits. But she was often like that. I find it so hard to tell."

Constable Priaulx nodded and said, "Oh, I know. Young people today!"

Contemptible Piggy left a few crumbs on a photo of Nic leaning over the railings on the Albert Pier.

"I expected better of little Vicky Senner." He sighed. "That party should never have got so out-of-hand."

"But Vicky's always been easily led," Mum added.

I glared at her. "That's not fair. You've always liked Vicky, and it wasn't her fault."

Mum pursed her lips. "I'm not trying to *blame* her."

"Well, it sounded like you were. Vicky didn't do anything. It's not like she told them all to go to the woods, is it?"

Constable Priaulx coughed up the last of the Viennese Whirls and pushed my album back towards me. Then he said he should be going and heaved himself up off the sofa. I must've been staring because he asked me what was wrong.

"Nothing," I said. "I was just remembering the last time you were here."

I hugged my little album and wanted to make him blush. We both knew it didn't seem so long since his last Routine Enquiry, when he'd come round to talk to Mum about Dad. They'd sat in the kitchen with the door closed, and I'd stayed in my bedroom. I suppose I should mention that a lot of people found Dad's death shocking and unexpected and other good words. But whatever their opinions, well, they were just opinions. It's wrong to gossip.

Constable Priaulx was still hovering in the doorway.

"You all right, sweetheart? Is there anything else?"

There was plenty as per always, but I shook my head and went back to the sitting room. I was staring at my photos when Mum came in and found me.

"*What* was all that about?"

I said I thought it was obvious.

"I don't mean about Nicolette. Why did you have to mention the last time he was here?"

I examined her more closely while sucking out the blood from a newly torn fingernail (a disgusting habit, I know).

"I didn't get a chance to say anything then, either."

Mum sat down beside me. "I was trying to help, and please don't do that."

I took my finger out of my mouth and stared at her silently, hoping I looked like a psychopath from one of her crime thrillers stacked up in the hall.

"I didn't mean to talk over you," she said. "Come on, I thought we were over all this. I thought this was a clean slate."

"It is," I replied. "It's fine."

She pulled herself up and headed for the door, then suddenly turned back around. "You'd tell me, though, if there was anything, wouldn't you?"

I smiled faintly (but still psychopathically).

"Of course."

Did she know I was lying? I can't be sure. It's funny how things have changed between us, and are changing still. Before Dad died I had her full attention and I was always pouring out my worries to her. I'd wait until it was officially bedtime and then insist we discuss the Meaning of Life or the End of the World, and she'd listen carefully and pretend to be bothered even if she wasn't. But after Dad died she stopped coming into my bedroom and I was afraid to ask her anything. I still had loads of questions, though, and they kept multiplying.

Why is it that the most important questions are the ones you ask too late?

Property of
Emile Philippe Rozier

The Editor
Guernsey Evening Press
23 South Esplanade
St. Peter Port
Guernsey
[undated draft]

Sir—

I am writing to you with regard to the article "The Unanswered Questions of the Nazi Occupation," which appeared in last week's Saturday supplement. As the owner and editor of The Patois Press, a publishing house dedicated to the documentation of recent island history, I have written to your newspaper innumerable times, calling for an inquiry into the "closed" Occupation files. I was surprised last week's article made no mention of my work. Perhaps your reporter was the victim of Selective Memory Loss, a condition widely noted in the wake of the Occupation?

Let me remind you, sir, my own attempts to compile a definitive and detailed history of the German Occupation have floundered due to pressure from the UK government and our local States deputies. I come under criticism from these same quarters because my books are apparently too reliant on informal and "idiosyncratic" sources, but given all the red tape what choice do I have? I readily accept that one person's point of view can differ wildly from another's, but this only makes it more vital that the official files relating to the Geheimfeld Polizei are made public.

The official line is that the release of "highly sensitive" archival materials would cause embarrassment to certain families in the Channel Islands, but surely it is time for the truth, the whole truth, and nothing but the truth to replace the gossip and hearsay. Once we know all the facts we will be better equipped to counter the many allegations that have been brought against us, and I am speaking from personal experience, as someone whose own family name has been dragged through the mud on more than one occasion. My father, Hubert Wilfred Rozier, was shot dead by the Germans whilst allegedly "trying to escape," my brother, Charles André Rozier, was then arrested and tortured by the Nazis at the notorious prison of Paradis before being deported to a German concentration camp, where he remained for the rest of the War.

As I wrestled to uncover the harrowing details of their story I grew to understand why so much had been repressed. Repression is a natural defence in the immediate aftermath of traumatic events, but it cannot become a way of life. It is time we faced up to our complicated history, and with that in mind I would like to launch my own campaign for an Unofficial Occupation Memorial. This would be a monument to be sited in a public place, and would list the names of all those who were imprisoned under German rule. For too long the bravery and courage of islanders has been overlooked, and I can remedy this situation with the help of your readers. It would go some way to counter the long silence from our States deputies.

But perhaps our States deputies are running scared. We all know that although many islanders suffered during the War, a great many more stood by and watched. Some had no choice but to cooperate with the Germans, others swapped sides willingly. In compiling a roll call of honour I might uncover this less honourable truth. Only a very foolish person would deny the existence of collaborators, informers, jerrybags, and black-market racketeers, whose behaviour during this dark period of island history was tantamount to treason. They might be few in number but they have left such a cloud of shame and guilt, and they still live among us, often coming from long-established Guernsey families and even occupying positions of authority.

On recently rereading back editions of this very paper I discovered that two-thirds of Guernsey's police force were accused of larceny on a grand scale in 1942, reputedly pillaging civilian food stores from 1939 onwards (see *GEP*, 2nd September 1942, "Bailiff Denounces Police Force").

It is no surprise that I have met with resistance to my research. Who says there was no resistance in Guernsey! Let us have an end to it. Guernsey is a tight-knit community and we wish to protect our own. Probing questions from outsiders deepen the already entrenched paranoia, but the absence of a proper inquiry only leaves a space for further distortions. We should do our own dirty washing. Just as the names of the brave should be noted, so should the names of the traitors be known. They should have been hunted down at the end of the War and tried in public, but they weren't. The guilt is thus passed from generation to generation.

Sincerely,
E. P. Rozier
Manager/Editor of The Patois Press
Sans Soucis
Village de Courtils,
St. Peter Port

P.S. I would be most grateful if any persons who recall friends, relatives, or neighbours who were arrested, or indeed if they themselves were subject to

14TH DECEMBER 1985, 5:12 P.M.

[BEDROOM, STILL WATCHING RAIN. SATURDAYS ON
GUERNSEY ARE SO VERY RIVETING.]

I used to think I was the only person Dad ever told off, but when I went through his old files I realised I was wrong. He was always writing letters, complaining about this or that. Nothing and no one escaped his scrutiny. He'd even been through our local telephone directory, making notes by people's names or occasionally giving them a star. I counted 245 Le Poidevoins, half of which were crossed out.

FYI: There wasn't much action on the Prevost pages, even though there were 247 listed. That's quite a lot, and it may explain why Therese acted so posh, if she felt she had a lot to compete with. I thought the fact that there were so many Prevosts was a sign of their success. After all, Therese had her own BMW and full-time cleaner who did all the dirty washing. By contrast us Roziers were dwindling year by year. We were dying out as per the panda bears. I mean, even Grandma (Dad's mother) had gone back to her maiden name after she was widowed. There was/is something wrong with being called Rozier.

But there are worse names you could have. Exhibit A: Donnie Golden. Yes, it's ridiculous, but then he was from England so what would you expect? I can't precisely remember when he moved into his swanky new home on the cliffs by Fort George. It was called the White House and he had a big party to show it off. Everyone from the Village* was invited, and even though Mum announced that she was far too busy, Nic and I persuaded her to go. We told her it was about time she went out and had some fun, and offered to come along for not-very-moral support. I think she felt flattered that we cared, and she even wore shoulder pads for it.

I should explain that for years Mum only ever wore long shirts and jeans and Nivea hand cream on her face, but when she took over the business she tried to smarten up. That's when she permed her hair and started wearing power suits. Mum and I never fought over clothes like Nic and Therese, but we did once go to Jersey on a shopping spree. We spent a hundred pounds in BHS. You can get a lot for your money in BHS, and I joked that I got a brand-new mum.

I should've been happy we were doing stuff together, and she looked almost presentable as we marched up to the electric gates of the White House. But she hadn't been to any parties since Dad had died, preferring to

* The Village=the Village de Courtils (see note on p. 45). The original occupants of these houses were turfed out by the Germans during the Occupation, and they became lodgings for lower-ranking German officers. Our house was the mess, which is appropriate if you look at my room. Donnie's house was built after the War, but the house that was there *before* was used by the German Field Police for orgies/interrogations/torture (apparently).

read P. D. James in the bath, and I could tell that she was nervous. I grabbed her hand and squeezed it tightly. I said we'd present A UNITED FRONT (meaning our neighbours were THE ENEMY), but as it turned out everyone was stupendously drunk and sliding down the wallpaper before nine o'clock, and they all agreed that it was good to see Mum out.

Of course, Guernsey people don't ever say what they mean. They are an excellent word called *fickle*. I know I said that when the Germans took over most people ignored them, but actually the population was split down the middle. Some people stuck their noses in the air and carried on like normal, while others made the Germans their friends and may have even helped them. Because of this, there was a lot of bad feeling, although it was never very clear who was good and who was bad because the collaborators covered their tracks, and even accused their neighbours and friends of the very things they'd done. So innocent people were arrested and suffered for no good reason. This is an example of how dangerous gossip can be.

Which means those people who said mean things vis-à-vis Mum's new career should know better. She shouldn't have to apologise to anyone. All she wanted was to make something out of what Dad left behind. If people thought she was quick off the mark, well, they didn't know all the facts and who were they to judge? Poor Mum. Perhaps I didn't support her enough. I didn't want to ask if she was A-OK because I didn't want to make her think she had to explain herself to me. When someone is arrested they're advised not to say anything because what they say might be taken down and used in evidence against them, and it was a bit like that between us.

Not that Mum was ever arrested.

I took lots of photos at Donnie's party, which annoyed and irritated everyone. There's one of the Senners with Nic making bunny ears behind them, and one of Mr. McCracken by the buffet. There's also a good one of Michael Priaulx and his parents. He's standing apart from them like he's embarrassed, which I suppose he should be. Michael hated having a policeman for a dad and was often called Piglet because of it. He obviously had a lot to prove, because he was always in trouble. It would've been interesting if he'd ever been arrested but, as I think I've already mentioned, our local law enforcers believe there is no crime on Guernsey. They therefore only stop people for speeding.

It's a fascinating fact that during the Occupation there was a very high number of speeding tickets issued. I think that's hilarious: the police didn't know how else to stand up to the Nazis, so they fined them for speeding. Of course, now it's the English who get fined, and Donnie got quite a few, but he didn't care because he was so *riche*. He had a nice face but I don't know how old it was, and he's almost impossible to recognise in my photos because he always looked different. I was impressed by his shiny skin and slick, black hair, and I thought it was amazing his teeth were so white.

"So you want to take my photo now, do you?" He

handed me a pitcher of punch. "You're a better subject, though, so much prettier."

He was the first person ever to call me pretty. Talk about giving candy to a baby (although in this case it was rum). I felt very proud of myself, especially since Nic was there and we'd coordinated our outfits perfectly. It was just after Valentine's Day and Donnie gave us each a rose from his garden, then we walked back into the kitchen, where Michael was helping himself to a beer from the fridge. He tried to open it using the door's hinge, and despite this failing spectacularly, I still thought he looked great.

Donnie asked him if he'd been sent any Valentines and he curled his lip seductively.

"Fucking stupid idea. What's the point in sending cards telling someone you like them and not bothering to sign your name?"

I blushed because I'd sent him one, as per always.

Nic pulled herself up onto a sideboard and kicked out her legs.

"Well, Cat's the one you've got to watch. She's got lots of admirers!"

As if on cue, in walked Mr. McCracken.

"Aha! John McCracken!" Donnie stretched out his hand. "So glad you came. Cathy's been trying to take my photo. Have you been giving her lessons? I see you out on the cliffs all the time. They are picture-perfect this time of year, don't you find?"

Donnie waved his glass towards his excellent sea view and almost bashed into Constable Priaulx.

"You're in a prime position," sniffed C.P., "but I'm not

sure I could ever live in a modern house like this. I suppose it's all you could get on the Open Market."*

Donnie told Constipated Piggy he preferred "all mod
cons" while quickly refilling his glass.

C.P. nodded and harrumphed back to the buffet.

"What's he got against the English?" laughed Donnie.

"Well," I said, "for starters you're a tax exile, so you're
basically just taking advantage. But more importantly, at
the beginning of the Second World War you abandoned
us and were entirely to blame for us being bombed and
then occupied by the Germans for five years."

Donnie pulled a face of what I would call mocky-
horror. "Oh, come on, the Occupation was a picnic.
Didn't everyone learn German?"

He winked at Mr. McCracken, who smiled and waved
his hands. "I'm staying out of this."

"Actually," said Nic, "half Cat's family were killed
by the Nazis so it's no laughing matter. She could show
you where the Germans buried the dead bodies of ex-
prisoners, too. It's pretty much at the bottom of your
garden."

Donnie froze. "What?"

I pinched Nic hard.

"Ow!"

Mr. McCracken shook his head.

"Ignore them. There are a lot of stories and it's mostly
built on gossip and hearsay. She's referring to an inci-

* There is no class system on Guernsey, only Open Market and Local
Market housing. Open Market houses are limited in number, very ex-
pensive, and deliberately ugly (so as to make the rich foreigners who buy
them suffer).

dent that was before my time, but I'm pretty sure it was a skeleton dating from the nineteenth century, and it was much further down the cliffs."

Nic gave me a nasty look, like I had somehow misled her, so I jumped in and explained how some of the poor people who'd been imprisoned on Alderney* had described watching Nazi guards herd fellow inmates off the cliffs. The men were often very weak and dying, so the Germans called it "suicide." They also shot some and claimed they were killed "trying to escape." I said it was highly likely that the same thing had happened in Guernsey.

I'd forgotten that Michael was still in the room, but suddenly he was standing right next to me.

"It's illegal to kill yourself on Guernsey." He raised an already-empty beer bottle. "But my dad couldn't even arrest a corpse. Ha-ha!"

Donnie was glaring hard at Michael (who scowled deliciously back). I pointed out that suicide was in fact the perfect murder since you couldn't catch the killer. Everyone was meant to marvel at my intelligence but didn't.

Donnie waved his hands nervously and asked if we had to pursue this most morbid of topics.

Nic jumped off the sideboard, flashing all of her thigh.

* Alderney is the island nobody likes to go to/talk about, because it was completely evacuated during the Occupation and the Germans built real-life concentration camps run by real-life SS officers. It was the only place in the Channel Islands that had SS officers, and these officers had been sent to Alderney as a punishment for being naughty somewhere else. So, in theory, everyone on Alderney was being punished (and it still feels like that now).

"Sir . . . I was going to ask . . . did you get a card?"

Mr. McCracken's eyes scrunched into raisins.

"What?"

"For Valentine's, sir! Don't tell me you didn't get one, a dish like you. I bet you get all the mums excited at our parents' evenings, and that's saying nothing about the pupils."

Before Mr. McCracken could answer Nic turned, cocking her head to one side.

"And what about you, Donnie, is there no Mrs. Golden locked in the basement?"

Donnie smiled his best TV smile and explained how he'd spent the last ten years nursing his mother, who'd only just died and was not locked anywhere.

"Between work and Mother I didn't have much fun these last few years. After she was gone I knew I needed a change. I've never settled anywhere in England for long and liked the idea of living on an island. Personally, I think it's good to be a little bit cut off from things."

Nic yawned. "Dead from the neck down, you mean."

Mr. McCracken ignored her and asked Donnie more about his work and Donnie gave a quick version of his life story, standing straight and keeping eye contact, so as to make a good impression. He knew some of his neighbours thought him suspect (and not just because he dyed his hair). Maybe that's why Michael liked him.

Michael Priaulx is a god, by the way. He was brilliant at football before his accident, and I'd often see his name in the sports pages of the *Press*. He's three years older than me but age is irrelevant. I'd watch him roar around Town on his motorbike and flick V signs at everyone and feel my heart beat faster. It didn't even matter when he started to wear eyeliner.

onnie said I didn't need makeup. That night he took me around his garden and talked more about his mother's slow and painful death, and how he'd brought her ashes to Guernsey and scattered them in his flower-beds, so they'd still be close. He asked me if I thought it was weird, and I assured him that it was, but that everyone had different ways of dealing with death. I then explained how Mum hadn't cried at all after Dad died, and how instead she'd acted like she was relieved.

"Well, it is a burden," Donnie sighed, "caring for some-one who's unwell."

I assured Donnie that Dad hadn't been unwell.

"Oh? Oh, I'm so sorry. I'm new here, remember."

I then explained how Dad had an accident when diving off the Moorings and had cut his hand quite deeply, and how the cut became infected. I said Dad hadn't noticed because he was completely focused on his (Un)Official Occupation Memorial, and unfortunately the infection spread quicker than malicious island gos-sip. It was the infection that most probably caused the heart attack. I also swore that it was true about the bod-ies buried on the cliffs and told him to be careful in his garden. Donnie just laughed and said Michael did all the gardening.

So I chatted more about Mum, and how she'd put all her energies into saving the family business, and how it was good for her to be busy and not have time to think.

Donnie looking genuinely disturbed, which I enjoyed. I'm such a champion storyteller! He listened carefully as I wittered on about how Dad sacrificed his health for the sake of the truth and how Mum just did as he said, and how I never realised because I was at school.

I tried to remember all the facts just like Mum told me and I think I gave an impressive performance. It's weird how I can learn things off by heart and recite them like a parrot but still not understand them. Dad didn't make it to my last prize giving on account of him dying and I did start to wonder why I'd worked so hard. There's no escaping death, not for any of us. With Nic it was over in a flash but at least when she was falling she didn't know that she was dying. Dad maybe did know, and Mum did, too.

My conversation with Donnie went on for hours and I felt very special to have all his attention. He told me he loved the company of young people and that if I ever wanted to talk I could come and find him. I said that'd be great since Mum didn't understand me and I wasn't sure I could trust her. That was the first time I'd said it out loud, to anyone.

And then she was tapping me on the shoulder.

"We should be getting home. Can you go and fetch Nicolette?"

I felt so ashamed and ran back into the house as quick as I could, grabbed Nic, and dragged her outside. I was thinking I'd find Mum looking cross and apologising to Donnie on my behalf. But instead she was chatting to him about the joys of the Guille-Aillez Library. We said our good-byes and drove Nic back to Les Paradis and

I wanted to tell Mum I was sorry and that I honestly didn't mean it. But she never said anything, so neither did I.

I suppose we were both trying to hide what we were feeling inside, although I don't know for sure if Mum was feeling anything. She was always as cool as a cucumber, never complaining about how hard she had to work, or her useless daughter. Perhaps nothing was as grim as the thrillers she read, and they helped her cope.

And perhaps that explains what happened between me and Nic, sorry, Nic and I.

I did what I did because, like Mum, I knew I could hide it.

And, like Mum, I knew I'd get away with it, too.

"The testimony of
C. A. Rozier"

*[Edits from transcript compiled and
corrected by E. P. Rozier]*

There is plenty our mother won't talk about, Emile.
According to La Duchesse it does us all no good,
this dredging up of what's been said and done. She
says if it is an eye for an eye and a tooth for a
tooth, then we shall all be blind with bleeding
gums. She has a point, truly I see it well, but how
can she forgive me?

She is a rare one, a rare and special case. You
know what she did in the days before the Germans
came? She put the whole of our house in order like
never before. She cleaned the place from top to
bottom and back again, she beat the carpets and
darned our socks. Everything was washed and swept,
scrubbed and pressed, and then she curled her hair.

"We are going to show these Jerries that we are
clean-living and respectable people," she said,

holding her chin up high. "I'll not let standards slip because of this."

She was a force to be reckoned with, that one!

She still wanted me out the way, but the only boats bound for England now were to be loaded with tomatoes. That's right, when we heard that our crops could be shipped out again we took it as a good sign. Of course, others weren't so sure. I remember it was 28th June, a Friday, and I'd come with Pop into Town to hear the Bailiff give another address. La Duchesse was at home with you, and I felt bad that she was missing the excitement: the High Street and Smith Street were packed solid with bodies and everyone was talking with their hands, the way only Guernsey folk can. The Bailiff was big with his "no need to panic" but the questions kept on coming.

"The English sent us troops and arms, and then they took them back, and now they're saying what? That we're too small to matter?"

"But they still want our tomato crops. What does it mean?"

That very evening folk were gathering at the harbour to watch the tomato baskets get loaded up onto boats.

"It is poltroonery," Ray said. "Whitehall should be sending guns. We fought for the British before, so surely they owe us something."

"There's no point in getting angry," someone replied. "They have bigger problems than this little island."

"And they might be on their way now," I piped up.
"A commando force to help us."

I thought I was being wise beyond my years and
you know, Emile, there were commando raids before
too long so it's not like I was wrong. Even so, they
laughed me down.

"Quai bavin!" Ray barked. "Are you the expert?
Maybe you should be up there with the Bailiff. Come
on everyone, let's have another tall tale from our
champion storyteller!"

A few people were turning their heads and I
shrank into my jacket, hoping the ground would
swallow me up.

"But—" I started.

"But nothing. Do me a favour and keep your big
mouth shut. At least until you're shaving."

There was a murmur of laughter, and the talking continued right over my head. Why did everyone
treat me like a kid? Ray was looking down his snout
at me, his hazel eyes twinkling. It made me so angry I had to do something.

And I did.

"Ow!"

Ha-ha! I'd kicked Ray hard, square on the shin.
Not big or clever, I know, but I didn't half feel
better as I burst through the crowds.

"Here, you!" I heard him shout.

Even if I was just a kid I mattered enough for
old Ray to give chase. But I hadn't done much damage since he was hot on my heels and closing in.
I didn't stand a chance against those long legs.

Still, you should've seen me, Emile, going Hell for leather down the Esplanade, sending other folk flying, and just as I reckoned I was done for a great big shadow swooped over. I threw my hands up and spun around, fists at the ready. Ray had lunged at me and was grappling me down, and I fell on my back, hitting the ground hard with a thud. That's when I saw it high above me. The swastika on a German plane, and a gunner standing at its open door, firing a machine gun.

"Rat-tat-tat," it went, like a child running a twig along some railings. "Rat-tat-tat!"

Next thing I knew Ray was on the pavement, too. I heard him cursing so I knew he was alive. We had both rolled onto our stomachs. Then came a deafening bang. Then another. I thought we must've been killed or bombed, but I didn't understand why I was still breathing. There was this buzzing in my brain and my ears felt like they was bleeding. I squeezed my eyes shut, pressing my face into the paving stones. Ray had turned around and was against the granite harbour wall.

Neither of us had counted on a fleet of German bombers interrupting our scuffle, and we weren't the only ones caught unawares. *Mais nen-nin.* The harbour was their target. They circled maybe three times in all. How many minutes I couldn't tell you. *Voomf! Bang! Crack!* I swear the whole island shuddered but I clung tight to it still. I smelled the smoke, I heard sirens wailing. Then I felt Ray tug at my collar.

We helped each other up, taking a minute to get our balance. It was like my ears were blocked but I could see the fear in Ray's eyes. So he's human after all, I thought. Then I turned my head and saw the blaze on White Rock. *Hé bian*, Emile, it was a terrible thing. People have forgotten about a lot of things the Germans did, but they've never forgotten White Rock. Nothing much had ever happened on our little island until that day. Lots of places got hit and lots of people, too. The tobacco factory near the bus terminal was up in flames, but it was the docks that got it the worst. They'd flattened the tomato trucks that had lined up along the Weighbridge and machine-gunned their petrol tanks so everything was in flames. There were thirty dead, if I'm right, but you should check that.*

Without saying a word to each other Ray and I headed straight for the smoke and the flames. Of course, everyone else was running in the opposite direction, crying out in shock and pain. I remember a woman clinging to an older man who was holding a bloody handkerchief to his eyes. Lots of people were cut from broken glass or had been peppered with shrapnel, and an ambulance had been blown to bits. The heat and the smell is what I re-

* E.P.R. notes thirty-four dead and sixty-seven injured, as in fact was later reported.

member the most, and the blood on the road. Well, I
thought it was blood but *p'têt* it was toms. Dozens
of crates were smashed open. The boats were on fire
as well. What a scene of dereliction! One man had
had his toes blown off and was staring down at his
feet with this puddle of red spreading outward. I
went towards him, then I realised Ray had left my
side and was heading down the harbour steps.

I would have followed—I swear it on my life—but
there was a clammy hand laid on my arm.

"How did you get here?" I'd never seen Pop so
wild-eyed and anxious. "Come. We must get home."

I thought I hadn't heard him right, but he told
me again that we had to get home.

"The bombers will come back."

"Wait." I looked about. "Shouldn't we help?"

His bony grip tightened. "No! There are police
and wardens for that. What about La Duchesse and
Emile?"

His voice was near to breaking. He tugged at his
shirt collar, choking from the fumes.

A policeman appeared at my side. "Get the old
man home . . . it's not safe," he told me.

I nodded, looking back at Pop. He was coughing
and there were tears in his eyes as he turned his
head away from me. He bent over, and I checked his
back for shrapnel, wondering if he'd been hurt.

"Pop," I said. "Are you all right?"

He shook his head and wouldn't answer me. Then
I looked again at the flames, the bodies, the dying and injured. I realised this was why he wept.

I gently took his elbow, steering him towards the
bus shelter.

"We'll go," I said.

He'd covered his face with a handkerchief.

"La Duchesse," he wheezed. "Don't tell her what
you've seen."

And to this day, Emile, I don't know if he meant
that I shouldn't tell of the men and women burned
alive, or of our father weeping like a child.

But either way I never did tell. How could I tell
our mother that?

15TH DECEMBER 1985, 7:32 A.M.

[SITTING ROOM, WATCHING BREAKFAST TV]

Of course Mum wouldn't like me talking about her, so it's better if I talk about Therese. Nic said Therese only cared about what men thought of her, but as far as I could tell Nic was just the same. *I* thought Therese Prevost was the Perfect Mother as per the Fairy Liquid commercials. Nic called her pathetic and sad, but I'm guessing she was mostly lonely. Mr. Prevost is the manager of Lloyds Bank so he was always working/entertaining clients with or at his golf clubs, leaving Therese to comfort shop at Little Red in Smith Street—Guernsey's most-expensive-ever shop. But half the clothes Therese bought she never even wore. They were hidden away in the spare room, which is where Nic always found them. I remember one Sunday afternoon I was gluing together my toenails with Nic dancing about in a slinky blue jersey dress.

"How old do you reckon I look?"

She pulled up her hair like she was modelling for a magazine. I pretended to take her picture and told her she looked old enough for anything, which was worrying but also true.

She leaned back against the window ledge, stuck out her little boobs, and stretched her swanlike neck. I thought this new pose was for my benefit until I turned to see Therese behind me, wincing microscopically.

"Don't you look glamorous! But take it off now. You'll stretch it out of shape."

Nic didn't budge. "I thought I'd wear it today. It'll look wicked with my denim jacket."

"No, darling, it's too old for you."

Nic had various ways of tormenting her mother. This time she pulled herself upright and stared hard at her reflection in the floor-to-ceiling mirror. Then she started fiddling with her hair. Therese repeated her request and Nic continued fiddling. (She could stare at herself for hours.) I sat in between them and tried not to breathe. Nic muttered something about someone else not dressing their age. I watched Rimmel Peachy Cream 90-Second Nail Varnish drip onto the arctic-white shag-pile.

"I said take it off."

"Why should I? I need some new clothes and you're always buying stuff you never wear—or at least, I never *see* you wear. Who's it all for? Who do you need to impress?"

"That's not true, I—"

But before Therese could finish her sentence Nic was out on the landing and running downstairs.

"Let me show Dad."

I jumped up to follow them but had to balance on my heels on account of the Peachy Cream Peril. I was therefore quite slow. All I saw was Therese at the bottom of the stairs, still clutching the banisters, with her knuckles turning white. She told Nic to stop making a scene just as I heard Mr. Prevost do a wolf whistle. I'm not sure if it's right for a father to wolf-whistle his daughter, but Mr. Prevost had recently drained the bar at the Royal Hotel.

He was standing in what I called the sitting room but they called the lounge, holding a glass of brandy, and he grinned when he saw me.

"Look at my two gorgeous women, am I not the luckiest man alive?"

Therese was standing next to Nicolette, staring down at her naked legs.

"Darling, you don't have to try so hard."

"What, like *you*, you mean?"

I can't be sure what happened next because I was worrying about my toenails, but I think Mr. P. told Therese not to fuss. Then he reached into his wallet and suggested that Nic and I go for a walk so he could spend Quality Time with his beautiful wife. Mr. Prevost was always wanting sex in the middle of the day because Therese was too tired at bedtime. According to Nic they were both having affairs, which must've been exhausting.

"It's no big deal," she said. "There's nothing else to do on this pissy little island."

Funnily enough, Dad had said something similar in a much more elegant way.

Three years back there'd been this big fight on White Rock one Sunday. It was between two rival gangs of boys from the Grammar School. The *Press* had printed a long article about the Vacuum of Authority and Dad had written a response, which they'd even-for-once published. Dad had said that the restlessness and frustration felt by young people on the Island was totally understandable, since it was an echo of what happened during the Occupation, when so many children were evacuated from the Island never to return, and those that stayed found it difficult to relate to their parents' passivity in the face of the enemy. Dad claimed that the Occupation had left A GAPING WOUND between one generation and the next. A lot of people disagreed and there were more letters saying so, but Dad was right as per always.

It's why we went to Pleinmont.

Pleinmont was important to the Germans because it's at the rocky southwestern tip of the island, which is why they built bunkers and gun placements and a watchtower* thingy that's as ugly as most Modern Art. For a while this was where all Guernsey's Dispossessed Youth™ did their dispossessing.

We used to meet in the car park every Sunday and wander up to the watchtower, which is over 50 foot high. It has rubble-filled corridors and dark narrow stairs up to the first floor, but after that there's just a rusty ladder and a strong smell of pee. The nearby bunker is for

---

* With its smelly and dark bunkers and blocked-up tunnels, it's probably the second-worst tourist attraction on the island, with the German Underground Hospital in St. Andrews coming first (because there they actually charge you an entrance fee).

glue sniffers and used condoms. It doesn't sound very glamorous and believe me it wasn't. The only thing that made it interesting was the graffiti, from which I learned some intriguing new words.

There's no point in mentioning names, but Jason Guille and Pete Mauger are important to this story— Jason is in the Sixth Form at the Grammar and has half a finger missing, Pete's his best friend and is missing his whole brain. There's also Marc Le Page and J-P, although they matter less. Pagey now works in a bank and wears leather ties, J-P is a stick insect with no obvious eyebrows. They don't talk to me anymore and I can't pretend to care. They probably still light their own farts and find it funny.

Nic and I would sit in the car park and watch them do wheel spins on their motorbikes or handbrake turns in their cars. It's funny, she had no interest in engines or electrics, but when it came to boys she was a brilliant mechanic. She knew just what knobs to twiddle.

She liked Pete Mauger the most at first. His dad worked in the off-licence on the Esplanade, which meant his car boot was often full of cigarettes and cut-price booze.* Nic preferred Silk Cut Purple because she could also steal them from Therese. Therese only smoked three-a-day-on-the-patio, but Nic could smoke a whole packet in an hour. Pete said it was like kissing an ashtray but obviously didn't mind. Nic would smile and pull herself close to him and blow smoke right into his mouth. She

* Guernsey does not have any Value Added Tax, which means you get 15% more alcohol for your money. This also means most people have a drink problem.

could be quite slutty like that. I'm sure that makes me sound spiteful and jealous, but I never tried to compete with Nic, I just sat in the corner and drank/talked a lot. Maybe it was because of the drinking that we first fell out. Or maybe it was because of tomatoes.

It was after five in the afternoon and as per usual we'd crammed into Jason's car to listen to the charts. Nic was in the front on Pete's lap and I was in the back by the only window that worked. I was trying to concentrate on the music but I wished it was just me with Nic, alone together. We used to sing along to all our favorite songs. I was also annoyed with Pagey, who kept moaning about how his dad made him work in his greenhouses* after school. I know sons are meant to hate their fathers as per the Ancient Greeks, but I told Pagey to show some respect. I then explained to him (and everyone else) how the tomato didn't arrive in Guernsey until 1834, and that it was initially grown as a decorative plant because people thought it was poisonous. How funny, then, that it became our major export and a kind of national emblem. And how tragic when, on 28th June 1940, German bombers destroyed an entire crop that was being loaded onto the boats for Southampton. What made it worse was they'd done so by mistake, because the stupid British government had never told them that they'd demilitarised the islands, and the Ger-

* Guernsey is made up of granite and greenhouses, and in these greenhouses grow mostly tomatoes. In 1940 two-thirds of Guernsey's population were growers. There is even a Guernsey Tomato Museum. (Not that I'd suggest you visit it.)

mans had mistaken tomato trucks for boxes of ammunition.

I told Pagey we should therefore hate the British and
not our parents, but he didn't agree.

"That's the most bloody stupid story I've ever heard,"
he told me.

"It's not a story," I replied, "it's *History*."

I saw Nic roll her eyes in the mirror. "We aren't here
for a fucking lecture, Cat."

I was a bit offended and opened the car door. "Anyone
fancy a walk?"

Nic laughed. "It's raining."

(I hadn't noticed.)

Pagey stuck out his caveman chin.

"For fuck's sake shut the door, you're getting me wet."

I stood there, feeling Stupid. I had wanted Nic to
make a choice but in fact she already had. Even if I was
her best friend, boys mattered more. Back then I didn't
especially like boys. They were far too rowdy/interested
in their own bodies. Of course, it was Nic who made
them rowdy/interested in their own bodies. I suppose
that means I saw them as a threat, but I never wanted
to grope Nic or stick my tongue in her ear. I just wanted
her to myself.

Instead of getting back in the car I decided I'd rather
be alone, so I grabbed my bag and a half bottle of Unlabelled Sinister Import and walked off up the slope towards the watchtower. I don't think I stormed off (like
Nic later said) because it was a steep hill and I had to
walk slowly.

Although the tower was dark and smelly, I liked the sound of the wind whistling through the narrow windows. I could walk around and watch the rain and create my very own music video, and I was having a lot of fun before I noticed Michael Priaulx leaning against the entranceway. That was more than embarrassing. I know I've just said I don't like boys but Michael is different, and you'll see what I mean soon enough. He was wearing his usual black leather jacket that skimmed his waist and had padded bits at the shoulder and elbow, and his face and hair were glistening from the rain. His flames-motif crash helmet was tucked under his arm, and a shadow fell across his face as he walked inside. Some people think his head is too big for his shoulders, and that he's slightly cross-eyed, but I swear he looks like Marlon Brando, even though I didn't know who that was at the time. I tried to act all casual but my heart was doing bunny hops. I assumed that was because of the music video choreography (which, of course, I'd stopped).

Michael didn't come close, but turned and squatted down, leaning his back against the tower wall. Then he reached inside his jacket and pulled out a homemade cigarette.

"It's pissing down. Hope I'm not interrupting."

I realised his cigarette was not actually a cigarette as he lit it and blew smoke out towards me.

"Those your mates down there?"

I nodded and realised I should try to say something.

I couldn't.

Michael reached into his other jacket pocket and pulled out a can of deodorant. I was quite excited because I'd heard how people had hallucinatory visions after inhaling deodorant (or Tipp-Ex). I was disappointed when I realised it was spray paint. Michael stood up and scanned the wall behind him. There was a large-ish bright red swastika bang-slap in the middle. He shook the can and wrote, "The Nazis Won." Only once he'd finished did he turn back to me.

"Your dad said the swastika was an ancient Buddhist symbol before the Nazis used it. It meant being at one with the earth. I gatecrashed one of his Occupation Society tours. Fascinating, it was. He knew every little detail, which was kind of weird, don't you think?"

I smiled encouragingly but also silently.

Michael held my gaze for a few seconds, then walked to the other side of the tower. He kept glancing out through the tiny windows at the rain, like he was willing it to stop. It made me think of the flea-bitten tiger trapped in its tiny cage at the Guernsey Zoo.

"If you want," I said, "I can lend you some of Dad's books. He knew everything about the German Occupation. It's hard to imagine now what it was like for the islanders back then, to be cut off from the outside world and to have no weapons or way of fighting back."

Michael smiled. "There's always a way of fighting back."

He'd stopped in front of the ladder that was bolted to the tower wall. I walked over to stand beside him and we were so close I could smell the leather of his jacket. Well, I think it was leather.

He was looking up. "You know what you see when you climb up there? *Everything.*"

I nodded and said things like "Wow" and "Amazing."

Michael sighed. "No it's not. It's fucking depressing."

"Oh"—I tried to smile—"so I'm not missing anything? What a relief, because I'd be way too scared to ever climb up there. I'd be afraid of falling."

Michael turned and narrowed his eyes enticingly. "Come on, I'll show you."

It was like he hadn't been listening! He jammed the can of paint back into his jacket and started up the ladder. Of course I went straight after him. We climbed and climbed. The ladder was so rusty it scratched my hands. I was definitely scared but I didn't look down or up, I just followed Michael as quickly as I could and thought about how relieved I'd be to get to the top.

I don't know how long it took but when I reached the ledge where the ladder stopped I was flushed. Michael turned to face me and there we were—stranded on this narrow ridge of cement that runs all around the tower. It felt very precarious.

"Be careful." He pushed me back against the wall. I tried to look as appealing as possible, like he could kiss me if he wanted to.

"Go on. Turn around."

I slowly turned and looked out of one of the square windows. It was terrifying to be so high up and to see so far, and I tried to grab Michael's arm for comfort, but he was busy relighting his large-ish not-a-cigarette. After a minute he offered it to me, glancing out of the window.

"So there you have it. That's all there is."

I couldn't focus too well but I stared down at the craggy slopes of Pleinmont. It didn't feel as vast or impressive as I thought it would, and there was a bank of fog rolling in off the empty sea. I suddenly understood what Michael had meant. Everything was too small. I looked back at him and tried to pout like Nic, but it was difficult because I'd singed my lips on one of Jason's B&H. Michael's smoke blew in my face and I vaguely wanted to kiss it.

"You know"—Michael gazed out at the view—"when you get up high like this you're not really afraid of falling—you're more afraid of wanting to jump. There's a pull."

I asked if he meant gravity, which we'd learned about in Second Form, but he shook his head.

"Nah, this is different. It's psychological, not physical, more the brain than the body. There's this town in Europe, it has even less taxes than here,* and it's built in a valley, and there's this road around it with lots of bridges, and people are always jumping off the bridges and killing themselves."

I told Michael how Dad had always liked to dive off the top steps of the Moorings, even though it was dangerous. Michael said diving was a lot like falling, and that falling was like being free.

"I want some of that, me. I'm going to travel the world."

"To anywhere in particular?" I asked.

---

* I now know Michael was talking about the town of Luxembourg, which is in the country of Luxembourg. Luxembourg is a bit like Guernsey, because it is also small and boring, has no taxes, and is full of rich people. You might argue that this is a good recipe for suicide.

He shrugged. "Maybe Australia. Mum's got a brother there she's not seen for years."

I wanted to tell him I'd be going there, too, one day, but before I could he'd turned and walked casually over to the other side of the tower. (He didn't hold on to the wall or anything!)

I'd drunk quite a lot earlier but that little walk sobered me up no end. When I caught up with him by the window facing the car park he put an arm around me, which made it all worthwhile. Then I realised he was trying to help me out of it. I looked at him like he was nuts.

"It's easy," he said. "Turn around and push your head out and then sit on the ledge like this." He demonstrated the manoeuvre.

"Not a chance," I told his thigh.

I'm glad to say he slid back in.

I stared down to the car park, where Jason's and Pete's cars were parked side-by-side. I cupped my hands around my mouth and called Nic's name, to see if she could hear me.

"You want to get her attention?" Michael bent away from me and rummaged in his jacket. "I know a way."

He'd pulled out another can of what I thought was spray paint, only this one had something sticking out of it. He flicked his cigarette lighter and I saw a little flame.

"And here's one I made earlier." He held it up to show me.

Before I could say anything he'd stuck his head out of

the window and lobbed it through the air. It flew in an arc and went bouncing off some rocks down below, and exploded with a crack and smoke. I looked at Michael, he was laughing, then he shouted, "You fucking loser!" so loudly I was scared. Jason had got out of his car and was shouting back. Michael nodded to me like I should scream, too. That's when I noticed his T-shirt: it was black with white letters that read "NEW ORDER." Most people think this is the name of a pop group, but as far as I know Hitler only liked opera. Anyway, in that moment, for whatever reason, I took those two little words as a sign to do exactly what Michael said. I screamed and swore my head off.

Then Michael took my bottle of Unlabelled Sinister Import and threw it out the window as well. It smashed on some rocks into lots of little pieces. I felt dizzy and ducked back inside. Then I heard car engines start.

"That's shown them, eh?"

I looked across at Michael and his eyes glittered darkly.

"What were we trying to show them?"

He frowned like he was irritated by my (perfectly reasonable) question. "Does it fucking matter?"

I was sitting down but I still felt like I was falling. I thought about Nic and Pete and Pagey and Jason.

I tried to smile. "The thing is, they're my friends."

Michael relit his cigarette and handed it to me. I took a long drag and held the smoke in my mouth. Seconds passed. I remembered to breathe. I tried again. My head felt hot.

"The testimony of
C. A. Rozier"

*[Edits from transcript compiled and
corrected by E. P. Rozier]*

Hé bian, Emile, we live so close on this little
island, friends and enemies live side by side. The
English must wonder how we do it. They have all
that open space whereas we are pocket-sized. So why
did the Germans even want us, eh? Why couldn't they
just bomb us and leave be? That would've been so
much the better. But instead they had to come and
live among us, they came and took our homes, they
got right under our skin, as close to us as our
own flesh and blood, so close we couldn't breathe.

Reckon all of us remember when and where we got
our first glimpse of the jodhpurs and the jackboot, and you know what shook me most? His hand-
some face. Underneath that queer-shaped helmet,
glittering in the sun, he had a fine chiselled chin

and greenish eyes. They was a colour I'd not seen before or since.

"Hello," he said, with a whisper of a smile. Then, "What are you doing here?" like I was the trespasser!

Cor là, that made my little head spin, all right, but then I was a good few feet above him and I've never had much head for heights. I was perched on that old stone wall at the back of the Royal Hotel, doing my own reconnaissance. I'd heard from our neighbour, Blanche Gaudion (that font of island gossip) that the Germans had arrived and were meeting with our local States deputies. That's when I saw the swastika for myself—they'd had one whipped up by Creasey's and paid for in full. I sat there for hours, keeping lookout, expecting gunshots and more bloodshed or drama, and to tell the truth I was disappointed. The only noise came from the planes high up in the sky. Over the next few days we saw hundreds of Junkers, Dorniers, Heinkels, and Messerschmitts landing at the airport. I was no mechanic, but I made it my business to learn the differences between them.

Whoever said Hitler wasn't planning an invasion is a fool. Just look at the guns, planes, and troops that poured onto this tiny island. The War Office reckoned we were of "no significance," but the Germans didn't agree. They covered the island in concrete soon enough, and anyone who has seen that very special species of vandalism blighting our beautiful coast cannot deny it. Look what they did at Pleinmont!* The Germans made this little rock their own and the Bailiff shook their hands and promised we'd offer no resistance. That's not what you'd expect from such a stubborn and independent people, is it? Of course, you could say that we had no guns to fight back, but we could have made our own bombs, or booby-trapped our homes.

Still, better to live a martyr than die as one. You know who told me that? That German with greenish eyes. His name was Unteroffizier Anton Vern,† and the next time I saw him he was standing in our parlour. He was tall and thin, but very dignified, not at all what I'd expected from my comic books. He called our father "Sir."

"You have nothing to fear as long as you do what we ask," he said. "We are required to print notices informing the population of the new military occupation of the island. The Bailiff and Attorney General have agreed to this new order. You are or-

---

* Aka Batterie Generaloberst Dollman. This covers a large area of cliff-top land and includes an impressive Naval Direction and Range Finding Tower with adjacent two-storey bunker. Nearby ammunition bunkers and personnel shelters were buried in 1948 during the island-wide tidy-up, as was a radar installation and radio room. All gun sites removed and rubble dumped over the cliff. (Sufficient evidence that Hitler could have been planning a major offensive from these islands?)

† Aka Anton August Vern: sent to the Russian Front January 1943. Later interned in a POW camp near Nantes. Now believed to be living in Vienna. E.P.R. to write again.

dered to assist us and I hope you can see it is in everyone's best interests."

We listened carefully as Vern moved about the room, light as air, making little gestures.

"We are not pointing a gun to anyone's head. We are all merely following orders. Yes?"

Pop slowly nodded.

"Good. We have control of the newspapers, but we cannot presume everyone will read them, therefore we shall display notices in prominent public places. I have yet to identify these places." He turned back and smiled at me. "I find your small and winding roads more than a little confusing, perhaps I need a guide?"

I was about to tell him to go to Hell when Pop spoke in my place, and I don't know what it was he said since to my shame it was in German. Maybe two or three sentences then passed between them, and I couldn't believe my ears. I later learned that Pop was explaining to Vern how he'd learned the basics as a prisoner of war. Of course, he was trying to unsettle this young sap and put him in his place, but I was wound up so tight, like the coil of a spring, so I didn't care a tuppence for Pop's motives. To hear my own father speak that foul language was more than I could stand for. I was flushed and well near choking with anger.

"Why should we take orders off of you?" I asked. "In a few months you'll be out!"

I felt a sharp dig in my ribs, courtesy of La Duchesse. "*Kique tu fais?*" she hissed. "*Tais ta goule. T es têtu.*"

I glowered as Vern blinked in confusion.

"Excuse me, madam?"

La Duchesse pulled herself up. "It is our local patois. I was calling my son here a blockhead. I presume I am still allowed to discipline my own son?"

Vern seemed amused. "It would be better you did so than I. But this patois you were speaking sounds quite French."

La Duchesse glowered back at him. "We have Norman blood in our veins, and it was the Normans who beat the English in 1066, as you should well know."

"Aha!" Vern's slight smile broadened. "Well, I understand a little French, so now we have several languages in common."

Languages in common! I looked from my parents back to this interloper, and couldn't for the life of me decide which was worse. It was beyond me. What could we share with this man? He was a greenfly, a slug, a filthy Hun. Is this who I'd be taking orders from now? Not that I was any good at taking orders before! And them Germans did love to tell us what to do. *Au yous*, Emile, all too soon it was "verboten" this and "verboten" that. Vern had us churning out red and black Bekanntmachungen, making curfews, banning meetings and dances, demanding we surrender our cars and our boats. They forbade the buying and selling of liquor and fuel, they closed down shops, they even banned the boy scouts. *Hé bian!* We heard that Hitler wanted to bring a "New Order" to Europe, well, here we was getting a "new order" every day.

And the fact that we had to work for them, to have their sickly green uniforms always in our sights. It was too, too terrible! I made plenty of noise about it, but La Duchesse told me to pull myself together. She said that if we didn't do what Jerry asked then someone else would.

"We'll lose the business and be out on the streets. Do you know what it's like to go hungry? I do, and I won't go through that again. We have to make do."

She was right, of course, but I didn't want to hear it. I watched planes take off from the airport, on their way to blitz London. Nobody fought back. Unless you call hiding pigs or pulling down the road signs good enough resistance. *Au yous,* plenty of folk would like to take the credit for pulling down the road signs but I reckon more people did it than there were ever road signs! These were dark days. I hated the Hun for many things but what I hated most was what they did to our parents. Young and old stood divided, and that was a rift that never healed.

"It isn't black and white no more," said Hubert. "The Germans are in charge and we don't know how long for. We none of us know what will happen next."

We don't know what will happen next! Was it a
game of Nuts in May where we could change sides as
we pleased?

"You cannot be serious," I told him. "You cannot
believe the Germans will win."

And of course he couldn't answer me because in
truth they already had.

15TH DECEMBER 1985, 1:34 P.M.

[FERMAIN, SITTING ON BENCH,
TRYING TO LOOK INTELLECTUAL]

was in the watchtower for ages with Michael, but I don't know what we talked about. I only remember three little words going round and round in my head. "The Nazis Won." Very romantic, it was.

I suppose I'd smoked a lot by then, which made it hard to climb down. Somehow I managed it, but by the time I got outside my head was spinning. No wonder I fell flat on my face and decided to stay there. The rain had stopped so Michael propped me on some rocks with my head between my knees. I think I stayed like that for quite a long time, which is obviously embarrassing. But it was more embarrassing that Mr. McCracken found me.

Yes. I know. This is another illustration of how small Guernsey is.

I never understood why Mr. McCracken was driving into the Pleinmont car park at the precise moment that I was hugging it. I certainly didn't have him down as a

Sunday Afternoon Driver,* but maybe he was lost in the fog.

I don't remember seeing him drive in, but I do remember his headlights were on. Then I heard his voice.

"What are you doing here?"

For some reason Michael got the giggles and said we'd been repelling enemy invaders.

I sat up and assured Mr. Mac that I was honestly A-OK.

Mr. Mac looked from me back to Michael.

"Has she been drinking? You know she's underage."

"Oooo! Are you a policeman?" Michael wiggled his fingers. "Like I'm scared."

Mr. McC told Michael not to be such a bloody idiot, but I couldn't hear most of it because my ears were ringing, and all I knew for sure was that my bum was getting cold. Michael had lent me his 100% acrylic Burton jumper (I still have it) but my legs had scary purple goose bumps. I stood up (a bit too quickly).

The next thing I knew I was in the McMobile, being bombarded with awful hippy music.

"Where are we going?" I asked. "You can't take me home."

Mr. Mac sighed. "Well, I can't leave you *there*. What were you doing anyway?"

* There are two types of Sunday Afternoon Drivers on Guernsey. The first are the Dispossessed Youth (see earlier), and the second are OAPs (senior citizens). They are most often found at Cobo or Vazon, sitting in their cars, staring at the low concrete wall (built by the Germans, of course). They do not seem to notice this wall, but this might be because they are half-blind/mad as per Grandma and therefore should not drive at all.

So I talked about my longstanding fascination with the Nazi German fortifications and how the guns the Germans had used at Pleinmont were manufactured by Skoda, which was the same make as his car, and wasn't that remarkable? I then admitted that the view from the top of the tower was quite disappointing, and therefore not strategic.

Big Mac said that it was very dangerous to go climbing the old German towers, but I explained that there was nothing else for young people to do on a Sunday afternoon on account of the GAPING WOUND/Vacuum. It was therefore inevitable that we would all turn into hooligans and do stupid and dangerous things that might eventually get us killed. At this point McCrack stopped at a filter-in-turn.* He squinted from left to right and seemed unsure about which way to go. I told him it was left.

"Bloody roads!" he muttered.

I explained how during the Occupation the islanders took down all the signposts so as to confuse the Germans and never put them back up because they realised it was the best way to cause endless suffering for holidaymakers. I thought McDoodle was enjoying my stories, I mean, that little nugget was right up the Rue-McClever. But he gave me such a filthy look.

"How did you let yourself ever get in such a state?"

---

* The States of Guernsey (our local government) has embezzled all the money it was supposed to spend on road safety and thus cannot afford traffic lights. This has led to a system whereby at certain crossroads car drivers are supposed to *take it in turns*. This means many excellent car crashes, but mainly among the tourist population, which of course doesn't matter.

I pretended not to understand, only McClobber wasn't having any of it. He told me I was far too young to be drinking and that I should know better.

"It's just as well I came along when I did. You could've got yourself in serious trouble."

But the trouble was now in my stomach. Mr. Mac had no inkling I might vomit in his car (and I didn't expect it, either). I was feeling all churned up (made worse by the gear changes). I opened my mouth to defend myself but before I could speak something else came out. He reached over to open my door as it spilled onto the road. Seconds later I was hunched over a hedgerow with McCrackers at my side. He asked what I'd drunk because my vomit was the colour of Radox tropical bubble bath. I admitted I couldn't remember, and continued to empty my stomach. Then I blew my nose and said sorry. Mr. Mac got a few more tissues from his car.

"You shouldn't be mixing with the likes of Michael Priaulx. I don't like to go by what I've heard but it's clear he's too old for you. Who else were you with?"

I was feeling so sick and hot and cold and scared. It's not good to feel so many things at once.

"What do you care?" I asked. "Are you worried I'll get you in trouble?"

"It's not that, Cathy. I *do* understand. I was young once."

It was round about then that I had a major freak-out. I went on and on about how I was more misunderstood than Hitler, and how I did miss Dad and how I got everything wrong. Mighty Mac put his arm around me and I snivelled on his woolly shoulder.

He was about to say something when another car appeared behind us and started beeping its horn. I wiped my nose and tried to look sane, which was just as well since it was Mrs. Senner. Mrs. Senner (aka Radio Senner) is Vicky's mum and Dr. Senner's wife, and is hard to avoid on account of her fluorescent fuchsia lipstick, which never comes off despite her kissing people in the Belgian way.* When she saw who was blocking the road she slowed down and asked if everything was "all righty." I thought for one terrible minute she might actually get out. Mr. McCracken panicked, too, and waved her along quite brusquely, saying everything was fine and I was just a little carsick.

"It's my fault." He shrugged. "I'm not used to all these narrow lanes and hidden turnings. It's all stop-start-stop-start with me."

Mrs. Senner laughed and told him he should have got used to it by now.

"I know, I know!" He rolled his eyes and smiled.

As she drove off I couldn't help but look at Mr. Mac with Super-Gluey eyes. What Mr. McCrack did was so noble and generous. He'd preserved what was left of my dignity. Mrs. Senner would've gone absolutely nuts if she'd examined me more closely/smelled/inspected my vomit. She'd have marched round to our house and told Mum all about it, and then Mum would've got upset about everyone knowing our business. But Mr. Mac had been my Knight in Shining Skoda, and he obviously

---

* Three times on each cheek.

really cared since he suggested we stop at Island Wide for a can of Coke and something to eat.

"You'll probably feel a lot better now it's all out of your system."

I nodded meekly, got back in the car, and he was right, after a few minutes I did start to feel better. I told him I was sorry for ruining his Sunday and he laughed and said there was nothing to be ruined.

"Truth is, I hadn't made any plans."

He then watched me guzzle two packets of Quavers and a Fanta, which kind of proved the point.

It was only after I'd scoffed the lot that I dared ask him what he was going to tell Mum.

He tapped his thumb on the steering wheel. "I don't know. Will she be at home yet?"

I shook my head. "She's at work. She's working all hours to save the business because you might not know this but Dad left us terrible debts. She's got enough on her plate, trust me, she needs this like a hole in the head."

Mr. Mac pulled a face.

"So, what do I do with you?"

I stared at my hands. "I'm meant to be at Nicolette Prevost's house. It's just round the corner."

Mr. Mac raised his eyebrows to make little quote marks over his face.

"You and Nicolette, I should've known. She was at Pleinmont with you, wasn't she?" He shook his head. "Bang goes my star pupil." But then, unexpectedly, he smiled. "I'll drop you back there now, shall I?"

was amazed/terrified/appalled. I couldn't understand why Mr. Mac would do such a thing, but I assumed he just wanted to humiliate me further. He found the way to Les Paradis with only two more gear crunches and when we pulled into the drive Therese was (thankfully) dressed and at the door.

She was very surprised to see me without Nicolette, and with Mr. McCracken.

"Is everything all right? Cathy, where's Nicolette?" There was a note of panic in her voice.

"I'm sorry," I said quickly, "Nic and I got separated, there was a mix-up over lifts, she'll be back very soon, I'm sure. Can I wait for her in her room?"

Therese frowned. "Yes, that's fine, go on up, but I'm cross with Nicolette for leaving you. Mr. McCracken, I don't know what to say. This is unexpected. How kind of you to go out of your way and bring Cathy back."

Mr. Mac smiled. "It was nothing."

Then Mr. Prevost came out into the hallway and draped an arm over Therese, who stiffened as per a post. Her eyes darted anxiously from me back to her husband.

"Roger, Nicolette's gone AWOL again. Poor Mr. McCracken here has doubled up as a taxi service. We have to talk to her, it's getting out of hand."

Mr. Prevost shook his head, still smiling. "She'll be back when she gets hungry, I don't doubt." Then he rolled his eyes at Mr. McCracken. "Kids, eh? It's like we talk a different language. I'm surprised you can be bothered."

Mr. McCracken was smiling at Therese.

"Well, I'm sure it's all just a silly mistake."

Mr. Prevost nodded. "Bound to be. I owe you a drink. If ever you fancy it, there's a gang of us who meet up at the Royal Hotel. A lot of the chaps at the bank are English and have come over on contracts. We go there on Wednesdays and Fridays and sometimes at the weekend. Ha-ha! I should probably move in. But seriously, I bet you'd fit right in."

"That's kind." Mr. McCracken was already Mc-backing away. "I'll bear that in mind, most definitely. Right now I must be off."

"Thanks again," I called. "I really appreciate it."

Mr. McCracken smiled at Therese with what I thought was sympathy. "I'm sure Nicolette will be back safe and sound, but if you're at all worried do call me."

Therese fiddled with a long gold necklace and looked all Lady Di.

"You're very kind."

And with that, Super Mac folded his long body into his car and started the engine without the slightest crunch or scream. He reversed down the drive and in a second he was gone. I couldn't believe it. He hadn't said anything about the state I'd been in or where I'd been or how illegal it all was. I was mystified. I stared up at Therese and Mr. Prevost like they'd witnessed a minor miracle. But once the shock wore off I felt a bit confused. I didn't want or need a miracle. I wanted a proper punishment. Or at least a proper parent.

I know Mr. Mac wasn't my dad, but he had a duty of care, or whatever you call it. As my form teacher he should've done something. Perhaps he didn't want to get involved, or perhaps he didn't want to make trouble. Either way, they made him a coward. And Mr. Prevost was no better. He thought Nic was his little princess and therefore could do no wrong. This is serious black-and-white proof that the adults on this island are utterly useless. They think Guernsey's so peaceful and perfect that their kids can come to no harm. Don't they consider the harm kids can do to each other?

If you give someone an inch they take a mile—isn't that what they say? Remember Guernsey's small; in fact it's only three miles wide.

15TH DECEMBER 1985, 4:30 P.M.

[KITCHEN, HAVING EATEN THREE LEAN CUISINES. THEREFORE "NOT LEAN."]

*T*raitor!"

It was Monday morning bright and early and Nic had just slammed her satchel on my desk. Her eyes bored into me.

"I can't believe you went off in a huff and left me like that. Have you forgotten who your friends are?"

The whole of the class went quiet and stared at us.

"I'm sorry," I replied, "I should never have climbed up the tower with Michael Priaulx. I had no idea he was going to go all nutty like that."

Nic folded her arms under her boobs. "How fucking *dare* you embarrass me like that! And what the Hell were you thinking, going back to my house afterwards?"

(I'd waited in Nic's bedroom for over two hours, and then Therese had driven me home.)

"I was looking for you and I thought you'd be there. What else did you expect me to do?"

"You could've gone anywhere. You had no right. And I know you went through my stuff. Where's my silver locket, you little thief!"

(She'd definitely said I could borrow it.)

I dug my nails into the sides of the desk.

"Look, I went there and waited for you because I wanted to say sorry. I thought you'd be back before too long."

"More like you were waiting for an excuse to suck up to my mum. I can't trust you. I didn't know what to tell the boys. And as if that wasn't embarrassing enough, you do your little Second World War reenactment with Monobrow Michael and act like a total spaz. *Jesus*, you could've hit the car!"

"We weren't trying to hit anyone, it was just a laugh."

"Were *you* laughing?"

(I couldn't remember.)

Nic shook her head and leaned in, lowering her voice a little but not quite enough.

"I don't know why I bother. Christ, I'd even set you up with Pagey, did you know that? I'd totally talked you up to him, told him to take it easy because, you know, you hadn't done much *before*. Then, *then*, you start spewing embarrassing facts about *vegetables*. Is it really any wonder we tell you to zip it?"

Anne-Marie enjoyed the reference to vegetables and muttered, "Cabbage" under her breath. I hissed at her to shut up. I tried to explain to Nic how I honestly hadn't been sulking. But she called me childish and annoying. She also said that I drank too much of everyone else's alcohol without ever supplying my own.

"You just want a free ride and if you don't get what you want you act like a baby. I mean, how dare you turn up at my house and tell my mum and dad you don't know where I am, and make out that I was the one who was in the wrong to go off and leave you in the middle of nowhere."

"I never said anything like that!"

"Well, that's what it looked like!" Nic glared at me in such disgust (as did everyone). "You're a fucking sneak. I *hate* sneaks."

"I'm sorry." I winced and tried to smile. "Did you get an earful?"

Nic curled her lip. "Of course not. *I'm* not some little *kid*. But get over yourself, the world doesn't revolve around you. Pete's my boyfriend and it's so obvious you're jealous. You're just embarrassing yourself."

My cheeks were like hot coals and everyone was whispering.

"So what was the plan? Was that little game with Michael supposed to get my attention?"

I quickly explained that Michael was a very interesting person once you got to know him, but Nic pulled the sourest face yet/ever.

"I bet he never told you he was, like, my stalker for a year. He used to follow me everywhere."

I was ever so slightly crushed.

"Let's not fight," I said. "I made a mistake and I won't do it again."

Nic frowned and pretended to think this over.

"I wonder if this is a bit of a warning sign. If you're going to be so weird then maybe I should find someone else to hang out with. I thought we could be friends but maybe I got it wrong. Maybe we *should* see less of each other."

I looked from Chantelle to Isabelle to Vicky.

My little world was falling apart. The bell rang and in came Mr. McCracken, clutching the register and his battered old briefcase. He told us to sit down but I couldn't. He was all clean-shaven and crisply ironed, but as he pulled out his chair I thought I'd faint. He sat down, opened the register, and started calling our names. I kept my head down because I knew I was going to start crying. I felt so stupid because I never-ever cried in public. My head was spinning and I didn't even hear when he got to "R."

"Rozier? . . . Catherine?"

I looked up and suddenly everyone was staring. All the blood was in my head. I pushed my chair back and it screeched along the floor. Mr. McCracken frowned and I didn't know where to look. So without saying anything, I ran out.

There were dots in front of my eyes when I reached the loos, which were only four doors down. Of course Mr. Mac followed me into the corridor, as did Nic and Lisa Collenette. Lisa came because her nose is the biggest part of her body, Nic came because she was (I think) worried. OK, she was probably more worried about what I was going to tell Mr. Mac, but even so.

"Are you OK?" Mr. McCracken pushed the door a little open. "Are you still feeling sick from yesterday?"

I clung to the basin. "Please go away."

I think it was at this point that Mr. Mac stepped back and saw Nic.

"Why don't you try to talk to her?"

Mackers went back to class, taking Lisa-Insect with him.

Nic pushed the door open with her elbow and stared at me. She had a medium-sized frown on her face.

"I'm sorry," I said, "I didn't mean—"

Nic held up her hand as if to stop traffic.

"What was that he said? Why did he mention yesterday? What does *he* know about yesterday?"

I swallowed. Nic was still staring at me. She looked more puzzled than angry.

"Why were you with Mr. McCracken yesterday?"

"Didn't they tell you?"

Nic cocked her head to one side. "Didn't who tell me? What are you on about?"

It was a pin-drop moment.

"Mr. McCracken was the one who took me back to your house."

"He *what*?" She blinked. "You're kidding me."

"No, I'm not."

Nic's little mouth gaped. "Fuck! You're serious. Who was there? Tell me *exactly* what happened."

I remember looking into the whites of Nic's eyes and knowing that I'd better make it good. This was my chance. Sometimes you have to twist the truth to make it interesting, and I *had* to make it interesting.

"Well, it was amazing, really. I mean, I can hardly believe that it happened. I was sitting at Pleinmont with Michael, and of course we were both pretty wasted by then. Suddenly, out of nowhere, up drove Mr. McCracken. He came over and asked Michael what we'd been doing and Michael laughed in his face. Mr. Mac then got all huffy and said he'd better take me home. I don't really remember refusing. Next thing I know he's bundling me into his car. I was giggling and mucking about, but he was so angry. I told him to chill out, only he said I was lowering myself to be getting in such a dreadful state, and what was I thinking, blah-blah. Then he asked me what would happen if it all went wrong and who would pick up the pieces? That was when I got upset. I told him he wasn't my dad and we had a bit of an argument. The windows of the car got steamed up and he had to stop driving. Then, the strangest thing happened . . ."

Nic's eyes widened. "What?"

I stared into her pretty face. It was like I was holding a loaded gun.

"*He* got upset. It was like he was really exasperated and at the end of his tether. He told me I was *precious* and *special*. I was freaked out. Then he said we needed to both calm down. We stopped at Island Wide and he bought me some food and we sat in the car park. After that we talked and talked. He really understood me."

"Seriously?" said Nic. "I can't believe it."

"Well, you always said he had a soft spot for me. He told me I was his star pupil. He even said something about how I was the one reason he still enjoyed teaching. He was leaning close and he had a tissue and he wiped my face really gently, and I could feel his breath on me."

Nic pulled back. "No way!"

"Yes way! Then he told me how lonely he was, and how his Sundays are just empty, and all he ever does is drive round and round the coast road."

Nic's pretty face crinkled. "That is *so* sad."

"Then"—I took a breath—"we nearly kissed!"

"No!"

I nodded frantically.

Nic's eyes started to shrink. She wasn't sure whether to believe me or not.

"Really!" I yelped. "He-was-being-so-nice-and-then-he-sort-of-leaned-over-like-to-give-me-a-hug-but-it-was-*definitely-something-else*. He hadn't shaved so it was bristly."

Nic shook her head, and I could see by her body language* that she wasn't convinced. That's when I told her about the projectile vomiting and Mrs. Senner.

"Yuck! How embarrassing. I'd have died."

"I know!" More mad head nodding. "That's why I asked Mr. McCracken to drop me round at yours. I was in such a state. He made me promise not to tell anyone what had happened, but I couldn't not tell *you*."

Nic sized me up with her eyes, it was like she was trying to see into my brain.

I gulped back panic. "I swear on my life this is the truth, Nic."

"Really?"

I nodded and blinked and waited.

A hint of a smile crept onto her face.

"You wouldn't lie about something this big, would you?"

"No way."

(And normally I wouldn't.)

She stared into my eyes and I still couldn't tell if she

---

* See *Jackie* magazine, January 1984, p. 12, "Boyfriends and Best Friends: How to Spot a Liar."

believed me or not, and I was rigid when she pulled me close and gave me a hug. It was a hug so tight that it almost stopped me breathing.

"Well, well!" she whispered. "We could have some fun with this."

And I thought it was just perfect. We were friends again, maybe better friends than before, and that was all that mattered. I was too happy to think about the lies I'd just told, or the damage they could do. I didn't think about what would happen tomorrow or the day after that, or the day after that, because it seemed so far away.

And now I get to the bit where I say kids tell stupid lies because they don't know any better, but actually I should know better, because of course I've read it all before.

"The testimony of
C. A. Rozier"

[Transcribed by E. P. Rozier]

Pour continua, Emile. You know the story of the
boy who cried wolf? He told so many lies nobody
would believe him when he finally told the truth.
I cannot excuse what I did but I shall say this:
life under the jackboot was no picnic. We thought
we'd be occupied for a few weeks and no more, then
weeks turned into months and the months dragged
on and on. Every day we printed out a new order,
or an amendment to an old order, or an addition to
it. They said they wouldn't take our wireless sets
and then they did, they said we'd be safe in our
homes but they took the best homes for themselves.

Seems the only thing they couldn't own was the
nonsense in my head. I'd lie awake each night,
listening as the planes hummed overhead, and I
pretended I was a pilot or a gunner. I felt the
bitterest hatred for the first time in my life,
and not just against the Hun. Certain Guernseymen,

and I could name them, were only too happy to fawn over the Germans and treat them like brothers, and some of the womenfolk were worse, their heads easily turned by a man in uniform—it didn't matter what uniform. It was more than shameful, Emile, it was treason.

To me it was the end of Guernsey and the world itself, to see my own people acting so yellow. Of course it's no excuse for what I did. I know I was wrong to lie, but lies were all I had since the truth was so stinking and rotten. Our father's reputation, our family name, all was lost.

Yes, yes. Now you tell me there were plenty of folk who were made to work for the Germans, but back then I reckoned on carrying the heaviest burden. I felt a hundred eyes on me when I went into Town and I was sure I heard whispers behind my back. Of course, it was all in my head, and the only trouble I had I went looking for.

And by trouble I mean Ray Le Poidevoin.

For a while I didn't see him and I wondered if he'd got away to France or to England, and was off on some adventure. No such luck, I'm sorry to say. Not long after the Germans arrived he'd been sent to Alderney—earning himself five months' hard labour for stealing groceries. That must've been a shock, as I'd see for myself soon enough. When we met again his young face had new lines and there were shadows beneath each eye. With his dirty hair and clothes he looked a bit wild to me, and I would've turned on my heel if he hadn't spotted me first.

"Well, well, if it isn't our new minister of Nazi propaganda!" he called out. "The last time I saw you, you were running away and it looks like nothing's changed. Do you remember? It was after the air raid on White Rock. There were wounded and dying everywhere and where did you get to, eh? You ran like a coward."

"That's not true." I stood firm. "We both know it wasn't like that."

Ray pointed a finger towards me. "*Je n'sie pas si cuite comme tu crai! Tu es caouard!* You did what your dad said, and we all know he's a Nazi lover. He even speaks the lingo."

I felt my pulse quicken. "There's no point in lamming into me. We've been forced to work for the Germans and we don't get treated any better for it. I hate those stinking Slugs as much as you."

"You are all bluff." Ray shook his head. He turned to the lads gathered about him. There was Jim Collard, Colin Turrell, Greg Mauger, all of them as tough as nails. Jimbo would trot after Ray like he was his pet spaniel. He later joined the army, he liked taking orders so much. Colin now works for the States. Greg Mauger died of typhus before the Occupation was out. They all enjoyed watching me squirm.

"I don't know why you think you're so much better than us," I replied. "What are you going to do now?

You'll have to work for the Germans like everyone else."*

Ray glowered at me. "Death before dishonour. Ray Le Poidevoin works for no one."

Jim and Colin nodded.

"We got plans," one of them said.

"I could help," I offered quickly. "I've got inside knowledge on the Germans. I know their new rules and regulations before they even happen."

Ray eyed me up and down like he was measuring me for a coffin.

"I was going to box your ears the last time I saw you and maybe I should do it now. What do you reckon, lads, is he worth it?"

They laughed.

"Run along back to your pop," said one of them. "You Roziers are yellow!"

I was furiously angry.

"Pop's not yellow, he's a braver man than all of you. It's not what it looks like. He's—he's not what you think."

Jimbo and Colin shook their heads and turned to go; Ray alone was listening.

"What's the old man up to then?"

I backed away. "I—I've said too much already."

Ray nodded. "If your father is a spy then you've just blown his cover."

"*Tais ta goule!*" I said, keeping up my bluff.

* E.P.R. notes: By 1942 it was estimated that three-quarters of the local population were working directly or indirectly for the Germans.

"You cannot tell anyone. Pop is gathering information for the Allies."

I know I was playing with fire, Emile, but you must understand, I was sick of these days without history, where history was being made somewhere else. I was sick of doing nothing and feeling nothing. I thought that if I said these things then I'd make them true, and my life wouldn't feel so shameful.

Jim and Greg were waiting on the corner but I wanted to keep Ray there. I told him that I was a loyal patriot and could easily prove my worth. I said I was prepared to do anything for the War effort. But he shook his head.

"I'm not ruining my good name mixing it up with the likes of you."

I was boiling up with rage. I pulled that little knife he'd given me from my pocket and lifted it towards him, but quick as lightning he'd grabbed my arm and twisted it behind my back.

"I don't need all this strife from a little kid like you. Where's your pop, now, eh, the war hero? I've seen him in Town, skulking about. He's no spy and you shouldn't say such stupid things. *Je ne sais pas*, maybe I should cut your throat now—at least it'd shut you up."

"Fine!" I choked. "Do that."

But he let me go, throwing my knife onto the paving stones.

"You're wasting my time!"

I was sick of Ray and his swaggering ways and

his motley crew of no-goods. What made them think they were better than me? I picked the knife off the ground and, without even thinking, pressed the blade to my arm.

"*Tu cré chuq t áeme à créer!* But I'll show you the colour of my blood and prove it's not yellow."

I dug in deep and the blood ran to my wrist.

"You got a screw loose?" Ray spluttered.

Tears sprang up in my eyes.

"You won't think that when I'm gone."

I met his gaze. He cocked his big head slightly. It was like the world had stopped turning on its axis.

"Eh? *Oueq vas-tu, man amie?*"

I waited a good few seconds before answering.

"Why do you care? I'm the big liar, remember? So I must be just imagining that boat that I'll soon be away on. Think what you like, *man amie*, but I'll be leaving you to rot!"

Mais vère dja donc, Emile, and so it is with that boy who cries wolf: he lies once, he lies twice, but when he finally tells the truth he'll get the punishment he deserves.

16TH DECEMBER 1985, 11:56 A.M.

octor, doctor, everyone thinks I'm a liar."
"I find that hard to believe."

It being a Monday I was supposed to be going to school, but then I nearly lost a finger. I was washing up the breakfast things and smashed a glass beaker in the sink. There was blood everywhere so Mum took me to Grange End surgery.

"You should've been more careful," she said, bundling me into the car. "And after our conversation last night I can't help but wonder if you did this on purpose."

Perhaps I should mention that last night I told Mum I was too sick to go to school. Trouble is, I've been (ab)using that excuse a bit too much just recently.

"You should see Roger," said Mum, as she pulled out of the driveway.

("Roger" is Dr. Senner, by the way.)

I wrapped the tea towel tighter round my finger. "Maybe I'm anaemic—I felt dizzy before it happened."

The windscreen was all frosted up so Mum leaned forward, frowning over the steering wheel.

"Maybe. But last week you said you had glandular fever. I don't know, Cathy. You're not eating properly, so perhaps that's it. And it doesn't help that you're always locked in your room, scribbling away. I don't know what you find to write about."

I stared out the car window. Guernsey's so small but everyone drives everywhere.

"There's only a week of term left, so no one will be doing any work," I said. "Can't I just stay off until next term?"

Mum watched me out of the corner of her eye. "I know you're upset about what happened to Nicolette but I don't think you should get special treatment. You weren't even that close to her."

(That's excellent proof how little Mum knows.)

Perhaps if I stop eating I'll get certifiably sick. During the Occupation a lot of people had weak immune systems because they were so undernourished, and once they got sick there weren't any drugs left to fix them. There were outbreaks of diphtheria, scarlet fever, typhus, worms, and all sorts of yucky things. When the insulin ran out diabetics died, and without disinfectant even the smallest of cuts would get infected and couldn't heal. They became known as Occupation Ulcers and sometimes proved fatal. But, on the bright side, there were noticeably fewer cases of depression. Presumably this was because people had real problems to worry about and no real time to obsess. (Although they had multiple, massive nervous breakdowns once they were liberated instead.)

Whatever the medical facts are, it would be best not to trust Dr. Senner with them. He is The Most Crap Doctor in the Whole World (or Guernsey). I don't know why Mum thought he could help me since it's not like he helped Dad. The one time he came round to our house to see Dad they had a big argument and Dad was Horrified-and-Humiliated-of-St.-Peter-Port (and went storming off). Dr. Senner was useless then, and I don't think much has changed. Besides, he's already decided I'm trouble(d). He didn't want Mum to leave us alone together, in case I accused him of sexual molestation.

"There's nothing physically wrong with you," he said, staying firmly behind his desk. "But obviously the mind is a powerful organ."

I shrugged. "Mum insisted I see you. She's obviously worried because of what happened with Dad. You should do some blood tests, or something. I think that'd keep her happy."

Dr. S. nodded absently, like he was playing along with a not-funny joke.

"And what would you expect me to find?"

"Hmmm, let me think." I tapped my chin. "Well, obviously not your homebrew since it all got drunk a few weeks back."

Dr. S. pushed his thumb into the top of his pen. He must feel pretty guilty that his homebrew was "Exhibit A" after they found Nic's battered remains in the sea.

During the War real alcohol was hard to come by, so people made their own, which was deadly lethal, and Dr. Senner's homebrew is no better. It was the first alcohol I ever tasted and I'm amazed anyone else would've willingly drunk it because it honestly tasted like vinegar plus floor cleaner. Dr. S. let me try some when I was only 10 because he had this theory it would put me off for life. Dr. Suck It Up knows alcoholism is a major problem on Guernsey, although Dad said the real problem was in Alderney.*

Dr. S. was watching me through the shrubbery of his eyebrows.

"So you don't want to go back to school? I know Nicolette was a friend of yours. What you're feeling, we are *all* feeling. Vicky is devastated. You should talk to her. If you sat down with your classmates, you could talk it through together."

Talk it through with those cretins? I don't think so.

Dr. S. twiddled his pen between his fingers. "Maybe you feel bad that you weren't at the party, maybe you think you could have stopped Nicolette."

"No," I said firmly, "I didn't care whether or not I was invited to the party. I feel sorry for Vicky, that's all. Nic used her like she used me. She called Vicky loads of horrible things, and even made jokes about when she'd have to start shaving."

* As per its traumatic History (see earlier note), there are more pubs than people on Alderney, which could be good but is in fact VERY BAD. It is often referred to as "25,000 Alcoholics clinging to a Rock."

Dr. S. frowned and I felt bad.

"Sorry, but it's true. I think it's important to be honest since there's been so much lying already. Nic used to make me lie. She was always egging me on to do bad stuff, and I know she was the same with Vicky."

Dr. S. nodded. "You seem angry."

"No." I sighed. "I'm disappointed. I'm disappointed that people aren't admitting what Nic was really like. At least now she won't be around to cause more trouble and upset, and I'm just saying what a lot of people are thinking. You mustn't go blaming Vicky for the party getting out of hand. It was Nic who invited half the island. And *you* should've guessed how it would end up. *You* are a grown-up, and grown-ups *should* know better."

Dr. S. sniffed in all of his nostril hair and stared at his pens.

"Does it feel better to get things off your chest?"

I glared at him. "There's a lot more I could tell you."

He opened his palms. "By all means. Whatever you tell me is in confidence."

How interesting. Dr. Suck Eggs Know-It-All could keep all my secrets, just like he kept Dad's secrets.

It was quite tempting, I'll admit. I could've reached over the desk then and there, grabbed Dr. S. by the collar, and told him to listen carefully. Then I could've confessed to all sorts of grisly details about my big fight with Nic. I could've said that I'd followed her out of the Village after the party and watched and waited in the bushes. How I'd maybe LURED her away from all her little friends in the woods and made her come to the Batterie, before BLUDGEONING her to death with a bottle of homebrew, and pulling out some hair as a trophy. I could've claimed that I'd pushed her off the cliff on purpose. Yes. I could've invented any old detail knowing he couldn't do a thing about it. Wouldn't that have been something? To spill my guts to Dr. Suck Eggs in his joy-of-beige office and then make him respect my privacy.

But I didn't, and actually I didn't need to. After half an hour he was telling Mum it wouldn't be the end of the world if I missed the last week of school. He said Vicky had been sent home twice already.

"It's nearly Christmas and maybe we should all take some time out." He smiled. Then he lowered his voice. "And I do think Cathy would benefit from some sessions with a counsellor. It would help her process things, most definitely."

Do you know what that means? I've got to go and see (drumroll, please) Mrs. Senner! Yes, Guernsey's that small: our local loudmouth is a registered psycho-whatsit and sits in a big room up at the hospital surrounded by abstract art posters and her certificates of depression. I was meant to go there once before to talk about what *did* or *didn't* happen with Mr. McCracken. Of course I got out of it, but afterwards Mrs. Sigmund Suck-Up was always round at our house, pursing her pink lips.

"If you ask me," she'd say, "there's no smoke without fire . . ."

In point of fact you can have smoke without fire, although it's more accurate to call it gas. Chlorine gas is greenish in colour and poisons the lungs. It was widely used in the First World War and nearly killed my grandfather. It's a pretty dirty weapon to use, but we all need good weapons.

I had to fight to keep Nic as my special friend, and I had Lisa, Anne-Marie, and Shelley all yap-yap-yapping at my heels. Even Vicky wanted in. I always felt outnumbered. After the War was over the Channel Islanders were heavily criticised for not resisting the Germans. The thing is, people never realise how many Germans there were on the Island. In occupied Norway there were about 1,200 Norwegians for every German occupier, and in France there were 120 French people to each German. In Guernsey the ratio was almost one to one! There was nowhere to hide or run to, and who was to know it wouldn't stay like that forever?

I wanted Nic to stay my friend and I would've done anything for her. I'm not just talking about the shoplifting and the drinking. She said that if I was serious about Mr. McCracken then I had to grow up and get some Experience. This meant doing things with boys, more specifically Marc Le Page.

We therefore spent whole days at Pete's house. It seemed so depressing to have the curtains closed in the middle of the day. Pagey and I would sit on the sofa and watch horror films while Nic and Pete disappeared upstairs. I generally liked horror films on account of the large number of cheerleaders who were beheaded. Pagey said he'd never met a girl who enjoyed scenes of dismemberment like I did. I suppose it took my mind off whatever was happening off the screen. I tell you,

French kissing just shows what perverts the French are, and as for the rest of it, it was worse than P.E.

I honestly cannot understand why God or Charles Darwin or whoever couldn't have made the penis more attractive. Maybe given it bright feathers that fan out like a peacock, or made it a nice colour and gotten rid of all that hair around it (although in theory the hair helps to hide it). I'm amazed the human race hasn't died out with penises looking how they do. I'm also amazed Marc Le Page doesn't prefer to keep his hidden.

Kissing him was like dunking my head in a puddle of spit. At least the sex part was over quickly, and sex was another reason why I started drinking more. Drinking helped me then like it helps me now, and if ever I drank too much I simply went to the bathroom and made myself sick. It seemed a whole lot easier to throw up and drink more than ever have to stop. Dad always blamed Mum's cooking when I found him in our downstairs toilet, making himself sick. Mum didn't like being blamed, although she got used to it. She'd crack two eggs into a glass and whisk them with tomato juice, then she'd make him drink it down in one. I presumed that was her most excellent revenge.

Dad wouldn't have liked Pete—he was definitely a bad egg and not one for drinking. I suspected Nic was with him just for show, since the other lads looked up to him and she loved the attention. He did weight training in his garage and he'd scoop her over his shoulder or twirl her around like a rag doll. He once offered to do the same to me but I promised him I'd crush him, and when I saw him fight with Michael I realised I could've done.

It was at André Duquemin's house one Saturday night. Everyone was there. Michael was sitting by himself in a corner, looking delectable/deranged, and I was drinking everything as per usual and trying to be hilariously funny. Eventually I gave up and went to sit by Michael. I remember he smelled of petrol and had a spot on his chin, but that really didn't matter. He was in a Joy Division T-shirt. I told him they were my favourite band and was keen to discuss their name, but he said they weren't a band anymore, not since their lead singer had killed himself. That didn't sound too joyous. I asked Michael if he'd enjoyed reading the choice selection of Dad's books that I'd dropped round at his house, but all he did was grunt. So I changed tack and complimented him on his careful tending of Donnie's flowerbeds.

Michael's furtive scowl deepened and he sucked on his Marlboro-Red-specially-designed-to-kill-you cigarette.

"You like Donnie, eh?"

I nodded and said that Donnie and I had become friends on account of our communal love of books. I then described Donnie's large-ish library of Catholic good-taste. I went on and on about Donnie's books, actually, and insisted that they were why I kept visiting him. But that's not strictly true. The real reason I went round to Donnie's was to stand by his kitchen window and watch Michael in the garden. Donnie joked that he could charge me by the hour. I don't know why I liked watching Michael so much. I liked the fact that he was so quiet and careful when he was weeding, and his face became angelic as he pruned. And occasionally he was topless.

Michael blew out a perfect smoke ring and asked what I was reading now and I told him I was working my way through the oeuvre of Stephen King.

He laughed.

"You're into real classics, then."

I bristled because I *had* read all the classics, actually. Dad had bought them by mail order from a *Daily Telegraph* magazine supplement, and I finished them before I turned 12.

But Michael found that hilarious, too.

"D'you know Donnie dropped out of university? He reckons they turn you into robots. He's got properties all over the world, time-shares and stuff. He's well rich."

Nic suddenly broke in. "Who's this you're talking about?"

I reminded Nic about Donnie's party and she hunched up her shoulders like she was cold (and she might've been, since as per usual she was barely dressed).

"That man is a total creep, living in that big house on the cliff. He's probably a serial killer with, like, weird perversions and a basement full of porn."

Michael told Nic not to talk shit, but she replied that talking shit was better than smelling of it.

He sneered brilliantly. "You just can't help yourself, can you?"

Nic laughed. "No, Michael, and neither can *you* from what I've seen."

She ran a finger down his arm, which I didn't like one bit. Then I noticed her bare knee pressing against his thigh. Nic always leaned in too close to people when she talked to them, like she was telling them a secret.

With a flick of her hair she turned back to me.

"Shouldn't you be with Pagey? He's getting the idea you're avoiding him." Her eyes jumped to Michael. "Don't you hate that, Michael, when girls flirt with you just to make their boyfriends jealous? It's not nice to feel *used*."

Michael smiled, but not with his eyes. "Those girls are slags, if you ask me."

"I wouldn't ask you, though." Nic shook out her hair. "You don't know much about it from what I've seen. And if you're going to let Cat down, at least do it gently."

Michael told Nic to fuck off and die.

She shrugged. "You don't know what you're missing. Cat's already a hit with the older man so you two have something in common."

Michael curled his lip gorgeously. "You are such a fucking bitch." And with that, he walked away.

I pretended that I needed the loo but I was really going after Michael. I didn't entirely understand what had just gone on. But then I got lost down a dark corridor, and realised that I did need the loo after all. I was standing by the back door that led into the garden. I'd drunk too much Curaçao plus Baileys plus cider and they were doing the "okey-kokey" in my stomach. So I stumbled outside, hoping the fresh air would do me good and there might also be a flowerbed to vomit in. I wandered down a little gravel path and lay down on the grass. I looked up at the stars and did my best yogic breathing. Then, after twenty or so breaths, I realised I wasn't alone. Jason was standing over me. Jason is quite worrying, by the way. He has big fishy eyes and pubic-curly hair, and the story is he bit off his own finger when he was nine.

"What are you doing?"

I told him nothing and that I wanted to be alone.

He crouched down next to me. "But you're crying."

I told him I was allergic to daffodils (which was a lie).

"Girls always cry when they're drunk. I reckon they only get drunk so's they can cry."

I told Jason he was ridiculous, although I wonder if he's right.

He sat down next to me.

"Want a smoke?"

I shook my head. He carried on sitting there, while I did yogic breathing. I'd counted to sixty before he asked:

"Is it true you're shagging a teacher?"

Of course I denied it, and Jason looked more fishy/ creepy.

"It's just what I heard. You know what this island's like, stuff gets around, girls, too."

"Well, it's rubbish," I replied.

I looked at Jason and he looked at me. He obviously misunderstood what that look meant because he tried to kiss me and stick his hand up my skirt. (Boys are just disgusting.) Unfortunately I was more drunk than I thought, so it took a few minutes for me to work out what was happening. I pushed him off and called him a pig.

"*Je-sus!* Pagey was right. You *are* all talk. What the fuck is wrong with you?"

A lot of things are wrong with me (that should be obvious by now), but I wasn't going to explain everything to Jason Guille. I also didn't need to, since at that precise moment Michael and Pete had come stumbling out into the garden.

With the splitting of a nanosecond Michael saw me on the grass and said, "What the—"

He couldn't say anything else because Pete grabbed him from behind and got him in a headlock.

"You say that again. Say what you said back there and tell me how much *you* like this!"

I knew Michael needed my help.

"Get off him!" I yelled, jumping up.

I think, in retrospect, girls shouldn't get involved in boys' fights. I'd also like to point out that when you see fights on TV or have them described in novels, they're nothing like the real-life version. Just by trying to describe a fight you slow it down with words, and string it out to make it more dramatic. And if it's on TV there's lots of different camera angles plus music. That makes it exciting. Real-life fights are very brutal. I tried to kick Pete and then Jason grabbed me round the waist so I elbowed him in the teeth. The next minute I was on my knees and I saw Michael flip Pete over. There was a cracking sound and I thought Pete's spine had snapped in two. Michael kicked him once and he yelped, curling over and calling out the "C" word. People were spilling out into the garden to watch but Michael staggered back, his breath and spit suddenly lit up by the house lights.

I suppose that's one good thing about boys: they get their fights over and done with quickly. With girls it's always longer because they fight dirty, and use their nails and teeth. My last fight with Nic was like that. I didn't have any secret manoeuvres like Michael, and I hadn't done any weight training like Pete, but I still managed to fight Nic to the Death. I never did bludgeon her, though. I only said that because I wanted to sound like Stephen King.

Dad had always warned me about this, of course. He used to say that if I was exposed to the language of sex and violence then I'd suck it up like a sponge. That's why he vetted my library books and threw the TV out and banned me from visiting Beau Sejour after dark. It's like he knew all along I'd eventually turn evil. It was only a matter of time. At least I've proved him right, and he did so like to be right.

"The testimony of
C. A. Rozier"

[Transcribed by E. P. Rozier]

Was I born rotten or did something make me bad? I never will know, and now it's my body that's rotten through and through. My kidneys are gone and my heart will be next. There's a weight pushing down on my chest so hard I cannot breathe. I can't even see right because of cataracts. Still, I've seen enough things that I can't forget. Men being beaten like animals, their legs twisted round and their skulls smashed open. Every day I watched men dragged off at roll call never to return, and then I dug their graves. *Emile, tchi que je vis te baillerais de mauvais saonges.* Once violence enters the mind it never leaves.

The bloodstains on my shirt were a warning to our mother.

"You have been fighting!" she cried. "Is this how I brought you up? Why don't you listen?"

My eyes were red-rimmed from crying and I hung my head as she bandaged up my arm. I promised her I'd be a better son and behave myself in future. I honestly thought I meant it, too.

"If you get hurt again there won't be no fixing you," she replied. "It's enough with one invalid among us."

It was the first time she'd mentioned Hubert's health, and now the cat was out of the bag. I watched as she sucked in her lips.

"He won't go to the doctor," she told me. "He seems to think that what medicine there is he does not deserve."

The winter months had taken a toll on all of us, it's the truth, but Pop had a terrible rattle in his throat and it wasn't getting better. When I watched him shuffle round the house I should've felt bad for him, but instead I felt the old resentments stir anew.

La Duchesse put on her armour plating and told me I was man enough for both of us. I tried to be, I really did. After that I pushed all thoughts of Ray out of my head and got up at seven each morning, so as to be in the office early, setting the inks. I resolved never again to go out at night or get into any fights. I even stopped giving lip to Vern and learned a little German. That stopped La Duchesse from quacking like a duck, and we all got a bit of peace.

The summer came and went, and then we faced another autumn. More and more slave workers poured

onto the island so there was less of everything to
go round. You cannot imagine how bad it got, Emile. I
didn't feel like I was getting much reward for being
good, as I sat in that office day in and day out. Vern
was always watching me, while Pop hid away in the
spare room, a shadow of the man he was. I hated Vern
for taking Pop's place and I'd dream of killing him
with his own gun, but he was just a sap, not built to
be a soldier and, like I said, I'd learned my lesson.

All this time I was a good lad, no trouble to anyone. People forget that. It was Ray who was stirring
and stealing and causing trouble. *"Y'a les impudents
qui vivent"** is what they say, and Ray was as impudent as any I knew. He'd carried on with what he
called his "Sab Squad," getting up to all sorts. When
I heard talk of water being poured in German fuel
tanks, or food being stolen from their canteens, I
knew it was down to Ray and his thugs. I wondered
how long they'd last, though, since the Hun was now
offering good money for information. Hunger loosed
all our tongues, you understand, and as a new year
dawned two of Ray's lads got themselves arrested.†

1942 was the hardest year yet. We was all a bit
closer to animals. By then everyone was stealing
from everyone else and blaming them poor bloody

* Translation: "Only the brazen thrive."
† E.P.R. notes: Jim Collard and Peter Woods were arrested
for disorderly behaviour at the Mare de Carteret public
house, 2nd January 1942. Sent to Alderney to work as fish-
ermen for the next ten months.

slave workers. *Emile, j'en sis pas à djotche!* Your neighbour would have the shirt off your back and the soles off your shoes if you didn't keep an eye on them, and the black market was big business—there was a thriving racket, courtesy of certain persons I could name.

And Ray was at it, too. Ah, yes, I've come back to that old rascal, or rather he came back to me. I was lying on my bed one Friday night when I heard some noises outside. I wondered what it was all about, but not enough to shift my bony backside. I rested my ink-stained fingers on my ribs and counted slowly to ten. It was an old trick—I just wanted to empty my head and get a bit of sleep. But then I heard a little tap at my window. I thought I was dreaming. Then came another tap, followed by more. Someone was throwing gravel at the pane.

I got myself up and went to the window, pulling back the curtains only a little way. I looked out onto the dark street and I couldn't see a thing. I leaned forward, peering left to right again, and then steadied my eyes on the shadows in the yard. That's when I saw something move. As I pressed my face against the glass he stood up straight, his outline lit up by the lemon slice of moon. I'd recognise them jug ears anywhere! It was Ray.

He gestured to me and without another thought I was pulling on my trousers and dashing down the stairs. I had no idea what it was he wanted, and a part of me wondered if it wasn't still a dream. War plays funny tricks on you, that's for sure. I

opened the front door with a great big smile, like
I was greeting an old friend. Only he wasn't the
chap I remembered. His lip was cut and one eye was
swollen shut.

"*Mon Dju!* What in Hell happened?" I asked.

"Them Slugs fight dirty." He was dancing from foot
to foot. "There's a do at the Gables, you coming?"

The Gables was a private house used for all-night
parties by some of Guernsey's wayward and not-so-
wayward youth. It was popular with the nurses from
the hospital. Of course I'd never been before. Of
course I went! Who wouldn't?

I can't name all the folk there but I was proud
to be in their number, and prouder still to walk
in with old Ray. I reckon I grew a good ten inches
in as many minutes and I felt more alive than I'd
felt in a year. It was a merry scene with lots of
drinking and laughing and dancing. You could've
almost made yourself believe the War was over, if
it weren't for that foul-tasting stuff they called
homebrew.

I drank it quickly to stop myself from asking
what I was doing. It was strange to have Ray slapping me on the back and calling me "*copain*," but
I guessed he was up to something. After a little
while he took me off to a corner of the kitchen,
checking all around that no one was in earshot.

"Listen," he says, "the time has come for us to
put the past behind us. We're all a bit older and

wiser. I've lost some good men and I'm sick of silly rivalries. We must make a firm alliance and stick to it. But I need to know I can trust you."

"You have my word," I nodded back.

Ray stared at me. "I've been watching you. You've been keeping out of trouble. Me? I'm on the German blacklist. I've managed to convince them I'm a bit touched in the head, but there's only so many times I can pull that trick."

"What are you planning?" I asked of him.

Ray winked. "First things first: I've got a tip-off that there'll be two lorries near La Valette. Both have fuel on board and it's ours for the taking. You ready to prove you're more than all that talk?"

I was on my feet already. *"Alaons!"*

This was what I'd waited all these months for, eh! My heart beat faster. I imagined that Ray and me were commandos flown into the island on a secret mission. I was the wingman or whatever you want to call it. It didn't matter that we were breaking the law and I didn't spare a thought for what would happen if we were caught. This is what I'd always wanted. So we headed off quickly down the narrow backstreets, winding our way into Town. The night was crisp and starry, and Ray moved quick, like a fox. He'd already sniffed out the hot spots and knew how best to avoid the patrols. Old Jerry was rigid in his habits, I suppose. Still, I was expecting to hear a "Halt!" at any minute, or feel the sharpness of a bayonet prodding into my back.

When we reached the waterfront the booze was wearing off, though. I was suddenly all a-jitter, and worried what was coming. I could see the trucks, but I could also see a German guard nearby, at the entrance to La Valette. His glowing cigarette end was hovering in the night air. Ray nodded to me and we crept up slowly, quietly, hunched over. Then he gave me the signal to stay still, and I was rooted to the spot. I watched as he lifted himself up onto the back of the first truck. I didn't hear a sound. *Ma fé*, he was a hefty bloke but he was nimble. I hardly dared breathe as I crouched and waited.

Minutes passed, then I heard the clip-clop sound of German jackboots, still some way off. I now know that sound better than anything on this earth. I skipped lightly round the truck and tugged at the tarpaulin so as to get Ray's attention. Then I tucked myself under it. The footsteps came closer and there was a rasping sound, like a cough. A new soldier was arriving to keep watch. I crouched low, holding my heart in my stomach, and I imagined Ray was doing the same. The guard walked past us and headed on towards the tunnel entrance. Moments later I heard him talking to his mate. I took a breath, pulled myself around and upright again, and wondered if I should take a chance and run.

One minute I was standing there alone, the next Ray was aside of me. I didn't hear or see him slide out from under the tarpaulin. He handed me a can that stank of fuel while reaching into his trouser pocket. He pulled out a knife, bent down, and cut the front tyre of the truck. Then he grinned.

"Slowly," he whispered.

We began walking quietly, almost on tippy-toe, sharing the weight of the petrol. I felt scared as Hell but for a long time the soldiers couldn't see us because the trucks still blocked their view. We were lucky, damned lucky.

The can was heavy but Ray bore most of the weight. We were halfway up Hauteville when I heard more jackboots.

"Quick! Down here!" said Ray, and we ducked down a side alley.

There was a commotion on George Street. We didn't see anything, just listened out for the smack of fists, the slipping and sliding of feet. I didn't dare look and I didn't dare move, but I'll bet it was a couple of drunk soldiers venting their anger on some poor soul. I was expecting Ray to signal to me that we should join the fray, but instead he crouched next to me, quiet as a mouse.

After a few minutes it was over. Ray and I remained.

"That was close." He straightened up. "I've had enough excitement for one night, eh?"

It was heady stuff. With my pulse racing and my heart jumping, we reached the Gables.

"Not bad for a night's work!"

Ray offered me one of his cigarettes and I took it gladly. He called me his second lieutenant, and I was choked up with pride. I didn't think to ask

what the petrol was for, and after a few drags I
was too giddy to care. Ray was laughing, smiling
his old smile and saying we should do it again.

I don't know how long it took before he told
me what he wanted. I think we were sitting in the
garden when it all came out.

"Now then, *man amie*," he goes, "these are the
worst of times. We've got to do something. Surely
you must feel it."

I looked across at him, not yet understanding.

He lowered his eyes. "What was it you meant when
you told me you had a boat?"

I swallowed hard. "What?"

"The boat. Were you serious?"

I didn't answer. I was like Zacharias in the
Bible, struck dumb through doubt.

"I need to get away," Ray says. "They'll have me
sent to France the next time I'm arrested. We'll
escape together, you and me, what do you reckon?"

I didn't reckon anything.

His rough face crumpled and he threw his cigarette on the ground.

"There's no boat. You were lying and I am a
damned fool to think you could help me."

It was like a game of poker when you never know
who's bluffing.

"*Ch'est pas vère.*" I jumped up. "I'll show you
if you want."

Tchi qu'il pense que j'sis fou? Je ne sais pas.
It didn't take much, did it? It makes my blood boil
to remember how I played into his hands. I get

into such a rage and I curse myself for taking a man like Ray Le Poidevoin at his word. If there is a pool somewhere down there that burneth with fire and brimstone, I hope he drowns in it. He was seventeen, don't forget, and I was barely fifteen year. *Cor damme, je m'en fou!* A stupid kid who didn't know better.

I should never have opened my door to that scum. When I walked out to meet him on that night I sealed my fate and that of our family. I wonder now if anything he told me was true, and if those bruises were as bad as he made out. He probably fell over drunk. He wasn't on no blacklist. He was no hero.

Knock and the door will be opened, seek and ye shall find. But I bolt my door now in case he comes back. One day I know he will. He'll be wanting to fool me into trusting him again, wanting to take my boat off me. The scoundrel! I see him everywhere with his laughing eyes and broken nose. *Au yous,* Emile, the only time now I'll open my door to Ray Le Poidevoin is when I'm in Hell. I'll open the doors of Hell all right, when I hear him banging to get in.

17TH DECEMBER 1985, 5:30 P.M.

Oh my God. You won't believe who just came knocking at my door! He didn't give up for ages, either. At first I didn't hear because the TV was on so loudly. (Yes, I know I said Dad threw the TV out but Mum went and bought a new one, which is bigger and better and even gets French channels (which are all quite filthy).

I was right in the middle of an episode of *Columbo* when I heard the banging and realised I had a visitor. I hate interruptions so I ignored it. Then Columbo got caught in a shoot-out and I was worried that whoever was banging would come and peer through the sitting room window and see me. So I went and hid behind the curtains. I stood there perfectly still like a Buddhist. But the banging sounded urgent and destroyed my sense of Zen. I wondered if it was the police, and they'd come to drag me off to prison, then I imagined it was Nic and she'd come to drag me off to Hell.

That's when I tiptoed into the hall to see what was happening.

"Come on!" I heard someone growl.

Our front door has a little window of frosted glass so I can usually tell who it is. I saw a big head, lusciously broad shoulders, a bit of a slouch. I stood very still and stared in wonder.

It was Michael.

MICHAEL PRIAULX!

Aaagh! (I thought).

It was as if he knew I was there, because he pressed his hand and face into the glass.

"Cathy? Are you home?"

SHIT! SHIT! SHIT! (I thought again).

I couldn't believe it! Michael. Michael! He's back.

But I wasn't going to let him in. I couldn't have him seeing me in such a state. I haven't had a shower for as long as I can remember and there's this spot on my chin that I've had to squeeze and squeeze. Peter Falk might be able to get away with looking like he's slept in a hedge but I'm not a famous TV detective (wearing what is surely a wig). A girl must have some self-respect/control/soap. Thus and therefore I pinned myself to the wall and tried not to breathe and hoped Michael would go away. He bent down and pushed the letter box open and stuck his nose right through it. I nearly had a heart attack and jumped behind our new pine bookshelf. Michael and I stayed like that for about three minutes, which is actually a very long time. Then I heard him straighten up. I knew the front door was unlocked (because nobody ever locks their doors on Guernsey), but I was 99% sure he wouldn't come in. I took my chance and darted up the stairs. It was definitely anxiety-making, because I wanted to see him but also didn't.

Then, when I heard him walk round the side of the house, I realised he was limping. It shocked me but it shouldn't have. After all, he's lucky to be walking at all. The accident nearly killed him and when he finally regained consciousness he couldn't turn his head or say his name.

I lifted net curtains an inch and there was Michael, inspecting the hydrangeas. He's still as good-looking although his hair's a lot shorter (they must've had to shave it to stitch his brain back in). He walked around the patio, examining the ornamental weeds and looking out to sea. Our house is at the bottom of the Village, which is also the top of a cliff. The garden runs down to meet scrubland, which borders the cliff path that runs to Fermain Bay. The whole of the Village is sort of toppling into the sea, but then if you live on an island the sea is always near.*

I wonder if Michael remembers the last time he was here. He might not because it was just before his accident and he's apparently lost some of his memory glands. Perhaps he needs my help. Or maybe he wants to talk about Nic. He's been in England for half the year, so he wasn't here when Nic went off the cliff. He wasn't here when everything went wrong. He was lucky, really, being in a coma.

A coma is a deep sleep before you die. I was often amazed at how deeply Dad could sleep, even in the

* Unless that island is Australia.

middle of the day. I used to want to prod him just to check he was still breathing. As it happens, he was in a real and proper coma when his heart stopped working. Dr. Senner told me that. Some people stay in a coma for a very long time, but this is not good for you (or for the people around you). I'm not sure if that means you are better off dead. Look at Michael. He's back from the dead in time for Christmas.

The last time I saw him was about a fortnight after his fight with Pete. By then I was definitely in love with him, and I'd also managed to convince him that Mum needed help with the garden. Mum didn't need help with anything, but she was out with her new best friends the Christian Aid Tin Rattlers, so I had Michael all to myself. I poured him a big glass of Dad's remaining whiskies and we sat on sun loungers, watching the powerboat races. At first I felt quite awkward and couldn't think what to say to him. I know everything about Michael so it's not like I need to ask questions. I know what bands he likes (Jesus and Mary Chain and The Cure), and where he bought his jacket from (Easy Rider in the Market Place), and what football team he supports (Arsenal Rovers). In the end I told him how impressed I was with how he'd handled Pete.

He sighed and stared at his hands.

"Pete Mauger thinks he's some fucking big shot. He walks into a room, expecting everyone to lick his arse. Fucking morons thinking they're special."

I nodded sympathetically but felt a bit scared.

"This piss-pot island does it to you. It's the same old crap, over and over. It's like a fucking net closing in.

These people, I feel like fucking squeezing the life out of them just to prove they're real."

He then had a demi-rant about Guernsey in general, which I found *très* worrying. He told me everyone wants to be a big fish in a little pond, and Guernsey's not even a pond, more a puddle. He said, "Bollocks to it" a lot. He also told me I couldn't trust anyone and I especially couldn't trust my friends. He said they'd fuck me over in a second, since that's what people did.

I wanted to tell him he was wrong, but couldn't. After all, during the Occupation lots of Guernsey people earned good money informing on their neighbours and friends.* The Guernsey Post Office had dozens of letters every month and Dad quoted cases all the time.

I watched Michael light up one of his red-packet-quick-death Marlboro cigarettes. He took a big drag and blew smoke in my face. I got completely sidetracked when I looked at his lips. He offered me the packet but I shook my head. He took another hungry gulp of whisky and I was convinced something huge was about to happen. I wanted to kiss him so much I thought I'd explode. I didn't know what to say or do. Michael rubbed his bottom lip.

"It's like with Donnie, yeah, he knows about the world and he's made all this money, but people hate him for it. They think he's dodgy. Of course he doesn't care,

---

* Cf. Blanche Agnes Gaudion's (generally dull) diary extracts first published in *The Occupation Today*, 1969, vol. 3. Wherein she reports "lowlife quislings" received a reward of up to £100 for informing on people. That's a lot of money, even now (unless you're buying French cheese and wine in Best Foods Ltd.).

he's got nothing to prove. I respect that. He's the only person around here who knows about *living*, but people have to go and shit-stir. Take your mate Nicolette—she turned up last Saturday out of the blue, pretended she was looking for you. She was *spying* on us. Then she was asking Donnie all these questions and calling me his 'pool boy.'"

I found it annoying that Nic had never mentioned this. I wondered what she was up to, but I had to pretend that I already knew. (I didn't want Michael thinking I didn't "know shit" as per usual.)

I told him Nic had a stupid sense of humour.

"Yeah, well, if she comes round Donnie's again I'll give her something to talk about. Tell her that if you want. Tell her I'll give her a private show."

"OK," I replied, not quite understanding.

Michael nodded and knocked back more whisky.

"She'll be stuck here, the one growing old and fat, and I'll be away, I'll be *gone*."

The words *away* and *gone* cut straight through me.

"Are you going soon?"

"Yeah." Michael lowered his eyes and shrugged. "I've got it sorted. My ticket out of here."

I sat very still and told him that I'd really, really miss him. Then I told him he couldn't and shouldn't go any-where, and that Guernsey wasn't actually so bad.

He laughed. "Wait a few years and you'll see what I mean. You'll get so desperate you'll do *anything* to get away."

I asked Michael to explain but he was too busy fin-ishing my whisky. Then he said he didn't want to talk anymore, so we just sat and watched the clouds move. I imagined us flying away together through them, but now I wish I'd made more of an effort to talk to him about his problems. I should've made him tell me what was bothering him so much. I feel a bit guilty about it all, and you'll understand why if I skip forward to the next morning.

I walked into my form room at ten to nine and found a crowd of girls gathering in the corner. For the first time in her life Lisa Collenette had an audience, but it was obvious why. Her face had turned purple and her eyes were swollen, and as she blew her spectacular nose Nic gently rubbed her shoulder. I don't like Lisa much and it's not because she can eat whatever she wants and stay skinny, or because she looks like a ferret, or because she beat me in Geography. I just don't like her. Furthermore I never understood how someone so genetically handicapped could be related to Michael. (Does third cousin twice removed* count?)

I asked what was wrong.

Nic shook her head grimly.

"You'll never guess! Michael Priaulx went off the top of Pleinmont Tower last night. They've had to airlift him to Southampton because his condition was so bad no one could help him here."

I was so shocked I nearly fainted there and then.

* During the Occupation the Germans made reports about the large number of subnormal people on the island, blaming it on the intermixing of resident families. Obviously this applies to ferret-face Collenette.

"I only saw him yesterday and he was OK."

Nic's neat little eyebrows jumped.

"What? You saw Michael? Where?"

"My house. He came round for a chat."

Lisa glared at me. "What about?"

"This and that." I shrugged. "We had a few drinks."

Lisa's eyes got big and scary. "Drinks?"

I thought everyone would be impressed but instead they were appalled.

Nic shook her head. "Christ, Cat, that's why he fell. He was pissed out of his brains."

I was standing there, feeling a lot like I was in court on trial, when in walked Mr. McCracken and told us to sit down.

"But we can't have a lesson, sir," Nic said quickly. "Lisa's cousin had a really bad fall and he might die and Cat's just told us *why*!"

"What? No, I didn't! I just said I *saw* him. You're getting ahead of yourself."

Nic stroked my arm like she cared, but the tone of her voice was all wrong.

"It's OK, Cat. We know you've had a hard time, what with your dad and everything, and I know you *really* liked Michael . . . only you shouldn't have given him *alcohol*."

The whole class seemed to hold their breath and stare at me. Mr. McCracken slapped his books down on the desk.

"What's this?"

Nic spun around to face him. "*Well*, sir"—she looked back at me—"we don't know the full story, but Constable

Priaulx found his son at the bottom of the Pleinmont Tower early this morning and apparently he'd been drinking heavily and had fallen from the top."

She then went on to itemise Michael's injuries, with lots of excellent gesturing. Apparently Michael's head had swelled up like a Giant Jersey Cabbage* and he'd nearly lost an eye. He'd also broken both his arms and legs, cracked several ribs, and blown a puncture in his lung. There was the suggestion he might be paralysed.

"And was he alone?" asked Mr. McCracken.

Nic swung back to look at me. "Who knows?"

"What are you trying to say?" (I must've been purple by now.) "I wasn't with him. I don't know anything. I don't, sir!"

I felt guilty for no reason at all, and was angry with everyone for staring.

Mr. McCracken gave me a curt nod. "Right, well, be sure to tell the police if you think you can help, Cathy. As for the rest of you, this isn't some kind of kangaroo court so I suggest you all sit down and let that be the end of it."

But it wasn't. The minute class was over, Nic grabbed my arm and hauled me off to the loos.

"What the fuck!" She was shaking her head as she steered me over to the basins. She then checked her

---

* *Brassica oleracea longata* (Acephala group) was principally a Jersey crop and looked nothing like the present-day vegetable to which I've been (most cruelly) linked. It grew up to 20 feet on giant stalks which were made into excellent walking sticks (see Southcombe Parker and G. Stevens Cox, *The Giant Cabbage of the Channel Islands*, Toucan Press, 1974. Yes! A book Dad didn't write).

mascara in the mirror. "Shit, Cat. What were you playing at in there? You really lost it!"

"What was *I* playing at? What were *you* playing at?"

Nic smiled at her reflection and dabbed under her
eyes.

"Excuse me, but I wasn't the last person to see Michael Priaulx in one piece." She turned to look at me.
"And if Mr. McCracken thinks you were getting all cosy
with Michael what's the harm? He might get jealous.
Don't you get it? It's a *ploy*."

I laughed nervously. "Right. But I wasn't having any
kind of secret *thing* with Michael and I don't like you
implying that I was. We should get our facts straight,
and find out what happened. And on that note"—I took a
breath—"where was Pete last night?"

Nic blinked. "What? Oh, you're kidding me. Fuck *off*!
You don't seriously think Pete was involved. He was
with me, of course."

I'll admit I was disappointed that Pete had an instant
alibi.

Nic laughed. "And you were just telling *me* not to
jump to any conclusions."

"I can't help it," I replied. "Michael said you were
bothering him at Donnie's the other weekend. Maybe
Pete got jealous."

Nic shook her head.

"You and your imagination."

It's true I have a brilliant imagination (which explains my high grades in Creative Writing) and I'm
embarrassed to admit I did imagine all sorts vis-à-vis
Michael and his death-plunge drama. Thank God he's

come back. He can explain things for himself. I think I've waited long enough—that's probably why he came round. He's been away all these months and now he's ready to set the record straight and tell me everything. And I can tell him everything, too. He's the only person who'll understand what I did and why. I hope he won't judge me. He might even be glad Nic's dead and thank me for killing her. Maybe he'll promise to keep my secret and maybe we'll get married.

He's obviously desperate to talk to me because he left me a note saying so:

Do you need a gardener?
If so, please call M. Priaulx on 237678.

How amazing is that? If I need a reason to keep living it's definitely Michael Priaulx. I love him, I think. Nic said I didn't know anything about feelings but now I do. I definitely understand what all those words mean. You *fall* for someone because you lose your balance. You have a *crush* on them because you've been *squished*. I love Michael Priaulx, for sure. He can honestly smash me to bits.

The Director-General of the BBC
Broadcasting House
Portland Place
London
W1A 1AA

Dear Sir,

I am writing with regard to the television documentary "Lying with the Enemy" aired on Sunday night last.

I was outraged and appalled by what I felt was a grossly inaccurate depiction of Guernsey and its people during the Second World War, pandering to only the lowest sensibilities. It would of course be impossible to convey the full tragedy of our five years spent under German rule in a mere sixty minutes, but you clearly approached the subject with an agenda, and the result was a crass simplification of a complex history. You stirred up the usual controversies but had no fresh material as the basis for your claims, instead hoping to titillate your viewers by dwelling on subjects such as the apparently "all too common" liaisons between local women and German soldiers.

Although I do not deny that these liaisons occurred, I would like to alert you to the presence of French prostitutes, brought onto the island for the sole purpose of "servicing" the troops. How lusty do you imagine us natives to be? For the most part Guernsey housewives devoted all their energies to finding ways to clothe and feed their families. My own mother, for example, was reduced to working as a laundress, pressing and mending officers' uniforms to earn extra money. When asked what she thought about this so-termed horizontal collaboration, she said most people on the island were too exhausted to involve themselves in illicit sexual liaisons. She pointed out that those that did were often the very young and naive, or the poor and ill-educated, and they were not won over by charming "officer gentlemen," but more worn down by their own desperate circumstances.

Most islanders had no idea when the Occupation would end. Many believed the Germans were here to stay. By 1942 we were surviving on less than 1,000 calories a day. It was a terrible time, but our personal circumstances were not nearly as pitiful as those of the foreign labourers brought in to build Hitler's Atlantic Wall, many of whom perished in the most appalling conditions. Your film was replete with lingering shots of the bunkers and towers, and yet barely made reference to the human cost of building them.

Had you taken the time to interview a diverse cross-section of islanders you might have come closer to the extremely complex truth, instead of making such extraordinary claims whilst consistently underplaying genuine acts of what you called "petty resistance" such as the harbouring of banned radio sets, or the theft of food or fuel. Let me assure you these crimes resulted in very serious penalties on more than one occasion. Perhaps they are not grand acts of heroism when considered against Great Britain's apparently impeccable war record, but they are memorable when set in the appropriate context, which is something you consistently failed to do. Guernsey is a tiny island, and with such a dense concentration of enemy soldiers it was impossible for any large-scale resistance movements to develop.

The hardship of life under German rule varied from household to household, but, generally speaking, the constant fear and deprivation led to bitterness, resentment, and exhaustion. By 1945 both soldiers and civilians alike were in a desperate and humiliated state. One German officer compared the island to a "sanatorium" for the sick and wounded. In real life people had lost their health, their livelihoods, and their property, children had lost the chance of a decent education, whole families had been destroyed.

Furthermore, I would like to point out that

Guernsey was six million pounds in debt after the Occupation, and there has been no compensation for islanders who were deported or imprisoned by the Germans. It is thus perhaps a drama, but one that is continuing.

I am appalled at how standards have slipped into the gutter and I have grown tired of these poorly researched, anti–Channel Island programmes, and therefore will not be renewing my television licence, since I cannot agree with providing financial support for things I stand firmly against.

Yours sincerely,
E. P. Rozier
Manager/Editor of The Patois Press
Sans Soucis
Village de Courtils
St. Peter Port

P.S. There were no GESTAPO on the Channel Islands—only Geheimfeld Polizei. Lack of proper research only entrenches stereotypes and deepens the resentments we islanders feel towards those so intent on judging us.

Sex! Drama! Passion! Who needs TV?

I've just been on the phone to Michael. I called him up after boiling myself alive in the bath, and applying three coats of The Body Shop Sage and Comfrey Blemish Minimiser to my entire body.

I welcomed him back to Guernsey and he asked me if I was being Ironic. I was impressed/surprised that he knew what it meant.

"I get the feeling people are avoiding me and I thought you might be, too," he said. "We should meet, have a catch-up."

Catch-up might be code for a Rampant Snog. (OK. Probably not.)

"I've only been back five minutes and I'm going mad. Mum's scared to let me out of the house and jumps whenever the phone rings."

I can't blame Mrs. Priaulx for being a bit anxious. She remembers her youngest son drinking meths/head-butting cattle/crashing his motorbike a trillion times, and she probably just hoped he'd grow out of it. At least she's letting him out of the house, though. We've arranged to meet by the old Military Cemetery tomorrow afternoon. Don't worry, that's not as grim as it sounds! The cemetery is actually very pretty and well-kept, with all the graves arranged in mathematical fractions, and the lawns neatly clipped, etc. Down the far end there's a big cement cross with flowerbeds beneath it. You never see anyone there, though, so whoever does the gardening must be embarrassed to be seen doing it, because most of the graves are German.

But not all of them. My grandfather is buried there, *par exemple.* He was a soldier in the First World War and for a long time I thought that was how he died. I can't believe he's too happy about where he's buried since he's stuck between a Jerseyman and a German. But the German was quite famous and his death caused a scandal. At first they thought a farmer had killed him, then they decided he'd killed himself because he didn't want to be sent to the Russian Front. Then they said he'd been robbed and stabbed by his own batman (who was promptly found down a well and so obviously *had* committed suicide). As this story demonstrates, Hitler only sent his youngest/most inept/injured soldiers to the islands because they wouldn't be needed to fight. They therefore mostly had a holiday.* Dad said it was a shame Syphilis didn't kill them all. Have I mentioned the French-style brothels dotted around St. Peter Port? And that's not to mention what the local women were up

* The rumour is that Hitler ultimately planned to make the Channel Islands "Strength Through Joy" holiday camps. They were going to be called Julius, Gustav, and Adolf. (No wonder people doubted his sanity.)

to. Inevitably there were frequent outbreaks of Venerable Diseases, as well as some suspiciously blond babies.*

Dad said the Occupation brought out the worst in everyone. One young soldier was shot because he didn't want to be a Nazi and tried to run away, and another was killed for milking a cow. Of course, that was in 1944 when everyone was starving or eating their domestic pets, and although his death was tragic, it wasn't his cow to milk. There's also the story of the soldiers who were drowned because they refused to leave the rock they were standing on, even though it was slowly being covered by the tide. No one came to relieve them of their guard duty and they refused to be helped by a local fisherman.

FYI: There were four or five suicides a week among the troops in occupied territories in 1943. This is widely attributed to low morale, local alcohol, and only pets to eat. Certainly by 1944 the German soldiers left on Guernsey were in a terrible state. They even tried to eat seagulls they were so hungry.

They never ate each other but I told Vicky they did. Unfortunately she believed me and dreamed there were flesh-eating Nazi Zombies lurking on the cliffs. For three weeks solid she woke up screaming and couldn't be left alone. Dr. Senner was understandably upset and came round to talk to Dad about it. He (wrongly) blamed Dad for putting "sensational" ideas into my head. At first I

---

* It's hard to know how many. Dad reckoned there were around 200 but mudslinging English journalists have pushed the figure into 1000s. (NB: In France the Germans claimed to have fathered 85,000 babies, so really, the English should just get over it.)

thought this was a compliment, but he then told Dad to "face facts" and "get a grip." It was very excruciating for Mum, who was left to apologise after Dad turned pink and then purple and stormed off to the Yacht Club. She whispered something to Dr. S., who mentioned seeing Dad at the surgery. I wanted to ask why, but I wasn't supposed to hear.

It was much later when Dad came back and loaded the TV into the boot of his car. He was staggering slightly from the effort and his eyes were red with fury. I tried to go and hug him but he pushed me away and ordered me to my room. He said I'd let him down terribly, and he promised me that he'd never tell me anything about his work ever-ever-ever again.

He kept to his word, as a matter of fact. He stopped taking me out in the boat, and when he was home he locked himself in his study until late. I'm sad to say we hardly ever spoke properly again, and it was only after he'd died that I went into his study and took copies of all his books and went through his files. That's also when I started learning them off by heart and inside out. I wanted to make sure that I never got my facts wrong again, and I wanted to make Dad proud of me. In case he ever came back.

Mr. McCracken would've found Dad's files so interesting, and if he'd ever bothered to look at them, they might've taken his mind off his messy divorce. Divorces can be time-consuming and traumatic, and I'm sure the Deadly Poison Pen Letters only made the trauma worse.

They kept appearing on his windscreen after school, and sometimes they were tucked between textbooks on his desk. I can't be sure when they started, and they were often only a word (although COCKSUCKER might actually be two).

Dad said you should always get your facts straight before you jump to hasty conclusions. He said everyone had the wrong idea about the Roziers, because they believed what they'd been told and never bothered to ask more questions. There was a lot of finger-pointing during the Occupation, as I've already said, and it didn't even stop when the Germans left. People were driven by money, malice, or just plain envious jealousy, and those who were wrongly accused had to move to Torteval.*

Par le chemin, the only reason I know about Mr. Mac's nasty letters was because I was with him when he found one. It was a few days after Michael's accident and I was trying to take my mind off things by helping him tidy the History library. I'd also got my first B- and needed to discuss this Greek tragedy.

"It's not the end of the world," is what Mr. Mac said, "but you have been a bit distracted. This is an important year, and I don't want to hear any more tales about you and Michael Priaulx doing whatever it was you were doing."

"Nothing was going on with me and Michael," I promised, "but I do feel bad that's he's ended up half dead."

Mr. Mac carried on stacking *The Tudors* onto a shelf.

---

* Torteval is on the northernmost edge of the island and is where the crazies live. They have a whole other language and never leave the parish, for their own safety.

"If Michael had been drinking and you saw him before the fall, you *should* tell the police."

Mr. Mac was frowning at me now, and I hated the feeling that I'd let him down again. It made me quite emotional. I'm not usually one to start crying in public, but that B- had really cut me up. I stood there, clutching G. R. Elton, and before I knew it tears were streaming down my cheeks. It was like I'd sprung a leak: my shoulders shook and my lungs heaved. How embarrassing. I didn't see Mr. McCracken's face because I was looking at my feet, but he gently rested his hand on my shoulder. I thought that was very big of him. I must've turned. He was close enough so that I could've pressed my head into his chest. I bet it would have felt like the most natural thing in the world (or Guernsey). I could smell his spicy cologne and I wondered if he had stubble. Sometimes when I saw Dad asleep on the sofa I didn't just want to prod him awake—I wanted to run my finger along his chin and feel his stubble. One time I did and he didn't even notice. I remember its smell quite distinctly.

Mr. McCracken was a lot taller than me so our faces didn't get close.

"There, there," he said.

After a few minutes I pulled myself together and tidied up my book pile and thanked him.

"Come on." He picked up his briefcase. "I'll give you a lift home, you're in no fit state to cycle."

So we walked to the staff car park, and that's when I saw the note on his windscreen. I could tell by his face it wasn't the first. Poor Mr. McCracken. Our melt-in-the-mouth moment was ruined. I tried to take his mind off it as we drove through the water lanes. We talked a bit more about Michael and his injuries.

"That boy had a death wish," sighed Mr. Mac.

I told him he was wrong.

I then explained the massive difference between death and dying (and this bit is very deep). Most people are afraid of death but are actually quite curious about dying. Dying is about experiencing something terrifying but also thrilling, where your heart either goes very fast or stalls. Dying is about seeing your life flash around you in Brilliant Technicolor. It's about taking a big risk: like driving at maximum speeds or stealing something precious or jumping off something high. It's about pushing your luck and getting away with it and deciding life isn't so bad. Death, on the other hand, is a big, blank space. You feel and see nothing. It's not even a colour. When you're dead people forget who you are and what you looked like. They carry on without you. I can't believe Michael wanted that to happen.

"You've thought about it an awful lot, haven't you?" muttered Mr. Mac.

I nodded back. "I used to hate thinking about it. I even developed this excellent theory that nobody ever died, they just went somewhere far away, like Australia."

He smiled. "Why Australia?"

"I don't know, although, coincidentally, Michael has an uncle who moved there after the War. He told me he wanted to visit him."

The McGears crunched and we shuddered into the Village.

"Well," sighed Mr. Mac, "the weather's nice but it's a funny sort of a place, no *history*, everything's so *new*."

I couldn't really imagine it.

We pulled up outside the house and I don't know why, but I imagined that Dad was waiting for me. I pictured him coming to the door to welcome me back from school. Maybe I'd been thinking about Dad as much as I'd been thinking about Michael. Of course, it would've been very unlike Dad to come to the front door to greet me. No, he'd be sitting in his study, completely ignoring/avoiding me. So I imagined him in his study. I wondered if he'd be secretly pleased to hear that I'd kept all his papers.

The car had stuttered to a halt and McCracky was staring at me.

"What?"

I tried to look calm. I hadn't realised I was speaking out loud.

"What did you just say?"

I shrugged. "Nothing."

"*I* see." He laughed. "You were talking to yourself. I know someone else who does that, apparently you get a better class of conversation that way. I don't suppose it says much about the quality of my company."

I opened the car door. "I don't talk to myself."

"Oh?" he frowned. "Who do you talk to then?"

I stared up at our house and of course I knew the answer. It was properly Ironic. I couldn't talk to Dad the whole time he was alive, but the minute he was dead I knew he'd have to listen.

"The testimony of
C. A. Rozier"

[Transcribed by E. P. Rozier]

The dead can't talk and it's a shame, since there's
one dead man I'd really like some answers off and
that's Jean-Pierre Duquemin. J-P was a chap Ray
knew, a mechanic at Falla's Garage, but he was also
a *crapaud*, which should've been an omen. I don't
like Jerseymen any more than the English, although
to give J-P his due he worked hard and only ever
said "*mais wai*" to everything he was asked. *P'têt*,
he agreed too much with what Ray said, and if
that's so he paid a heavy price for his goodwill.
I cannot think of a worse way to die.

He's buried next to Pop at Fort St. George, and
I like to keep their graves tidy in case we ever
get visitors. Not that Ray Le Poidevoin would be
welcome. He can stay on the other side of the world
and that is still too close for comfort.

Three isn't ever a good number, is it? I knew it

from the offing. But we needed J-P, since it was him who got us the Seagull outboard motor and it was him who found us some good black paint.

"Have you got a death wish?" laughed Ray when he clapped eyes on *Sarnia Chérie*. "Escaping on a bright red boat? We'd have been sitting ducks."

I hunched my shoulders and blushed from shame.

"I was going to paint her, of course I was."

"Well"—Ray nudged Jean-Pierre—"now we all can."

I knew I was out of my depth, but once old Ray got going he was like a dog with a bone. He told me to get to work on mapping a route to Southampton, meanwhile J-P caulked the boat and he found us a half-decent trailer. Planning an escape, I soon realised, was a serious business. I had to find an embarkation point, get to know the shipping routes, work out the timings of night patrols.

In case you're curious, Emile, I'd done a good job of hiding *Sarnia Chérie* for two long years. Old Mess. Chardine* had a boatshed not used for nearly a decade, over at Hommet Bonnet. It was so overgrown you couldn't see it till you were in it and nobody imagined it was ever worth bothering with. To tell the truth, the Krauts acted like they knew every inch of this island but they didn't know their Jaonniere from their Jerbourg, and they'd never get their nice boots dirty! So J-P was working there at night, under cover, and I started

---

* E.P.R. notes Charlie is referring to Leslie Chardine (1880-1946). For property maps see 23/45/AVTTH at Greffe Registry.

scouting further up the coast. It was a good few weeks before I settled on a slipway, just north of Bordeaux Harbour.* There were mines in the fields all around but the track was safe, since fishing boats still used it. From there I reckoned we'd have a safe run out to sea.

But I was in over my head all right, sweating over my Channel Islands Pilot and pretending I knew the ropes. Ray called me "the brains of the operation." *Si l'bouan Dju I'l pllais!* I feared in my heart *Sarnia Chérie* wouldn't get us halfway across the Channel and that was the God-honest truth. Some folk later said I was lucky the Nazis stopped me. *Bran-d'iaeux!* What do they know but the lies Ray peddled for his five minutes of glory. They call me bitter, but there's good reason I'm bitter, eh? Think of all the tripe that's been written.[†]

It was a foul winter but Ray was hell-bent on leaving once the boat was ready, giving no heed to the weather. We argued about it plenty, and he always

* E.P.R. notes: during the Occupation, fishing boats were permitted to leave from Bordeaux, Portlet (Torteval), St. Peter Port, and St. Sampson, although no boat was allowed to leave without a German soldier present.

[†] C.A.R. is referring to the articles that appeared in the *Guernsey Evening Press* on 6th and 10th May 1957, which gave details of Ray Le Poidevoin's "heroic" escape from Bordeaux. A longer version of the story was subsequently published in a national newspaper.

used the same cheap tactic. He'd say I was too
chicken, just like my old man. I never knew how
to answer him. In truth I found it harder and
harder to defend old Hubert. He barely spoke or
looked at me, and he moved about the house like it
wasn't his no more. I knew he was sick, but he'd
always been sick. He'd lost weight, but so had we
all. The skin was hanging off La Duchesse and I'd
catch her sometimes, standing in front of the mirror and pinching at her cheeks so as to give them
a bit more colour. She was run ragged, and she'd
even started taking in soldiers' uniforms to wash—
not' mémaon—enne lavresse, pensaï donc! Of course,
I saw plenty of local women lower themselves in
all kinds of ways. Not that I'm suggesting anything about La Duchesse. She was always the hero,
holding things together. No doubt about it.

But Ray was all about a different kind of hero.
He had decided that if we were going to England
then we couldn't go empty-handed.

"We take intelligence with us," he said. "We
should map out the island, the new fortifications,
estimate the number of men and weapons at each
base. It will help the Allies win the islands
back!"

He expected a lot of me and I did my best, in
truth I did. I started work on my own version of
Festung Guernsey. With scraps of paper taken from
the office I drew maps, dividing up the island
into sections, and I started noting down all the
strong points and billets in St. Peter Port and

St. Martin. I wandered all around the east coast,
scribbling as I went, and as my scrapbook grew, so
did my anxieties. I couldn't think where to hide
it. I stashed it under my mattress, then I hid it
in a drawer, then I kept it in my satchel. *Hé bian,*
it's nearly funny since, for the first time in this
story, I lacked imagination. The trouble was, wherever I looked I saw them German swines. They were
always in the office and the office was next to
our house. La Duchesse said we had nothing to hide.

"I take people as I find them," she'd say. "If
this is what my life has come to then I'll make do.
And at least those Germans show me more courtesy
than other persons about."

It was a dig at me, her errant son, but what
could I reply? This was Hell's own nightmare. I
felt sure I'd be caught out, and I remember the
day I found La Duchesse at our front door, waiting
for me.

"Where have you been?"

I told her nowhere but I felt so guilty. I
would've made a rotten spy.

She looked me up and down. "I have things to do.
Your brother is next door with Blanche. Will you
fetch him in an hour?"

I nodded silently and galloped up the stairs,
feeling her eyes burn into my back. When the front
door slammed I turned around. Was silence better
than lies? *Je ne sais pas.*

The pressure was too much for me to take alone.
Without even thinking I was tapping lightly at the

door of the spare room, hoping Pop would answer.

"Pop," I whispered. "Are you there?"

I imagined him slowly opening the door, seeing the worry on my face, and I saw myself walking in, ready to tell him everything. But back on the landing I tapped again and waited and heard nothing. After another minute I pushed the door open. The room smelled stale and the curtains were half drawn, but what I saw on the wall in front of me made my hairs stand on end. It was a crumpled map of Europe pinned up high, with small flags dotted over it, marking what I realised were the Allied positions. Eh me, it was a sight I hadn't expected. I walked over to the dresser to get a better look and there was one of the old leaflets from before the Germans came. The words "Why Go Mad? There's No Place Like Home" stared back at me.

It was like Pop was talking to me, trying to tell me something, and I sat on the bed with my tired eyes watering. I stared at the map and wondered where Pop had got his information from. I wanted to ask him, and I waited and I waited. I didn't know where he'd gone. Still don't, in fact. I sat there with my old school satchel resting on my lap. I toyed with the dust that danced in the air in front of me, I flicked through the pages of his prayer book. On the back page Pop had written some numbers and I wondered if it was verses of the Bible. Then the door slammed and La Duchesse was calling for me. Over an hour had passed, I had let her down again.

That is when I did it, Emile. I was in a hurry and

I had to hide my scrapbook. I quietly pulled the
dresser away from the wall and lifted the floorboard. I remember thinking someone had pulled the
nails up once already. I slid my scrapbook underneath Hubert's strongbox, and off I went to fetch
you.

*Malin haen? Oui, J'étais si malin, mais saber-
dé-bouais j'sis gnolle auch't'haeure?* Is it any
wonder nobody wants to hear my side of this story?
They cannot imagine I could do something so stupid. They'd prefer I just went away. Well, I'd have
liked to get away and that was always the plan. We
were meant to be off on 12th December, a Thursday.
It was going to be me and Ray and J-P to Southampton for Christmas. *Au yous*, my goose was cooked
all right. We reckoned on departing before eleven
o'clock at night, and after that we had plenty of
hours of darkness to get some distance from the
German Water Police.

I'd tried to convince Ray to wait because I was
scared about the weather, but I was also worried
what would happen if I was gone. I knew there'd be
a payback and my family'd be for it.

"I'll go without you, then," Ray offered. "Maybe
it is different for me. My sisters are safe in England and my mother's as tough as a boot. Just get
me the intelligence and I'll take it without you."

I wasn't sure if he was joking. Should I let him
go without me and take all the glory?

"No, no, I want to come," I remember saying. "I stand by my word."

But later I got so worked up I made up my mind to stay. I was battling so many emotions, turning this way and that. If I'd had more time to think on it, if I'd known how it would end, I'd never have done it. Trouble is, I'd made a pact with the Devil himself.

Who knows what would've happened if the 12th had ever come like we'd planned it. But it was just before eleven o'clock at night on 9th December, year of Our Lord 1942. That's when the Feldgendarmes came to our house, kicking in the door with their rifles.

Je m'en fou! For years I went over this stuff, again and again, Emile. I blamed myself and so did everyone. Guernsey was and is my world, but they still think I'm that silly boy whose father died instead of him. But I say to them now, sometimes the wrong folk get the blame and sometimes the blame must be shared. After our so-called glorious Liberation there were unanswered questions going round my head. When the Krauts came to our house they knew just where to look—how *is* that? Who told them? I've been fed all sorts of lines by them in the States who keep a tight hold over those secret German records. I know you've tried to get them opened, Emile. Perhaps they'll listen to you. I want to see those files, the names of those lowlife informers. You say there's a Human Rights Law that says we're not allowed to. What about my rights, eh? How come the lowlife who informed on me gets away with murder?

And it is *murder.*

Es-t à écoutaïr, Ray Le Poidevoin? Jean-Pierre has paid his price but when will you tire of the hero act? You were no brother to me. You hung me out to dry, you did. Hypocrite! Traitor! I've been over it enough: who else knew where I hid my precious notes? I told you because I trusted you, but you gave me up to the Germans all the same.

The Bible is wrong, Emile, it isn't the sons who pay for the sins of their fathers, but fathers who pay for the sins of their sons. How else could it be, when the Germans went straight to our father's room and ripped up the floorboards? They knew what they were looking for and they found it, soon enough.

18TH DECEMBER 1985, 5:30 P.M.

[SITTING ON SOGGY DECK CHAIR ON PATIO,
HYPNOTISED BY FOG]

I didn't know what I was looking for when I first went into Dad's study. I suppose I wanted proof, and I don't just mean proof that he was dead. I needed proof that he'd lived at all. Don't get me wrong, he'd definitely been here—all flesh and blood and hair—but he'd also *never* been here. I was sure he was always meant to be somewhere else, which is why I'd dreamed that he was dying and/or dead. Maybe that's why I didn't cry when it finally happened.

I wonder if some people are dead before they've lived. These are the same people who won't play Snakes and Ladders because it relies too much on chance, and have to colour-code the contents of the fridge, and insist that cucumbers should be peeled.

It was when I was searching through the drawers of his desk that I found the bottle of Glenfiddich. I'd never had Dad down as a drinker, but then I found another bottle in his filing cabinet—this was Famous Grouse. I remember the first time I unscrewed its top and sniffed it. Before then I'd thought all stubble smelled like whisky.

It's funny, when Dr. Senner drinks he tries to hug and kiss everyone, and once I saw him cry, but Dad was never like that. He hated going to parties and the few times we got invited to any he'd hover by an exit, ready to make his escape. He wasn't like other drunks—he never told rude jokes or fell over—he'd never be caught out.

Although there was that one time at White Rock. I've mentioned Dad's (Un)Official Occupation Memorial, but not its grand unveiling, which was a disaster. Dad had lobbied the States for centuries (almost) to get them to approve of this plaque. It listed the names of islanders who'd been accused (rightly or wrongly) of misconduct under the Germans, and there was a space at the end for more names to be added, when new information came out. This list proved (Dad said) that Guernsey people didn't just SUFFER IN SILENCE* during the Occupation.

The plaque is now part of the harbour wall, and I should feel very proud of it/Dad, only I can't be because of what he did.

I was in the crowd with Mum, and Dad was on the platform with the Bailiff.† After a little introduction by said Bailiff, Dad was meant to give a speech about the bravery of families during the War and the unsung heroes who were put in prison for no good reason, and how

* It would be REMISS of me not to mention that my grandparents and Uncle Charlie are all named on the Memorial and Dad would've been, too, only he was given to a neighbour to look after because he was three years old, and the Nazis were (rightly) scared of toddlers.
† The Bailiff is in charge of local government and gives long and boring speeches, just like the English Prime Minister, but not like English bailiffs, who are scary and go round collecting debts/kneecaps.

the past was not behind us but all around us and still shaping us, etc. Only he totally embarrassed himself and the Bailiff had to jump in front of him, giving the cord a quick tug and going: "How splendid! Look at that!"

Dad disappeared behind the camera flashes, leaving me with Mum in the crush of people. She dragged me off to the car because she was so embarrassed, and I was too scared to ask her what was wrong. Then she told me it was nothing and that Dad was just Emotional because of the big unveiling.

It was only when I found the bottles that I realised Emotional was code for Drunk.

I know drinking is bad for you. Nic and I both drank too much but she was the hypocrite—blaming me for giving alcohol to Michael. I *did* call the police and tell them about the various whiskies he'd drunk before his accident and I'm very *très* glad I did. The duty sergeant promptly told me that an empty bottle of Absolut had been found in Michael's jacket. I went and reported all of this back to Nic and do you know what? She told me I was acting very guilty for someone who'd done nothing wrong.

I don't know if she fancied Michael. I don't know if I care. He's not the reason I killed her, but I need to tell him that I killed her. Michael's the one person I can 100% trust. I met him today, just like we'd arranged, and it was amazing. He was waiting for me by the cemetery gates, looking ruggedly sinister. I was wearing one of Dad's old shirts which I'd tie-dyed dark purple. It matched my Clobber Box leggings and cropped denim jacket. Michael was meant to notice how much thinner I looked and how much longer my fringe was. I wanted him to make some comment about how he hardly recognised me. But he didn't.

He just said: "How are you?"

His voice sounded different to how I remembered.

"Fine, and you?"

"Oh, you know."

Of course I didn't know, but he shoved his hands in his pockets and hunched himself over like a tortoise going into its shell.

"When did you get back?"

"Last week. So I missed all the excitement, eh?"

I nodded.

He kicked at the ground.

"Shall we walk for a bit? I'm slow but the doctors say I've got to walk every day."

I said that was fine, and that I was in no hurry.

We took the path down through the cemetery and climbed over the low fence at the back to get into Bluebell Woods. Michael managed really well. I asked him about Southampton and whether he'd liked it there and would go again, and what hospital food had tasted like, and what parts of his body still hurt. He answered back in a quiet voice, and sometimes paused and looked about. It turns out there's a big cinema in the town centre, he didn't like it much, hospital food was mostly wood pulp, and he might need another operation in a year.

"We all thought you were going to die and Nic and Lisa blamed me because I saw you last. I'd given you a lot to drink but you maybe won't remember. I wished I could've done something. All I could think about was how I'd climbed up the Pleinmont Tower with you that time and what a long way down it was."

Michael nodded. "They reckon I was lucky but after all these months it doesn't feel that way."

"Well, you missed a lot of really bad stuff, what with Nic dying so horribly."

Michael laughed a bit too loudly.

By now we'd walked down to where the cliff path starts, it was quite uneven and I was hoping he'd want to take my arm or lean against me. He didn't. I suppose I should be glad he can walk so well. The only time he hesitated was when we'd gone a little further to where the main path forks, left takes you into Town and right goes to Fermain. The path into Town goes past Soldier's Bay and Clarence Batterie.

Michael stared at me and it was megawatt electric.

"You plan to go that way?"

"I thought you'd want to."

"Why?"

"I don't know, I just assumed you'd want to see it."

We stood facing each other. It was like High Noon in a TV Western.

Then Michael smiled. "Most folk want to keep me away from sheer drops."

The place that Michael did/didn't want to go to was the Clarence Batterie (aka the scene of the crime, aka where I killed Nic). If this was one of Mum's dog-eared thrillers such an important location would've been described in detail much earlier on, but Dad has already written about it endlessly, and even drawn a map and floor plan. I therefore don't have much to add. The Clarence Batterie has always been and (despite everything) still is one of my favourite places to walk to on account of its stunning panoramas. It was no doubt because of said stunning panoramas that the Germans decided to make it one of the island's coastal defence units. At least here the Germans did most of their building underground so there's only the old gun positions visible on the surface, but if you refer to the excellent and comprehensive *Bunker Baedeker,** you can get some idea of what was going on under the surface. It's a shame that the tunnels are blocked up (but that also proves what the States are trying to hide).† The guns (of which there were five) were sold for scrap after the War. There is a notice explaining this, plus three dilapidated benches that are bolted into the cliff edge. Beyond that there's mostly a sheer drop down to razor-sharp rocks and rabidly foaming sea.

Michael tried to force the lock on the tunnel entrance. It's an ugly wooden door with lots of bolts. He stared at it for a long while.

"This place always gave me the creeps."

We climbed together up to the slope to the benches,

---

* Pages 74–76 to be precise.

† The theory was that the underground tunnels were intended for a far more sinister use than the British government/States of Guernsey/Guernsey Tourist Board would have us think. (Yes! Gas Chambers!) See also the testimonies from former slave workers vis-à-vis their brutal treatment (and tunnels being mass graves), E. P. Rozier, *Guernsey Gas Chambers and Other Myths*, ibid., op.cit., blah-blah, pages 1, 4–6, 23–56.

but Michael carried on, right to the cliff edge, which made me nervous. I dithered behind him, talking about "suicidal" slave labourers, etc. He nodded like he was listening. I'm not sure that he was. He was looking very dramatic, peering downwards. It's ridiculous they never put railings up, but I'm sure they will do now. I stood very still and watched Michael loom and brood (and other good words).

After a minute he turned so that he was looking straight at me.

"Come closer and see."

I went and stood right up next to him.

He whispered, "*You hear her voice, she's calling your name . . . the sound is deep.*"

I wondered if he'd become a Nazi Zombie, but he was actually reciting lyrics by The Cure (who may actually be Zombies now I've seen their album covers).

He gripped my hand. "*You hear her voice and you'd better run . . .*"

I listened to Michael's mad whispering, and the wailing of the seagulls around my head, and I couldn't run anywhere. It was more frightening than exciting, and it took me right back to that last night with Nic. My heart was beating full throttle ahead as I remembered how she'd grabbed me round the neck. I stole another nano-look at Michael, who was swaying now, and still glaring down into the oblivion into which she'd plummeted. He glared for an unnecessarily long time. I focused on him and tried (and failed) to mind-read, then I couldn't cope and had to step back. Michael lifted up his head, stretching out his arms on either side of him so that he looked like Jesus on the cross. It was all very weird. I was worried he'd jump and I'd get the blame.

"What are you doing?" I tugged hard at his jacket. "Stop it! Stop it!"

"What the fuck!" he toppled backwards and turned. "What the fuck is with you?! I wasn't going to jump. I just wanted to know what it felt like."

I looked into his burning coals/bottomless pits/eyes and I didn't know what to say.

He wiggled his hands in my face, pretending to cast a spell. "Don't worry. I can jump off anything and survive!" He walked over to the nearest bench. "Fair enough you're freaked out, though. You actually *liked* her."

It took a minute for me to catch him up.

"So did you. It was obvious. Don't try and deny it."

Michael stared at me for a second, then burst out laughing. His laugh was like a bark. "That's a good one." The frown twitched back and he looked around. "Couldn't stand her. Who cares if she's dead. One less to worry about."

I was shocked (but vaguely pleased).

"So"—he kicked at the ground—"your mum's still working too hard to look after the garden. If she needs help, tell her to name her price. Tell her to call me."

"OK."

He stared at me, so I stared harder.

He shrugged. "What?"

I was sure he'd want to hear more about Nic. I thought he'd want me to tell him about Vicky's stupid party and how, after Dr. Senner closed it down, everyone went off to Bluebell Woods. I thought he'd want all the blood and guts of it. But I suppose he's probably heard it from his dad.

So I sat down on the grass next to his feet and said Mum could definitely give him a few odd jobs, blah-blah, but surely too much lifting and carrying wouldn't be good. I asked if he needed a helper, etc. It was massively frustrating and boring. I wanted to tell him the important stuff (i.e., the-truth-the-whole-truth-and-nothing-but) only I wasn't sure how he'd react. He says he's not sorry Nic's dead but that doesn't mean he'll want to hear how I killed her.

"The garden's taken quite a beating because of all the storms, and it was because of the storms that everyone thinks Nic fell."

"At least they can't blame me. I suppose I should be angry, though, I've been upstaged by a fucking airhead like *Nicolette Prevost*!"

I turned back and saw Michael smirking in what I'd call a most worrying way.

"So come on, brain-box, you can't really think she was swept off the cliffs by accident." He nodded towards the cliff edge. "She'd have had to get right up close to the edge and she'd only have done that if she was going to jump."

My heart went into reverse and stalled. I wondered if Michael was trying to trick me.

He was glowering expertly. "No one likes to imagine she'd do something so *fucked up*, eh? She had it easy, why would *she* want to die? Just shows you never know what's going on in people's heads. We're all a bit twisted under the skin."

He was now staring at me in an officially mad way, so I bobbed my head happily.

"Yes, we're all twisted, I absolutely agree, but I really think you've got it wrong. The Senners' homebrew is lethal. She could've got lost in the dark and she wore such stupid shoes."

Michael made a huffing noise, then he brushed his hands on his jeans. "Nicolette Prevost was *never* on her own, so why the fuck was she on her own here?"

I shrugged. "Accidents happen. People get drunk and make stupid mistakes. After all . . . *you* did."

The minute the words were out of my mouth I wanted to take them back. Michael was already on his feet.

I scrambled after him. "Hey! I didn't mean—where are you off to?"

I tried to grab at him and he staggered forward, and because of his weak leg he almost lost his balance. It's quite a steep slope and I was honestly just trying to slow him down. Then we got entangled. I'm not sure if I was holding on to him or if he was holding on to me, but as we tumbled onto the grass he doubled up and reached for his knee.

"Fuck! Fuck! Fuck!"

A real-live tear slid down his cheek and his whole face creased like paper. I felt the soggy earth press through my leggings, I tried to put my arm around his shoulder. He looked up and his eyes were all over me, which was strange but also great. I imagined us rolling around in the mud together (although he clearly didn't).

"I'm really sorry."

He winced as he hinged his leg back and forth.

"Yeah, yeah. It was *an accident*."

I didn't know what to say so I just sat there. Michael rubbed his knee for a little bit longer, then he stared at the ground in between his legs. After a while he took up a stick and started breaking it into pieces. I waited and picked at my fingers (I know, I know, a revolting habit). Minutes passed. Then, finally, he asked me to help him get back on his feet.

I stood up and held out my hands to him.

He smiled up at me and didn't move an inch.

"By the way, I jumped."

I blinked.

His smile broadened. "It was no accident, I was off my head and I thought, 'What-the-fuck!' I felt really strong and powerful, not like I do the rest of the time. It was really something."

"Wow," I said.

"Yeah. I felt like I'd been taken over and before I knew it I was up, up, and away. Fucking brilliant. *I was free.* There's something about this island makes you go a bit mental, I reckon. It's hidden, I don't know where. Maybe it's in these bunkers and tunnels and towers, eh?"

I grabbed his hand and hauled him up. "Maybe."

"Accidents don't just happen, Cat. People *make them* happen."

I was totally amazed and enthralled but also slightly scared. Michael's eyeballs were all over the place and I was worried that they'd escape out of his head. I wanted to ask him if there was anything else he had to tell me—if there wasn't some other reason why he'd jumped. He rubbed his forehead like he had a headache. I couldn't help but wonder if he'd done something very-very bad. Then I wondered if he'd done something worse than me. Then I realised no one could've done something worse than me. I wondered how I could tell him that.

I looked into his diesel-oil eyes and wanted to tell him everything, but it was so confusing. There was a time I thought I knew everything, but the truth never comes out like you want it to, it's just like Liberation Day.

But that needs a whole other chapter of explaining.

[BACK IN BEDROOM,
WITH WET BOTTOM BUT BETTER PEN]

Liberation Day is important on Guernsey, but not always for the right reasons. Officially it's a public holiday when we are meant to celebrate being freed from German rule.* Trouble is, anyone who remembers this momentous and long-awaited event will tell you there wasn't much to celebrate. By the end of the Occupation most islanders were starving, and they were furious with the British for making next-to-no effort to help them. They had to wait ages for France to be liberated and Hitler to go mad and the Germans to surrender before they were freed. This was because the British had decided that the Channel Islands were a bit of an embarrassment and islanders no better than collaborators.†

---

* 9th May 1945 was the day Guernsey was officially set free. (NB: This is some time after the War was won.)

† Although it could be argued the British were only going on what they'd been told by islanders themselves. This is because the ones who managed to escape slagged off the ones they left behind, and this tale telling got worse as the Occupation went on (see *The Occupation Today*, vol.17, 1978).

They therefore deliberately kept references to the Occupation out of the national newspapers and off the airwaves in case it put a dent in Great British Morale.

Then, when the Liberation finally came Winston Churchill didn't. Apparently he wasn't too keen on associating himself with ill-will, and there was a lot of that from the evacuees who came back to find their houses plundered. But the people who'd been put in concentration camps or prisons (like my Uncle Charlie) were in a much worse state, and they were never compensated. All in all, life in Guernsey was/is grim. Thus it's probably right that on our day of supposed celebrations everyone ends up getting blind drunk and brawling, or jumping into the harbour wearing fancy dress, and swimming in what is essentially their own sewage.

And Liberation Day last year was especially disastrous, because everything went officially wrong with Nic. Let me elaborate (good word): I was meant to be meeting her and Pete and Pagey and a few of their friends and second cousins from the Grammar. It had all been arranged weeks in advance. We were going to meet at the Vale Castle* with buckets of out-of-date booze and a mega-ghetto-blaster. Everyone I knew (even vaguely) was going and it was a V.B.D. (Very Big Deal).

---

* Vale Castle aka Chateau du Val. No one knows how old it is, so it obviously dates back to a time when no one could write. It was garrisoned during the French wars of 1793 and 1815, and the proof of that is the graveyard next door. The Germans also used it during the Occupation (and added ugly new concrete bits as per typical). It is now only good for local rock concerts, which sadly involve local rock bands.

I thought it'd be the most excellent party and it was just what I needed after all the bad feeling re: Michael.

The only thing that was still bothering me was Bloody Lisa Collenette, the in-bred ferret/weasel.

After Michael's accident the Lisa-Ferret was always hanging around Nic, as per a bad smell, and it slowly drove me demented. Three is never a good number—I should've known that—and Lisa had an amazing talent for turning up in Town whenever and wherever I'd arranged to meet Nic. The trouble was, Nic didn't seem to mind, and I started to get the feeling that she even wanted her there.

"What's the problem?" she'd say. "It doesn't have to be just us two, and Lisa's *up for anything*."

Did that mean I wasn't? I tried my best; I stole and drank as much as I could, I had my ears pierced three times, I lied to Mum and stayed out late. It wasn't enough, though. I was out of my depth and not a good swimmer.

And Michael didn't help matters. There he was in his coma/Southampton, pretty much forgotten about by everyone. Lisa pretended to blame me for what had happened and she used it as an excuse not to invite me to her house. Of course, it was nose-on-face obvious that the real reason Lisa never invited me was because she wanted Nic to herself. I tried to ignore it, but Nic went round there more and more. And then Lisa had *that* party. It turned out her parents were getting divorced and the house was going to be sold, so her mum wanted to trash it to spite her dad. Or maybe it was the other way around. Anyway, Lisa decided to have her party in secret and not invite me, and what was more upsetting was that she had it on Liberation Day, knowing full well what we'd already got planned.

So, there's me at Vale Castle, all alone on a lovely, sunny day. I waited and waited and waited, but there was no sign of Nic. There was no sign of anyone. There was only pug-faced Dickie Guille from Sark and a rough-looking girl he was probably wanting sex with.*

Eventually I asked him if he'd seen Nic, and he squinted at me (because, in fact, he always had a squint).

"Everyone's at Lisa Collenette's from what I heard. She's having a barbecue today. Didn't you know?"

I blushed tomato-red so it was obvious I didn't.

"Oops," Dickie laughed. "N.F.I., is it?"

(Which means "Not Fucking Invited," in case you didn't know.)

I was gutted. I couldn't believe Nic (and everyone) had stood me up, and I was especially angry with Lisa. She'd done this out of spite, to make me look moronic. Talk about Lowlife! Talk about Two-Faced! I jumped on my bike and cycled at top speed in first gear to the nearest phone box. Then I looked up Lisa's number and dialled it.

It rang for ages, and I could hear the sound of a party the instant Lisa picked up. There was laughing and screaming and (terrible) music.

---

* Sark is very small and has worse TV reception than Guernsey, therefore everyone sleeps with everyone else from a very early age and at the same time, and often in public. There is a special Summer Clap Clinic because of it.

"Lisa," I said, quick-as-a-flash, "are you having people over? Only I arranged to meet Nic at the Vale Castle— is she there? Can I talk to her? I must've got my days muddled."

There was the sound of muffled laughter, and I'm sure someone said, "Shit."

"I'm sorry! Sorry? *Helloooo?* I can't hear you. Who is this?"

Lisa's voice was loud and clear to me.

I tried again. "Can I speak to Nic?"

"Hello? Is that *Cat*?"

(Honestly, Lisa's a terrible actress—I knew she was only pretending not to hear me.)

"Yes," I replied, trying not to get angry. "Can I talk to Nic, please?"

"Sorry? Did you want the animal shelter?"

Someone barked in the background.

"Very funny. Please can I talk to Nic?"

"There's no one by that name here. You must have the wrong number. Go and get a life!"

The line went dead before I could argue. I stared angrily at the mouthpiece and thought about smashing it as per a hooligan. Then I tried to imagine what was happening at Lisa's. Had Nic been listening in on my call? Probably. Maybe. I bet it was a big joke to them. H.I.L.A.R.I.O.U.S. Lisa was poisoning everyone against me. I was so angry I cycled straight over to Lisa's to see exactly what was going on behind my (stabbed-in-the) back. I also needed to know for sure that Nic was even there. Maybe she was sick. Maybe something else had happened. I mean, we'd made plans, the two of us.

She wouldn't just change them without telling me. She couldn't. Could she?

Yes.

I got to Lisa's house just after 3 o'clock and there was Nic, in the garden, gyrating to what I think was Jesus and Mary Chain (because it sounded like someone killing themselves and then a cat). As per usual she was flirting with the nearest boy to Pete who wasn't Pete, which was greasy Caz Mitchell. Pete was sitting a little way off, clutching a six-pack of lagers and resembling unaccompanied luggage at an airport, the kind that might just explode.

I walked in through the garden gate and tried to act casual and not trip up, then I tapped Nic lightly on the shoulder.

"Hi. You look like you've been at it for a while. Did you forget we were meeting?"

Nic wasn't surprised to see me. She shrugged just like she always did. "Shit, yeah. Sorry. I thought I could get away but, you know, things got a bit mental here. It's a cool party."

"I can see that. You could've told me, though."

Nic wrinkled up her nose. "How could I? I didn't want to hurt your feelings and it was all a bit embarrassing. Pete wanted to come here and I did *ask* Lisa if I could tell you, but you know what she's like." She shrugged again, like she was embarrassed for me. "What could I do?"

I was staring at Nic, arms folded, and I think I was tapping my foot.

She sighed. "It's only one party!"

But it wasn't just that. Half of Guernsey was in Lisa's garden and they were all giving me funny looks. Guernsey's so small and everyone knows everyone, and when someone doesn't like you, well, it'll easily make the pages of the *Guernsey Evening Press*.

I remember Pete's ugly sneer.

"Couldn't keep away, eh? I told Nic you'd turn up. *Desperado*."

Nic was pretending not to hear.

"I can't believe you're letting this happen," I told her. "You're supposed to be my friend. What right has Lisa got to make me feel like I've done something wrong? I'm getting the blame for what happened to Michael, but it had nothing to do with me!"

Pete stood up, waving his beer can at me. "No one's interested in your opinion. I heard what you said to Nic about me. You think *I'd* go after Michael and push him off the tower? Je-sus!"

"I never said that!"

The veins on Pete's thick neck were pulsing like a disco beat.

"We all know Michael Priaulx jumped off Pleinmont because he was a nutjob. P'raps you should do the same."

Lisa was suddenly standing beside me. (Her sharp, pointy ears meant she had good hearing.)

"Who's the nutjob?"

I turned to her ferret/weasel snout.

"Nothing. This has nothing to do with you."

"Yes, it has!" Pete snarled, nodding to Lisa. "Cat here is really looking forward to your cousin coming out of hospital. She reckons if he's brain-damaged she might finally stand a chance with him."

That was just about the meanest thing anyone's ever said to me.

"At least I care about Michael," I replied. "The rest of you obviously couldn't give a shit what happens to him." I turned back to Lisa. "You don't. All you want to do is have a party!"

Lisa scrunched up her mean ferrety eyes. "I can have parties whenever I want, and you're just jealous because you're not invited. You'd better leave now or I'll get Pete to throw you out."

She then said some really mean things to me (which I shan't repeat) along the lines of everyone was bored of me, I wore terrible clothes, and I was a big, fat cow. Of course I answered back and told her she should stop butting in and trying to take Nic away from me.

That's when Nic burst out laughing.

"I'm not your personal property. You're totally over-reacting."

I thought that was unfair, and told her so.

"Come on!" I said. "We're friends. You don't mess friends around."

Nic glared at me. Her eyes were hard as glass (but also twinkling). "Is that right? Well, we're obviously not friends then. A good friend wouldn't turn up here and embarrass me like this. Snap out of it, Cat. You want things all your own way and if you don't get what you want you sulk and try to make us all feel guilty. But guilty for what? Christ! You're stuck in your own little world! No wonder Lisa didn't invite you. She's not the only one who thinks you're weird."

I should've expected that, really. I was becoming the weirdo everyone said I was. And why did Nic matter so much? She didn't care about me, so why did I let her hurt me? It's a question I still can't answer.

Maybe I need THE WISDOM OF HINDSIGHT.

As I cycled away from Lisa's my heart was in my mouth. I wasn't crying but I felt so rotten and I didn't want to go home in case Mum caught me crying. I dumped my bike at the Vale Castle and went for a long walk instead. I climbed onto the low wall that borders the beach and followed it as far as I could. It's strange, because it wasn't a route I could remember taking before, but it felt weirdly familiar.

Bordeaux Harbour isn't really much of a harbour anymore since most people now keep their boats in Town. I counted the yachts bobbing in the water and listened to the chink-chink sound of the rocking masts in the wind. That's still the most soothing sound I know. I sat down and hugged my knees in tightly, feeling nearly hypnotised. I could've stayed like that all night. I don't know. I'm the first to admit that I hated sailing, and I hated Dad for making me do it. It was boring, and it took forever, and I never tied the sails up right. But as I sat at Bordeaux and watched the sunset all I wanted was to be back in my sleeping bag, curled up at the bow of our boat, looking through the hatch at the big, darkening sky.

I never thought you could miss the things you didn't like, and miss them so badly, but it turns out that you can.

"The testimony of
C. A. Rozier"

[Transcribed by E. P. Rozier]

I was in the shit, all right, if you pardon me.
I was on my way to Bordeaux when it happened.
Ray had suggested I check the times of the night
patrol once more, and that meant staying up all
night. It was cold, I remember, and I was walking
quickly along the coast road by Vale Castle when
I met crazy Esme Le Messurier. D'you remember her,
Emile? She's the one who was dead in her bed a
whole week afore anyone noticed, and I can never
forget the pickled smirk on her face as she waved
me over.

"*Wharro! Kique tu fais ichin?*" she says to me.
"I just heard from your neighbours that the Germans have turned up at your place. *Hé bian*, I
always knew your lot were friendly with old Fritz
but I didn't know they were giving them a party!"

I looked at her like she was mad. "What in Hell are you talking about?" I asked.

Then she pushed out those once-cherished bosoms and simpered: "Lie down with the enemy but you won't get no sleep, 'tis what I reckon! You'd better get home, boy."

Sapré conaons! My blood ran cold if it ran at all. The Germans were at the house! It couldn't be! *Quaï terrib1le nouvelles!* I thought of my notebook.

There is only wisdom with hindsight, and that's no wisdom at all. I was running as fast as my legs would carry me, and my heart was hammering in my chest as I asked myself the questions that would haunt me all my life. What had happened? Who'd informed on us? Was this my doing? I burst through the open door of our house, well near to exploding. I don't know what time it was, but I was too, too late.

There was maybe five of them, four or five filthy green Slugs in our tiny home. Ma and Pop were standing closer than I'd seen in many months. I've no idea what they were thinking or if they was scared, and I'll give her her due, La Duchesse, she was good at putting on a face. You could never tell when she was scared or when she was lying or when she felt guilty and I believe she must've felt all those things at one time in her life. As for Pop, well, I still can't tell you what was behind them haunted eyes.

What I do know is this: by the time I was marched

into our front room the Germans had found what
they'd been looking for. Happened Esme was right,
and there had been some little party I'd missed
out on. Vern was there, but talking German so I
couldn't get a word of it. That was no, no good.
Then I saw my scrapbook lying flat down on the
table next to Pop's strongbox. My heart stopped. I
moved forward to grab it—or I tried to—only there
was a jab right between my shoulder blades.

"Stand still!"

That was the first time Pop even noticed I was
there. He blinked and said something to the officer in front of him. This chap was obviously senior
to Vern. He turned, tapping his hand lightly on
his gun holster. In that moment I wasn't sure what
was happening.

"You must be the son," says the officer. "We are
arresting your father on suspicion of espionage
and we will want you for questioning also."

I felt sick to my stomach. It was all my worst
nightmares come true.

La Duchesse rested a hand on my shoulder.

"Keep him out of this, he's only fifteen, you
can't be taking him!"

Vern muttered something to one of his chaps.

The other officer shook his head.

"These are serious allegations and we'll have to
question all of you."

I heard a gasp from our mother. "With a baby in
the house! You cannot be serious."

"What are these allegations?" I asked.

Vern cleared his throat. "We have evidence."
Then he gestured to my notebook.

"That's mine!" I said.

Au yous, Emile, I wasn't ever going to let Hubert take a bullet for me. I was the real culprit, the one they wanted, and I needed them to know it. The senior officer, a cold fish if ever there was one, keeps staring and staring at me.

"Whatever you've heard is lies," I tells the senior officer. "My father's no spy." And then I glanced to Vern. "You must know it," I says to him. "I'm the one you want. What I said, I said only once, just as a joke. I said that my father was a spy, but I lied. I made it up!"

The chief Kraut blinked in disbelief. "Why would you do such a thing?"

Pop gave me the smallest shake of his head. I took no heed.

"Because people were saying he was a collabo, because of what you made him do! I lied to people so I wouldn't, so he wouldn't-"

I was going to say "so I wouldn't feel ashamed" but I'm glad I shut myself up.

The big German officer stared at me for a minute. His cold eyes twinkled and I thought he believed me, but then he smiled widely and nodded.

"A good performance if only your father had not already confessed. If you wish to confess also, be my guest."

I called him filthy lowlife Hun and plenty more things I won't repeat, and as a result I felt the

full force of a rifle butt. It split my lip and I
fell to the ground, but I wasn't down for long. I
jumped up and lunged at Vern. Got a nice bit of
blood on his shoulder.

"This does you no good!" he says. "Stay calm."

"It's stupid talk!" I shouted back. "It's all
lies! Are you so blinkered you cannot see that?"

What a sight that must've been: my fifteen-year-
old self squaring up to them Nazis! The thug behind
me smacked me down.

"Enough," says Pop, spreading his thin hands
wide. "It's only me you want. My son talks big but
he's a child. You know what I've done and I'd do
it again. Heil Churchill, I say, and Hitler go to
Hell."

I looked up into Pop's eyes and it was like
they'd come alive again, but all too soon the spark
was gone. We were bundled into the back of a black
Citroën and I tried to whisper to him.

"Keep quiet," he replied, staring straight ahead
as we drove into the darkness. "They're taking us
to Paradis."

That's right, Emile, that's where they took us:
the big house with a view out to sea. It was called
Paradis, which almost seems funny and I suppose
it was the place plenty of folk met their Maker.
You've heard the stories from others, eh? I can
still remember the smell of it and how the floorboards creaked. There was men flogged from the
banisters, left to starve, beaten to pulp. Who
knows where all the bodies went.

They might've torn the old house down, but you cannot escape them ghosts. New bricks and mortar won't make a difference. Whoever lives there now won't last—they never do—since they'll never get no peace.

[On the patio,
almost dancing]

F reak out! I've just been on the cliffs with Michael again. I saw him head out earlier this morning and pretended it was a big coincidence. I think he was pleased, though. This could become our new routine! I could be his personal assistant, physical therapist, and stalker rolled into one.

Malheureusement he's still going on about how there's nothing to keep him on the island. I think he's upset because Donnie's gone AWOL. The White House is all locked up and there's a big firm that now looks after the garden. We were walking through Bluebell Woods when Michael told me. From the path we could just glimpse the side of the house through the trees. It was sitting there, all gleaming and empty.

"Bloody typical," Michael mumbled. "They buy a house, spend a fortune doing it up, and then bugger off to Monaco. Half the houses on Fort George are empty. Tax status, my arse."

I told Michael it was probably about time Donnie got

his tan more realistic. I mean, if he has houses all over the world why should he stay here for winter?

"He won't be back."

I felt a bit let down, and then a bit itchy. It had just stopped drizzling and there were midges all over us. Michael grabbed at one, then pulled his fist into his chest to take a closer look.

"I was meant to go with him."

I watched as he rubbed his fingers together.

"That's what he promised. He said he had a job for me. I was going to help him manage his properties."

I tried to work out if I should be happy or sad—I couldn't.

"That's amazing!"

Michael stared up at the trees.

"It won't happen now. Get a chance and I blow it. There's a fucking self-destruct button hardwired into my brain. I'll never get away. I'm a liability, a fucking waste of space like everyone says."

I felt really sorry for him and gave him a nudge. Perhaps too hard because he staggered forward.

"You could still find Donnie if you wanted to. He's not been gone long and he could've left a forwarding address at the Guernsey Post Office."

Michael shrugged. "I'm not going to break my neck." Then he grinned like that was a joke.

I smiled back and he shoved his hands in his pockets and carried on squelching up the path. I tried to loop my arm through his, but that made his limp more obvious.

We'd walked a short way before I realised Michael was watching me out of the corner of his eye.

"You didn't know he was going?"

"No," I said quickly, shivering in the cold. "Why would I?" Then I remembered a few things. "But . . ."

Michael faltered. "But *what*?"

We were now moving slower than two snails on crutches. I wasn't sure if he was doing it on purpose or if he was getting stuck in the mud.

I stopped and turned to face him. "I did see Donnie quite a bit."

"Yeah?"

I nodded. "When things were getting tricky between me and Nic I'd go there on the weekends. He needed help with the garden."

Michael raised his luscious eyebrow(s).

"Course he did."

"He talked about you all the time. He knew you'd pull through. He said you reminded him of how he used to be as a teenager."

Michael made a little snorting noise.

"He likes teenagers, or hadn't you noticed?"

I thought this was a stupid thing to say. Of course I'd noticed. Headline News: I Am Not an Idiot! But I'd always felt sorry for Donnie: he was lonely and no proper adults would talk to him. He told me often enough that he had no family of his own. He regretted this, most definitely, and having young people around made him feel young. Personally, I never really noticed the age difference. Mum was fifteen years younger than Dad, and nobody ever said anything bad about that (within my ear-shot).

But Michael was looking so sly/smug, like he knew something I didn't.

"Did Donnie tell you anything else?"

I was totally stuck in those pools-of-treacle eyes.

"Is this an official interrogation or am I allowed a phone call?"

For the (police) record, my friendship with Donnie was always totally innocent. I liked spending time with him. He made fresh lemonade and had big deck chairs to sit on. That's it, I swear. Well, that's not entirely it. Nic was always with Lisa and I needed somewhere/one to escape to. I was tired of competing with Lisa or Pete or who-ever else came along. Plus, Nic had gone and got herself a part-time job at Etam. Mum said I was too young to work so Donnie gave me a bit of money to help him with the weeding. Most of the time I'd just sit in the kitchen and watch him clean. He had a housekeeper but he still loved to clean. He'd dismantle his yogurt maker or Magimix or SodaStream and line up all its parts under the window and check how it gleamed in the sunlight. Then he'd sit me on one of his high stools and tidy his fridge and say things like "Fat is a State of Mind" and "The Universe has an Order." We'd talk about Fate and Karma and Life-after-Death, and have all sorts of intellectual-style debates.

It was a very meaningful time for me. We talked a lot about Michael but we also talked about Dad. Don-nie had never met Dad so he was interested to hear about his wide-ranging achievements/obsessions. I even showed him my press cuttings file, which included the article about Dad's (Un)Official Occupation Memorial. Of course the photo's no good because Dad's hiding his bad hand and squinting. Donnie joked that Dad looked like a war veteran himself, but Dad was just a baby in the War and, like Mum said, age didn't matter.

Nic knew I went to see Donnie because I didn't try to keep it a secret. I also wanted to show her that I had other friends. I told her about his wine cellar and video library, and fitness studio with its instruments of torture. I wasn't trying to make her jealous but I (sort of) hoped she was. I thought it was funny that she'd be stuck in a shop all summer whereas I was going to get paid for having fun.

But I need to make it clear that I never invited Nic over. I'm sure I never did. And if I did, well, I didn't mean to. Honestly and truthfully, it was the last thing I expected when she came barging through the door. It was a Saturday afternoon so she should've been working.

"Hope I'm not interrupting." She smiled.

I was gobsmacked, as was Donnie, who eyed her rah-rah skirt and said nothing.

"So! What are you two up to? Got anything good open? Come on, Golden Boy. You going to get us drunk?"

I felt so embarrassed. I didn't want Donnie to think I'd been telling tales about him.

I asked Nic what she was doing here.

"I missed you, that's all. Can't I stay?" She turned back to Donnie. "You wouldn't mind, would you?"

Donnie shook his head. "Of course I wouldn't. It's nice to see you again."

His tone was very clipped and formal.

Nic wandered around the kitchen, picking up various utensils and putting them down in all the wrong places. "It's a great pad. Perfect for a party." She parked herself on a bar stool and started swivelling round. "I really enjoyed the last one. When was that?"

Donnie smiled. "If I have another you'll be the first to know about it."

"We could have one now!" Nic stopped spinning and stared at him. "We could have cocktails."

He nodded. "Help yourself. I'm sure you remember where everything is." His voice tailed off, and Nic lowered herself onto his lino and sauntered towards the door.

Once she was in the hall I told Donnie how sorry I was and crossed-my-heart that I'd never invited her over.

"Don't fret." He tilted his head back and rolled his eyes skywards. "Nicolette is hardly a girl one needs to ask."

Before we could say anything else Nic had waltzed back in, twirling a little paper parasol between her fingers. She pointed the parasol at Donnie and speared him in the chest.

"I need you to come and help. I can't decide what to have and you're much better at mixing things than me."

Donnie looked at me. "Would you like that?"

I shrugged but also nodded.

Pretty soon we were back in the kitchen with various coloured potions and three types of rum. Donnie started chopping up strawberries and Nic and I sat there, eyeing each other. But after the first cocktail we relaxed, and after the second we were laughing. I suppose half of me was glad she was there. I thought it meant she cared. Then we started playing this game where Donnie would invent a cocktail that we'd have to name. I'll admit it was a lot of fun. Nic told Donnie that he made the best cocktails ever and he was really pleased.

"You know," he said, "this is better than a party because I haven't had to invite my tedious neighbours when I know they'll never ask me anywhere!"

Nic knocked back her drink. "It's nice for us to have some grown-up company, too. I can see why Cat likes you so much, but you probably know she's got a thing for older men."

That sobered me up a bit.

"Don't be shy." Nic giggled. "Donnie approves, don't you, Donnie? It's like you once said to me, girls mature quicker than boys so it's only right we don't waste time on them."

Donnie was crushing ice for our Fruity Booty Transgender Sex Fiend.

"You are both very mature for your age. Did I really say that about boys and girls? I'm no expert. All I know is everyone's different and they should take their time doing whatever it is they choose to do."

Nic stood up and leaned over the breakfast bar.

"You're so wise. We could learn a lot from you, couldn't we?"

Donnie stopped.

"I don't think you two girls need any help from me.

I'm past it, wouldn't you say?" He winked at me. "Trust me, that ship has sailed."

I focused on the polished lino floor and waited for it to swallow me. Nic told Donnie he wasn't that old but he promised her he was.

"You wait till you hear my taste in music. I'll put on some music, shall I?" He headed for the sitting room. "I've got this new stereo from De Gruchy's and they fixed speakers in every room. The whole house vibrates!"

While he was out of the room I told Nic not to be such an embarrassment.

She laughed as per usual. "What? You afraid I'll tell Donnie your dirty secrets? Don't tell me you've got a crush on him as well!"

I didn't have any kind of crush on Donnie but I was worried Nic would go and mention Mr. McCracken. That was the last thing I needed. My grades were back on track and I was trying really hard again, and because I'd dented the front wheel of my bicycle I was relying on Mr. McCracken to give me lifts home from school. Of course, whenever Nic saw us together she pushed her tongue against her cheek, which was really quite revolting. I kept hoping Mr. McCracken would give her a proper telling-off. At least now I know why he couldn't. It turns out no one is quite who you think they are.

Even Donnie. I can still see him trying to set the volume on his remote control with Nic wiggling her hips all around him. He was obviously distracted—he preferred sitting down and listening to music properly. We'd already done alternate weekends of Jazz and Blues music, and I had enjoyed sitting in Donnie's greenhouse and discussing the difference between "Form" and "Content." It's a fascinating fact that even though the Blues consists of old men singing about dead dogs or wives, it can still sound remarkably upbeat.

Donnie and I had never danced together before, so I felt a bit awkward when he started shaking himself. Then, very quickly, Nic guided Donnie's hands onto her waist and made him dance with her. But he wasn't very good at it. He kept kicking his legs out at right angles for no obvious reason, then he pulled away and started twirling his hands in the air and pretending to beat an invisible drum. He didn't embarrass easily so I blushed for him. Nic was too busy concentrating on her own routine to notice. She drifted down the corridor and into the sitting room.

"Come on!"

Donnie clapped and did a twist manoeuvre and looked so ridiculous that I had to laugh. We were North Show prize turnips but it was good not to care, and the fact that Donnie was waving his hands all over the shop made me feel a hundred times better. We twisted into the sitting room where Nic was and then jumped between the sofas. Donnie and I kept watching Nic and smiling to each other, and at one point Donnie jumped off his sofa and onto mine. He grabbed my hand and rocked me back and forth, and I imagined we were in *Grease: The Movie*. I did a twirl and landed on the floor.

Nic had always told me that dancing was like sex. She said that if someone was a bad dancer, the chances are they'd be rubbish in bed. Donnie and I were enthusiastically rubbish, and Nic danced like she was having sex already. She was throwing herself at Donnie, grabbing his hands and pushing them against her bottom. She wanted him to knead her like bread dough. I didn't know where to look. Donnie was sweating a lot and getting red in the face, and his eyes went glassy like they were sweating, too. It scared me, if I'm honest. Nic was grinding herself against him and lifting up her hair, and then she started to unbutton his shirt. She was smiling as she looked at me.

I hated seeing Nic like this and I didn't understand it. I mean, no offence to Donnie, but the man wasn't exactly a Greek Adonis, and even if his teeth had new crowns the rest of him was massively older than Mr. McCracken.

Nic grabbed my hand and pulled me over to him, like she wanted to watch us dance together. She manoeuvred herself behind me and pushed me closer and closer. I pretended not to mind being caught in this human sandwich, but I could see Donnie's hairless chest plus one nipple. Then he took both my hands and tried to pull me down onto the sofa. I dug my heels into the carpet. He smiled a little pleadingly. I shook my head. He sank back onto the sofa and Nic was suddenly in front of me, leaning over him. They'd started kissing and I watched his hand move up her skirt. The music carried on and I stood there, not really believing what was happening.

"Fuck!" said Michael.

(Yes, I was telling Michael all of this.)

"Fuck—that's mental!"

He stared at the ground and called it "Jesus." He was obviously impressed by my Compulsive Tale Telling. We were walking up through the Village and had nearly reached his house but he had to stop and swear a lot.

"Nic and Donnie? That is fucked-up. But I shouldn't be surprised."

"Well, I was," I replied.

Michael made a regrettably piglike snorting noise and shook his head.

"Donnie-Donnie-Donnie. You naughty boy!"

I think Michael must've misunderstood to find it all so funny.

I hate being laughed at. I really do. Nic laughed in just that same way, like she knew some joke I didn't. She called me a "Frigid Little Freak." She spat the words out so they stuck on my face and then she grabbed my arm and dug in her nails.

"Donnie's not interested in you, so why don't you just get out."

I pulled her away from the sofa and we had a little tussle, and she slammed into some china dogs on a sideboard. Donnie went hysterical.

"No! Not the Wally Dogs!"

He stared at me with blazing eyes and I felt so confused I went running out of there. I ran and I ran (and I ran) but once I was back home I knew I couldn't run anymore. There was nowhere left to run to. I couldn't go forward and I couldn't go back. Nic had ruined everything for me, and she'd ruined me. I felt so dirty. I stared at my hands and wondered if they were capable of killing. Then I imagined how. I punched my bedroom door and kicked the skirting board. I wished I'd killed her already. It was the beginning of the end. Yes, sir-eee. It was WAR.

"The testimony of
C. A. Rozier"

[Transcribed by E. P. Rozier]

War is not a means but an end. It makes violence respectable and makes sadists look like heroes. Them Nazis had sadists aplenty, Emile. I've still got the scars from that first beating they gave me, and that was just the start. I was locked in a little room, all alone, and that made me proper anxious. Then I was led down this corridor and taken into what looked like an office with a wide, wooden desk. There were three bad-looking blokes sitting behind it. I'd not seen them before—the ringleader was named Wessel, but known to many as the Weasel.*

He tapped his finger on the desk.

---

* Aka Major Klaus-Michael Wessel, formerly of the Gestapo. Wessel was well-known as a sadist, whose hobby it was to flog his victims with a rope. Died of a brain haemorrhage 1962; see PRO (Public Records Office) WO 23.34.43.

"So," he said, "should we shoot you now or let you rot in prison?"

I felt sick in my throat.

The Weasel laughed like a typical German, thinking he knew better than me. He got up from his desk and came round to stand in front of me. I took the biggest gulp of air as he stared downwards. He had big, popping eyes so I knew he was a crazy one. Quick as you like, he slapped me. I thought he'd used a bit of leather and not a human hand at all.

"We know all about your father's secret activities, he has given us a full confession. He was easy."

"What do you take me for?" I replied. "If he was that easy why are you questioning me?"

Vère dja, Emile, the Weasel was a proper Nazi—all pent-up to be away from active fighting on the Front, spoiling for a good scrap right here with little me. He went on and on.

"We have our sources. Very serious allegations have been made," he said.

"Rubbish!" I replied.

"Your own people have turned on you, my boy."

Dju me pardson! That sent a chill like a dagger through my heart. I wondered if he meant Ray or J-P.

"I know nothing and I'm saying nothing."

The blood was pumping fast.

The Weasel hovered horribly close to my ear.

"A pig about to have its throat cut squeals, Charlie. Will you not squeal?"

Those were his very words, I swear. Then he

grabbed me round the neck and pushed my face into the desk. For a second I couldn't breathe. You tell me that he bleated like a lamb when the British military got hold of him after the War. I'm glad for that. I'm glad he got a taste of his own medicine. *Quaï maonstre qu'il étaï!*

I don't know where I got my strength from but I held it together. When I did finally start talking I didn't tell him what he wanted to hear. By then I was fighting back all right. I told them they were wrong and that Pop was a more honest and truthful man than the whole Kraut species put together.

The Weasel shakes his head.

"You are a good tale teller, but do you expect me to believe you are working alone? What were you going to do with the information you had gathered? Swim to the mainland?"

I wouldn't answer him so he got his henchmen to pull me to my feet. Seconds later I felt a sharp pain in my crotch. Those swine knew how to hurt you, that's for sure. They talked about a "secret army" and I laughed like the village idiot. I focused on different corners of the room, pretending not to understand. They repeated the same stuff over and over, then I decided to turn the tables and started asking questions back.

"Who sold us out and how much did you pay them? Did they want food or did you give them blood money?"

We went round and round in circles, like a game of cat and mouse, and the only thing that sticks in my head is the Weasel saying I should choose my friends more carefully. Did he say it so plainly? I reckon he did.

I told him I had no friends.

"And what about your father? Who are his friends?"

"He has lost them, thanks to his work," I replied. "My father's only friends are Germans now."

The Weasel snorted like the pig he was.

"And I presume that is the same for your mother."

I would have answered with my fists if he'd let me.

I've since met a good many army types so I know what it can do to a man. In my own opinion, the army attracts the very dustbin of society, people who need a uniform to hide behind, and the Germans have that sort in abundance.

I don't remember the interrogation ending, only that I spat out blood and a tooth. But I didn't stop asking who it was who'd sold us out. Reckon that was the only thing I clung to.

"There must be someone with a grudge," I said. "Father has cooperated with your lot up until now. Unteroffizier Vern will vouch for that. Perhaps it has made some locals bitter."

Wessel nodded and smiled his sadist's smile.

"And who might those locals be?"

Si l'bouan Dju I'l pllais! Ray's name was on the tip of my tongue. After all, I was only human. But I never uttered it. Do unto your neighbour as you would have done unto you is what I was taught, so I kept my trap shut. If I had my time again I'd do it

different, mind, and I wouldn't think twice about
our supposed bond of trust. I should've pulled old
Ray Le Poidevoin down with me. But back then it was
all a fog, what the Krauts claimed to know.

What else can I tell you, Emile? The whole day
must've passed. By nighttime they'd done their
worst on me and I was left alone in a cell with
only a tin can to pee in. One eye was swollen shut
and my lips were puffed up like pigs' bladders.
Even though I was worried for Pop, I was so tired
I had to sleep. Hours passed and the next thing
I know it was morning time—the morning of 11th
December. It was when a young officer came in. I
didn't know him and thought I was being carted off
somewhere else. I started kicking but my body was
so stiff! I was taken back down the long corridor
and into another room. I found old Hubert waiting.
There wasn't a scratch on him, and of course I was
glad he'd missed out on a beating, only I had to
wonder what he'd said to get off so lightly.

    The officer in charge signed us off in a book
and said that we were going to be released. We had
to show ourselves at the Girls' College next week,
and after that we'd be formally charged and seen
by the Military Court. I was chuffed they were
letting us go free, but Pop's face brought me back
down to earth.

    "It's because the prison is full." He sighed.
"We'll be sent to the camps."

I looked about but I didn't see anything. Honestly and truthfully, Emile, the whole world of Guernsey vanished in that instant. It was as if we were taking part in a film and the scenery was falling away. *Mon Dju*, I thought, is this the ending credits? I stumbled forward and, blinded by the light, I went straight into a woman. She was taller than me, with a wide, hard face and eyes that glinted in the morning light.

"You there." She looked past me and pointed to the officer. "Where is my son? What have you done with him? I know you've got him. *Tu n' peut pas me trompai!*"

The officer told her to calm down but she wasn't having any of it.

"*Bouger-dé!* What have you done with him? Where is he? I want to know what you've got him for."

I looked into her dark eyes and knew her name before she spoke it:

"I'm Florence Margaret Le Poidevoin of Les Capelles, I am the mother of Raymond Le Poidevoin, and I want to see him now!"

I grabbed Pop's arm to steady myself. There we stood, on the steps of a place they'd called Paradis, not yet dead but surely damned.

19th December 1985, 7 p.m.

[In the kitchen, having eaten ten fun-sized Mars Bars. No idea why they are "fun" since they're so small you have no "fun" eating just one, but then you eat ten and feel shit.]

felt terrible after Nic and I had that fight at Donnie's. Everything was falling apart and I didn't know how to stop it. The rest of the weekend passed in a blur. I went round and round in circles (in my head), and I really wanted to talk to Nic about it. I called her up on Saturday night and even cycled round to Les Paradis on the Sunday morning, but nobody answered or came to the door. I had to wait until school on Monday for our Mexican standoff.

This time, though, I was ready for her. I had all my arguments written down in note form and carefully rehearsed. There was no way I was going to be called nasty names in front of the whole class. Oh no. I was in school early and waiting for Nic, smiling fakely at everyone, and I tried not to bristle when she came in with Vicky of all people. They were laughing so loudly, like they were having a good joke about something/someone. I wanted to tell them to shut up but I knew better, stayed calm and said nothing. Then everyone went quiet for Mrs. Carey, who announced that she was standing in for Mr. McCracken, who was stranded at Gatwick because of fog. Mrs. Carey is our French teacher and the daughter of a slave worker who bought his freedom from the Nazis. He did this by helping them burn the corpses of his comrades. It's an unbelievably nasty story and Mum was very shocked when Dad told her at a parents' evening.* She also thought it was rubbish since Carey is an ancient Guernsey name, but Dad pointed out that women change their name when they marry, and wasn't that convenient.

But let's get back to roll call: Mrs. Carey was working her way down the register and when she called out my name I shouted, "Yes." I was ready for a catty comment from Nic or Lisa, but nothing happened, and when I looked around everyone was staring into space or stacking up their books. The bell went and we filed out for the first lesson and I was worried someone might trip me up, so I stayed back to let everybody go ahead. Nic filed past without looking my way. I was surprised and then annoyed. Vicky gave me a nudge and asked me what was wrong.

---

* Dad didn't like foreigners but he wasn't a racist. There is no racism on Guernsey. This is because there are no proper dark people, only the Spanish and Portuguese, some of whom are descended from the slave laborers brought over by the Nazis. P.S.: There were also Russian and Ukrainian and Alsatian (not the dog) slave workers, and Polish and Czech Jews, although no one wants to talk about Jews ever ever ever.

I eyed her carefully. "What were you talking to Nic about?"

She shrugged and said nothing.

I didn't believe her.

"Whatever she says isn't true."

Vicky frowned. "Like what?"

I glared at the doorway.

"If she's got anything to say to me she should say it to my face."

But she didn't. Nic ignored me brilliantly. All day. It was the last thing I expected. I tried to convince myself that being ignored was better than being shouted at (cf. Past History ref. Dad) but it didn't feel right. I'd wanted shouting and screaming and when I didn't get it I felt cheated. Nic was pretending I didn't exist. She made me feel like nothing. No. She made me feel like less than nothing (which is quite impressive).

The only thing I was glad about was the fact that nobody else knew what had happened. Nic had obviously been too embarrassed to tell people. Phew (I thought). But still, she carried on ignoring me the next day, and the next. I tried to talk to her but she'd just turn her back on me, and I didn't want to make it look too obvious. Eventually I gave up and wrote her a long and detailed letter. I said we'd all been very drunk and that we were both a bit to blame. Perhaps that was my big mistake. No one likes being blamed. After Liberation there was a lot of talk about justice/revenge and who'd done what to who, but in the end that's all it was. A few slutty women got chased and threatened, but they didn't get their heads shaved/chopped off vis-à-vis the French.

Dad said if you live on a small island you can't get back at each other, you have to get along. He also pointed out that Guernsey has too many glass houses for folk to go round throwing stones.

I was excellently eloquent in my letter to Nic. I tried to smooth things over and say it was a silly mistake. Then I also got quite emotional and said I wanted to die. I begged her to stop ignoring me, etc. Howsoever and forthwith, none of the above matters because Nic never even bothered to read it. When I went to hand it to her she batted it back and made a tight fist.

"Come on," I begged, "I'm trying to say sorry!"

She wouldn't even look at me.

The Bitch.

That's how it was the next week as well, right up until the end of term. Everyone noticed and lapped it up as per fat cats and Guernsey cream. Nic surrounded herself with Lisa and Shelley and Isabelle and even Vicky, and I was ignored and shut out in the cold. I tried to pretend not to care and suffered in silence with bells-on dignity. But it was like I didn't exist. It was like I was dead.

When my uncle was shipped back to Guernsey after the War he wasn't given much of a welcome. When they saw how pale and ill he looked, they got scared. Even his own mother—my grandma—didn't know how to act. More Guernsey people than you'd guess were put in prisons and camps by the Germans. A lot of them didn't survive but Uncle Charlie did because he was young and fit, although he wasn't especially fit after three years' hard labour. The Nazis had starved and beaten him, and put him to work in a quarry, making him dig with his bare hands. You'd have thought, after what he'd been through, his friends and neighbours would've been sympathetic, and cooked him a proper meal. But people said he'd been very foolish for causing so much upset, and it was his word against theirs so he never stood a chance.

I never met Uncle Charlie because he died before I was born. He lived the rest of his life in a tiny cottage at Icart. For years he could never talk about the terrible things he'd been through. Dad said it was the same for a lot of locals who'd suffered under the Germans—they'd been through Hell once already and talking brought it back.

But Dad was obviously very determined to go through Hell as well, which is why he wrote all those letters, and why he campaigned for his (Un)Official Occupation Memorial, and published his pamphlets for next-to-no-money. And which is why he had to drink himself unconscious all the time.

In History, alcohol was widely used as an anaesthetic. Boots the Chemist actually prescribed remaining stocks of brandy to old people during the Occupation, to ease their aches and pains. However, although drinking a little numbs you from feeling, drinking a lot makes you feel worse. The day we broke up for the summer holidays I took myself off to the Moorings with a half bottle of whisky. I watched as the tide went out and waited to feel better about life/Nic, but soon I started to think about Dad/jumping. Mum won't talk about how much Dad drank, but I've often wondered if he was drunk when he dived off the Moorings and cut his hand on the rocks. He was always so careful: he'd check the timings of the tides in the *Press*, and even if he didn't, he'd judge the water level on the side of steps. So why did he dive in when the tide was so low? I've asked Mum over and over about it, and she's told me to leave it alone. She says Dad made one mistake and that's it. He was embarrassed, so he bandaged the hand himself and pretended it wasn't serious, and she took him at his word.

Of course Dad was wrong to be so proud. He should've known more than anyone that you can't ignore A GAP-ING WOUND, but for the first time ever he didn't make a fuss and blame someone else or write a letter. Perhaps he almost wanted it to happen. I don't understand it, I really don't. I think it's pretty clear that all this SUFFER-ING IN SILENCE is just a massive waste of time.

Property of
Emile Philippe Rozier

The Editor
Guernsey Evening Press
23 South Esplanade
St. Peter Port
Guernsey
               WITHOUT PREJUDICE
RE: *Flight from Fortress Isle*

Dear Sir,

It has been some months since I first wrote to you regarding the forthcoming publication *Flight from Fortress Isle* by Raymond Le Poidevoin, but my letter remains unanswered and I find this silence greatly troubling. I am eager for us to meet at the earliest opportunity and discuss the matter, since I am aware that the book shall be based on a series of short articles first published in your newspaper in 1957. At the time they were well received and widely talked about, but please appreciate many years have now elapsed and serious errors and inconsistencies in Ray Le Poidevoin's account of events have subsequently come to light.

I am sure you would agree that inaccurate stories regarding our Occupation rob true accounts of their authenticity, and it is the responsibility of us all to ensure that misrepresentations are not perpetuated. My brother, Charles Rozier, was imprisoned and deported as a direct result of the same escape Ray Le Poidevoin has glorified. Charles endured three years of mental and physical torment at the hands of the Nazis, only to return to his island home and find himself perceived by many as "the guilty party."

Only now, with his health deteriorating rapidly, has my brother made efforts to divulge to me his own version of events. He has not done so, I should stress, in an attempt to clear his name or to counter Ray Le Poidevoin's claims, but rather to set the record straight once and for all.

I hope we shall be able to meet and discuss the various points of departure and controversy vis-à-vis the Le Poidevoin account, but in brief I shall now enumerate key issues that I feel are in need of immediate clarification (and apology).

In his first article dated 6 May 1957 Ray Le Poidevoin [hereafter R.L.P.] stated that it was Charlie Rozier who first broached the idea of escaping, and offered him his boat, calling it "a ticket out of here."

My brother absolutely refutes this and insists that Ray had landed himself in trouble with the German authorities and needed to escape. Although Charlie had hidden the boat just before the Germans arrived in Guernsey, he had no clear plan for it until Ray began to pressure him.

In a subsequent article dated 10 May 1957 R.L.P. asserted that, although my brother had initially intended to escape with his father, he radically altered these plans due to the latter's ill-health. I would like to state quite clearly and unequivocally that there is no evidence to suggest that Hubert Rozier knew about *Sarnia Chérie*, or about Ray and Charlie's activities. Charlie never confided in his father. Furthermore, although it was suspected that Hubert had tuberculosis, there was no diagnosis. It was certainly not the reason the boys altered their escape plans.

In an interview published in the *GEP* and the *Jersey Tribune* on 23rd and 25th August 1957 R.L.P. suggested that my brother had most probably "tripped himself up with his own loose tongue," since Charlie was known to have a vivid imagination and had already spread a story about his father being a spy. Although there is a grain of truth in this last statement, it has been taken out of context. Charlie grew up quickly during the years 1940 to 1942, and by the time of the proposed escape he had learned how to keep a secret. Such an accusation from R.L.P. seems grossly unfair, especially considering the comment three paragraphs later where

R.L.P. deigns to thank his "little friend" for enduring hours of Nazi interrogations but still withhold-
ing any information regarding the boat.

To speak plainly, Charlie Rozier might have started
the War as a "puny kid who told tall tales," but what
he ultimately had to endure would have broken the
spirit and will of any full-grown man. Despite repeated beatings he stayed loyal and true to both his
friends and his relations.

    The pain and suffering these articles caused my
brother is inestimable but he remained silent out of
respect to his mother. However, I am greatly vexed
by what effect the publication of a new book would
have on his fragile health. Whilst he is alive you
have my assurance I will do everything in my power
to ensure Ray Le Poidevoin's story is never printed
in its current form.

Yours sincerely,
E. P. Rozier
Manager/Editor of The Patois Press
Sans Soucis
Village de Courtils
St. Peter Port

20TH DECEMBER 1985, 9 P.M.

[SITTING ROOM]

Dad was cremated, in case you ever wondered. So was Uncle Charlie. I don't like the idea of incineration so I've planned my funeral carefully.

I did it during my Long Summer of Torment. I'd spend hours in my bedroom imagining how my classmates would be devastated by the shocking news of my death, and would write poems in my memory. They'd bind them in an album to be read at my graveside but the rain would smudge the ink (because it would be an open-air service). There'd be a trillion different-coloured freesias on my antique mahogany coffin, and Vicky would probably faint from grief and fall into my grave. I was going to be buried in the Military Cemetery with trumpets and cannon fire and Donnie leading the tributes. He'd have named a rose after me and would be holding this great, big wreath with the thorns digging into him, dripping blood. Then he'd put on a Miles Davis record and everyone would be amazed to find out that I liked jazz. After that we'd play Tears for Fears ("Mad

World") to symbolise my tragic waste of life, and then would come the Elaine Paige/Barbara Dickson classic "I Know Him So Well," just to make sure everyone cried. Nic would weep uncontrollably and maybe sing along and then tell Mum how sad she was that we'd not had a chance to make up. Mum would say amazing things about my wit and intelligence (which had been so unfairly overlooked).

Let me tell you, it was B.R.I.L.L.I.A.N.T., far better than my miserable reality, which involved leaving my bedroom every two days to mooch into Town and hover outside Etam, looking for but avoiding Nic and her cronies. I was now a vast size 14 and needed some new clothes, but the idea of facing Nic in a public place made me melt like ice cream. In the end I stayed indoors and watched repeats of *Dallas*, specifically the episode when Bobby Ewing is run over by a car.

Then I found out from Bridget Falla (the biggest mouth in the Sixth Form) that Nic had gone to France for the whole entire month of August. I was upset for all of five seconds, then came this tidal wave of relief. It was a temporary solution to my problem. I knew I wasn't totally off the hook but then I had a new daydream of how I could be: all Nic had to do was die. I imagined she'd fallen off the ferry to France, or been run over on a French motorway.* I visualised her death in various excellent ways and picked out flowers for her funeral. Does that sound so awful? I suppose it was quite morbid, but

---

* French drivers are notoriously bad, plus they drive on the wrong (i.e., German) side of the road.

I'd often imagined that Dad was going to die and then he did. So surely it could happen again, and to Nic.

Death was something to take my mind off the summer, which, unlike every other Guernsey summer since 1940, was horribly hot. I don't like sunny weather one bit. This is because of my vast acreage of Persil-white skin, which has been known to reflect the sun and blind people. I could be a superhero, only I burn and bruise easily, plus I'm too wobbly for Lycra. I don't know if I ever got as fat as I felt, but after Nic's Cold Shoulder/War Treatment I was eating and eating and eating. I had to ask Mum to ration my food.

During the Occupation, nobody had a weight problem. Strict rationing meant the islanders got stick-model thin. What most people don't know is that Winston Churchill was against sending Red Cross food parcels to the islands. This was because he'd heard that most islanders were lowlife collaborator types and therefore deserved to suffer.* But people survived one way or another. Dad always said it was amazing how little a man could live on, and he proved this fact regularly with his rabbit food.

Mum started buying me diet meals, but I was always sneaking off to Les Riches and stockpiling chocolate and sweets. Then I'd go and eat them on the beach at Fermain. I'd sit in an XL T-shirt and stuff my face and

---

* "Let them starve . . ." was what he scribbled in the margin of a liberation plan. (Quite outrageous, considering his belly.)

pretend I was a common English tourist. Well, I did that until Mr. McCracken found me out.

There I was, surrounded by Fanta plus crisp packets plus Lion Bars, when along comes McCracky, wandering-lonely-as-a-cloud along the water's edge. He didn't look half bad with his shirt off, unlike me, the Human Pavlova. I wanted to run away but I didn't dare get up in case that was more frightening.

Mackers waded into the sea like he was going to go for a swim, but his arms were up at right angles so I knew he was feeling the cold. The water was icy, even in August, and I think he must've lost his nerve. He was hobbling back up the shingle when he saw me. I waved while trying to hide Bounty wrappers.

"Hello." His eyes darted over the wrappers and crisp packets. "Are you having a picnic?"

I was still eating so I put my hand over my mouth. "Oh, don't worry, it's not all for me! I'm meeting Vicky and some of the other girls." (I looked up and down the beach and acted exasperated.) "I don't know *where* they've got to."

Mr. Mac nodded. "You must be missing Nicolette. She's in France with her family for the whole summer, I hear."

I had to swallow hard and some Lion Bar got stuck in my throat. After narrowly avoiding a choking fit I looked up at Mr. Mac.

"It's not like she's my *only* friend."

He smiled. "Of course." Then he turned back to look at the sea and I did the same and there was a long enough silence for it to feel awkward.

A few kids ran past us. When they dipped their toes in the sea they jumped and started screaming.

Mr. Mac chuckled. "I was trying to build myself up into going for a swim but it's still so cold! I don't know. I think your dad had the right idea about jumping in off the Moorings. Are you still clearing the stones out there?"

"Oh no," I said, "I stopped doing that ages ago. Nobody else dares to dive off there so what's the point?"

Mr. Mac blinked. "Oh! That's good to know."

I advised him to go to the west coast, since the water is definitely warmer there, and Vazon kiosk has home-made ice cream. He said he might definitely try it and told me to take care. That was my last Mc-sighting of the summer. OK. So I did go to Vazon a few times but I don't know if he took my advice, and NO, I didn't go to check. I went because cycling there was good exercise, and I needed a change of scene. I certainly wouldn't have bothered if I'd known I'd see the Lisa-Ferret. I was sitting on the slipway, minding my own business and reading That-Genius-Stephen-King when she came along. Actually, it was quite funny, since I was reading *Pet Sematary* and Lisa does have the look of the undead.

Bloody Lisa-Ferret-Face Collenette. I suppose I should be glad she came over to sneer in my face, since she also told me that Michael was out of his coma. It was Wednesday, 20th August—I remember writing a big "X" on my Guernsey Museums wall calendar.

"The doctors are really pleased with him. He'll need physio and stuff, but all things considered it's amazing."

"That's fantastic." I smiled so hard it hurt. "When will he be home?"

Lisa shrugged her bony shoulders. "Just count your-self lucky. He says he doesn't remember a thing about what happened so you're off the hook. *We'll never know* what really happened."

I thought about calling her a loony but knew there was no point.

"Thanks for telling me."

Lisa sniffed and walked down the slipway onto the beach, and I watched her go, waiting for her to be a teeny-tiny speck and not matter anymore. Then I stopped smiling. I closed my book and stared at the horizon, hugging my knees and folding up my belly. I should've been happy that Michael was OK, but instead I felt weirdly disappointed. I suppose I'd already got used to the idea of him being dead, as per Shakespeare's Ro-meo. I was looking for a chance to weep and wail, and pull my hair out. If he'd died then I could've wished that I'd done everything differently and told him I loved him before it was too late. It would've given me the best-ever reason to cry. I could've even made up for not crying over Dad.

Perhaps I also prefer it when people are dead because that's when they become History, and what I like most about History is how you can change it. Yes, that's right. Don't think it's set in stone. Just look at what happened with the Occupation. Once it was over, most islanders decided that it hadn't been that bad, and even called it character-building. Dad used to get so cross about how people chopped and changed their views, and forgot about all the atrocious things that happened. Of course, I'm now doing the exact same thing to him. I like Dad so much more and I've even started wishing he'd come back.

Dad, for the record, I'm finally very sorry. I never understood you and I didn't even try. If it's any consolation, when I'm walking on the cliffs I pretend I'm talking to you (although, of course, you're not walking with me, you're walking ahead of me because you always walked too fast and never made allowances for my short legs).

Anyway, now I'm a bit older I think sailing would've been fun. I'm also sorry for all the times I left doors open and didn't do the washing up and thumped up and down the stairs. If I could do it all again I'd do it differently and be quieter. I'm sorry I didn't look or sound more like you, as per a shadow or an echo. I'm also sorry we weren't total opposites, like the pieces of a puzzle that could be put together to fit. It's really annoying that I think I love you now you're gone. Even your weird habits have become quite special (although I still don't understand why cucumbers should be peeled). I tell everyone you were a champion swimmer and a hero and a genius, even if you weren't.

And at least I know why I'm doing it.

It's called Revisionism, isn't it?

"The testimony of
C. A. Rozier"

[Transcribed by E. P. Rozier]

"History will be kind to me, for I intend to write it." That's what Winston Churchill said. The pompous fool! Well, Emile, you don't need to be kind to me. I know I don't deserve it.

You'd think, by now, I'd have told our father everything, but there was still this deafening silence between us. We took the path back down towards Town. I kicked at the stones under my feet and thought about Ray Le Poidevoin and what I'd do to him if I caught hold of him. The Germans swore blind they didn't have him, but the minute I saw his mother it was as clear as day. Ray was the cause of my undoing. He had set me up.

I was too vexed to spare a thought for Pop, and I was striding on ahead and leaving him far behind. It was only when he called to me that I turned, and looking back I saw this frail figure who barely

cast a shadow. I hurried to his side, holding out
my hand. I knew then in that instant I had to talk
to him about everything, confess my sins, and beg
to be forgiven, but still I was wondering when I'd
be able to get over to check on the boatshed. It
was all a jumble in my head and I didn't know what
to think first. But I knew one thing for sure, I
wasn't going to sit around and wait to be tried
without judge or jury. And neither was Pop.

Hubert looked up at me and his dark expression
was like a mirror to my own. Then he ducked his
head and coughed painfully. I swear I felt it, like
a hammer against my chest. We'd both aged about
twenty years within a night and day. Enough was
enough. I opened my mouth to speak.

"Don't." Pop raised a hand to stop me. "No need
for you to tell me. I know what you've been up to—
all of it—and I won't judge you neither. But let's
stick to the story."

"You know I can't do that," I told him.

The old man grabbed me and hugged me tightly to
him. He was not the kind of man who ever did such
things, and it scared me half to Hell already.

"I love you, son, and I'm sorry you got mixed up
in this."

I pulled away and suddenly the tears were
springing from my eyes. "*Eh me! J'sis guerre de
fou!*" I said. "*T'chi qu j'ai fait?*"

Pop sighed. "It's not just you. We've all done
things we regret. I should've acted sooner. It's my
time, though, son, and I am ready."

I swear those were his very words.

My mouth was hanging open, I clung to him and wept like the child I still was. I'd called him a coward, my own father, but he was ready to lay down his life for me. *Quaï haomme*, Emile!

I reckon that's what gave me strength, in fact, because not long after I was gripping him by the shoulders, telling him we still had a chance. "*Si nous ne peut pas s'ecappaïr, nous moura a éprou- vaïr!*"

Of all my daft ideas.

Pop shook his head and hugged me close once more.

"It's the guilty who run away, and we aren't guilty."

And he was right, eh? He was ever right.

Our father was a man of few words and never was one wasted. It took us an hour to walk home and I counted every minute. He talked to me hon- estly, like never before. He told me about the best friends who'd died alongside of him in the trenches and the chaps he'd met in the prison camp. He told me about good Germans and bad Germans, about the prison chaplain who'd died for his men, about the young lads screaming for their mothers. He told me what it was like to live in mud and fear.

"You've got to believe in God," he said. "The world is too wretched for there not to be something beyond this. Believe there will be justice in the next life. We should fear no evil, eh? 'Though I walk through the valley of the shadow of death . . .

thou art with me; thy rod and thy staff they comfort me.' "

As I tell you this, Emile, I feel so choked. I wish this were all a dream. I wish I would wake up. *Not' poure père*, he was a dead man before I did this to him. But that's no comfort, there is no comfort. What a curse I had brought on this family. La Duchesse couldn't look me in the eye. They'd arrested her, too, but she'd been released without charge. When we got home she was clutching you tightly in her arms, staring at the fire. I expected her to shout at me but she couldn't even speak. She was in shock and it was more than I could bear.

As soon as I had the chance I couldn't help myself: I ran over to Chardine's place. My brain was on fire and I didn't know what I'd find. I prepared myself for the worst but it was still a mighty blow—an empty boatshed! *Bran d'te*, Ray Le Poidevoin! (is what I thought). I turned on my heel and headed straight for Mess. Falla's garage to find J-P and sort him out. I don't know where I got all that energy from, but I was running faster than the Germans in their motorcars, and I was stomping hard on the ground like I owned it.

Reg Falla shook his head when he saw me, and his long face almost tripped me up.

"*Ossa*, the dog comes back to its vomit. I thought they had got you."

"They did, they have." I looked about. "Where's J-P? Have they got him, too?"

Reg Falla was rough around the edges but butter underneath. He had no sons of his own and he'd taken J-P right under his wing a few years back. He had tears in his eyes when he told me what had happened.

"*Eh me, ch'est énne terrible chaose*, Jean-Pierre is dead. He was killed by a land mine in the fields by La Fontenelle."

This, I didn't expect. I felt like I'd been punched hard in the stomach.

I asked when it had happened.

"Two nights back. He had a bag of supplies with him, the Germans reckoned he'd been planning something."

My ears were ringing! I asked Mess. Falla what time the body was found but he wasn't too inclined to talk more.

"What's it to you? What were you hatching? If you've been stirring up trouble for the rest of us you won't make any friends. People round here just want to live as best we can. They'll have us all shipped to some camp in France because of this. What were you thinking?"

You see how it was going, Emile? It's a lot easier for folk to put all the sin of the world onto one pair of shoulders. They did it then and they do it now. I must have the Devil on my back, or else it was Ray. And where was he? I thought about going back to Paradis but didn't know where that would get me. The officer in charge had sent his mother packing, calling her a madwoman. I went to

Ray's home to check, and then I went to Le Brun's
farm where he used to work, and then I went to the
Salerie Inn, and then I went down to Petit Bôt,
and Bon Repos and Pleinheume and all around Fort
Doyle and the Vale. I think I walked all around
the island looking for Ray, and then I went back
into Town and asked at the police station and the
prison. Nothing. Ray had gone.

The next day was the night of our supposed exo-
dus. It was raining nonstop and I stayed indoors.
I could never forgive Ray for deserting me, and
that's what I knew he'd done. But had he managed
it, or had the boat sunk? Had him and J-P been
plotting secretly behind my back all this time or
had Ray done the dirty on J-P, as well? Pop told me
to pray for my so-called friends, but I couldn't
pray. I hated God as much as myself. The miserable wretched sinner that I am! Don't waste your
prayers on me, Emile, pray for our father instead.
    On our last night together I begged and pleaded
with him to go and see the doctor. Everyone knew
the Germans were terrified of TB and that cough
was a right bone-rattler. They'd never send him
to the camps if we could get a diagnosis. Pop finally agreed and I went easier to my bed, knowing
he might be saved. I didn't see him walk out into
the night, but in my head I see him now. He never
does go to the doctor. Instead, he's making his
way slowly down to Belle Grève. I don't know how

he climbs over the wire but he does and then he's staggering quickly down over the shingle. He probably never expected to make it through the mines, but on he goes, drawing closer to the water's edge.

Our dear father couldn't take his own life because he knew what a sin that was. He carried on walking even when he heard the shouts behind him. Perhaps he quickened his pace. He was a broken man but he didn't turn back, and there was no begging for mercy. It was just him and the waves as the bullets drilled into his back.

That was how it ended, Emile, there on that north beach. The Germans won the War and I lost everything, every ounce of love, hope, and faith, I lost a father and a mother and a baby brother. That was when I died and there's but one reason I hang on so. Whilst I still live and breathe I can think of our father, and I can love and I can miss him. Once I'm gone he's gone.

Emile, *you* will see our father in Heaven, and you tell him that I learned my lesson, tell him he was always in my thoughts. You two shall be together one day and I'm sorry I won't join you. I will miss our talks. I've tried to tell you what I can and I hope to God it helped some. I love you, dear Emile . . . and I hope, I hope I was a better brother than I ever was a son.

[In bed]

michael doesn't believe in Heaven or Hell. He's got closer to death than most living people and he tells me there was no tunnel of light or dancing angels. I'm a bit disappointed, to be honest. It means I won't see Dad again and be able to say sorry in person. It's good I've got Michael to talk to, though. I've just got off the phone to him. I know it's a bit late to be making deep-sea intellectual phone calls but he picked up straightaway, like he was telepathically waiting for me.

I told him I'd been thinking a lot about Life-and-Death.

He wasn't too sympathetic.

"Thinking about topping yourself, eh? That'd be good. I told my dad that Nic jumped off the Batterie and other kids were bound to copy her. He's had his head in the fridge ever since."

"The poor man is comfort-eating."

"Nah. He feels guilty. Guilt is the only reason anyone does anything."

I said most probably and suggested we meet tomorrow night for further discussions at the Fermain Tavern. Unfortunately Michael doesn't want to be seen with me in public—presumably because I'm underage. He therefore proposed that we meet on Monday night at Donnie's.

"We can't!" I insisted. "It would be breaking and entering."

I heard Michael snort and cackle. "Come on, how about it?"

I wasn't sure at all. "But if it's all been packed up, what on earth do you want to do?"

"I dunno. Snoop about. I'll bring some matches and you bring the drink. We can have a séance if you want. Bring your little friend Vicky Senner and we'll try and contact *the dead*."

"No!" I said (to the séance and to Vicky). "I'll come alone, we've got important things to discuss, just us two."

I've got to tell him about Nic, about how I killed her, etc. I must! I'm off first thing in the morning to buy a brand new bottle of whisky (to replace the one I've almost finished). I know for a fact Michael's been banned from all Island Wides courtesy of Deputy Dad, so he'll be dead impressed if I supply the booze. It'd be good to get it off my chest. The more I think about it, the more I realise that I couldn't have done anything differently. I only ever wanted Nic to be my friend, and I never meant to kill her. I loved her so much. I didn't love her the way I love Michael, but love comes in all shapes and (plus) sizes, and it involves great dollops of pain and suffering. I've suffered plenty for Nic.

All last summer I was counting down the days to September. It was like I was serving a prison sentence, without even looking forward to my date of release. Before then I'd always got excited about the start of the new school year: the shiny new textbooks, the baggy cardigans, the comedy fringes and home perms. This time, though, it was different. Mum couldn't understand why I wasn't going hyper about being in the Fifth Form. I'd always thought fifth-year girls were so grown-up. But when she dropped me at the school gates that first day back I wanted to run away. I remember walking down the corridor to Assembly and wishing I was somewhere else, and when I first saw Nic it was like I'd been punched. She had a lovely tan and bleached-blonde highlights from the sun. People were swarming round her as per bees and a honey pot. Then she saw me and there was this strange magnetic tug-of-war with eyes. She put her hand to her mouth and whispered something over her shoulder. Lisa laughed and Shelley turned to look at me.

So Nic wasn't exactly ignoring me anymore, but I wouldn't call it an improvement.

"I'm amazed they could find a uniform to fit her."

"Christ! *The embarrassment!*"

Yes, yes. I should've expected it. Why would I think things could be any different? There was Nic and Lisa and Shelley, and the way they shut me out reminded me of how I'd always felt shut out of things. For the longest time it hadn't mattered. But now it did matter, because I knew what I was missing. I was like one of those people who'd been famous for all of ten minutes, and then had my dreams cruelly crushed or snatched from me. There'd be no more glittering invites to VIP parties, and my usual table in Le Swanky Restaurant du Choix had been taken by somebody else.

Lisa was now with Pagey. What a joke. And Shelley was with Jason. Oh-the-horror. They thought they were so special—they'd sit round the back of the music block and talk about all the exciting things they were doing after school. They'd link arms and giggle and flick their glossy hair. Of course I did my best to avoid them. I'd sit in the cloakroom or work in the library, and inside I was dying.

Nobody knows this, but by the middle of that first week I'd locked myself in the science lab loos for the whole of the lunch hour, clutching a bottle of bleach. I 100% wanted to drink it. The next day I stole a scalpel from Biology so as to gouge out my wrists. I actually managed one good-ish cut before I chickened out. I felt guilty for wanting to kill myself and guilty for not trying harder. I imagined my next school report. "Catherine should apply herself more. We all know what she is capable of."

The whole thing was Epic and Titanic. I wanted to show Nic that she was wrong to drop me, but I had no idea how.

Let's be clear about this next bit. It wasn't something I planned. I didn't sit in my bedroom and plot ways to get Nic back. Maybe it looks like that now, but remember looks aren't everything. I was getting more and more depressed and I just needed a friend. I needed someone to give me a bit of perspective. And History just happened to be the last lesson on Friday. I'd been back at school all of two weeks and was in the worst state ever. I was dreading the weekend. I kept it together for the whole of the Poor Laws and then the bell went and the classroom emptied. Nic and Lisa were chatting about another big party at André Duquemin's that Saturday night. They'd always talk so loudly just to rub my nose in it.

"It's going to be wicked!" said Lisa. "Everyone's going." Then she looked back at me and smirked.

Nic flicked her ponytail. "*Careful.* We don't want gate-crashers."

I sat quietly and watched them leave.

A minute passed and I wondered whether to try to cycle home. Then I heard a sigh. Mr. McCracken was still in the classroom, tidying up his books. When I saw him standing there it felt like a sign. He was The Only Person in the World (or Guernsey) who didn't laugh at me. The Only Person Who Liked Me (even a bit). He wasn't my form teacher anymore and I missed him. I missed how he always smoothed out old book jackets and lost pages from his Filofax. I didn't have anywhere to go to and I was pretty sure he didn't, either. We had nowhere and nothing, the two of us. I hated it and I wondered if he felt the same. He certainly didn't look great. His eyes were tired and his hair was unwashed and his new beard didn't suit him. I was already crying but I tried to do it quietly. He was about to pull on his tweed jacket when he noticed me.

"Come on, Cathy, home time."

I looked up into those friendly hazel eyes.

"I can't go home," I told them.

Mr. Mac arched one eyebrow as per James Bond. "Whyever not?"

The tears came more quickly. "I've got nothing and no one to go home to."

"That's not true."

"Yes, it is. I may as well be dead and in fact I wish I was."

Mr. Mac looked shocked.

"Don't say such things."

I got the feeling he wasn't too thrilled about me crying on him again. He'd started fiddling with his papers, as if they were in need of his Instamatic attention. I was a bit put out and shoved my books into my satchel as noisily as possible. Then I shuffled to the front, head hung low.

"Come on," he said, "nothing's that bad. You've had a rough time, but—"

"But nothing! Nothing ever goes right for me. It is unbelievably bad and crap and shit *always*. Everyone hates me. They think I'm a freak no matter what I do. It's like everything has already been decided. My life is set on this crap course of crapness."

Mad Mac's lovely face set into a frown. "What do you mean?"

"You know! Nobody likes me, so what else can I do? I should do what they want me to do, which is just go away and *die*. Maybe *then* they'll be sorry."

Mr. Mac had put his hands on his hips and seemed to be genuinely concerned. I was getting quite hysterical.

I think I was somewhere near his desk but I really can't remember.

"I try my best, I work hard and try to do the right thing, but I'll always look like this and therefore be a *reject*."

"Oh, Cathy. You're putting too much stock on how things look."

"It's how it is," I replied. "It's the *truth*. I hate myself."

The McFrown reached Olympic-sized proportions.

"Where's this coming from?"

"From me." I jabbed my finger to my heart. "Me! I can't be me any longer. I'm hideous. I have to stop it, I have to stop everything!"

There was an awkward silence as Mr. McCracken tried to think of what to say. He stared down at his desk like he might find some good words there. (I did like how he paused before he said things, it made him seem more intellectual.)

"You're in a right old state." He steered himself to-wards me and laid a hand on my shoulder. "Have you talked to anyone about this?"

I drew myself up. "I'm talking to you."

"Yes, but—"

"I want to talk to *you*, I want *you* to help me."

Mr. McCracken lifted his head and dropped it again. "Cathy"—he pushed out his bottom lip a micro-inch—"how can I help you? What do you want me to do?"

I glared red-hot at him. "Tell me you care. Tell me I'm not nothing."

I remember how he smiled very especially.

"Of course you're not. You're very special."

I nodded and gulped down my tears.

Bollocks. I'm trying to write this down as accurately as I remember but I've also tried hard to block it out. What happened next? I think I sort of took Mr. McCracken's hand and maybe pressed it. Then I pulled myself up onto tippy-toe and leaned forward. Yes, that's it. I knew Mr. Mac wouldn't like me leaning in so close but I couldn't help it. I was sort of carried away in the emotion and I didn't care how it looked, I just wanted a bit more contact. Did I plan to kiss him? No, not him. I was just sort of imagining anyone with a head and hair. I pressed the palm of my hand flat on the McChest so as to feel his heartbeat. I suppose it was the sort of thing I'd seen before on TV. Then I tried to put my other arm around his neck and tilt my chin towards him.

I may as well have prodded him with a poker.

"Cathy!"

He stepped back and I lost my balance—talk about destroying the moment!—I had to grab him so as to steady myself. Then he took me by the shoulders and tried to hold me up. For a split second the eye-to-eye contact was intensely smouldering, but not in a good way. We were close enough to kiss and I tried wrapping both arms around his neck this time. Then his hands were on my waist.

He said something like "Stop! Huuuh!"

It was over in a flash, and all I can now picture is the terror on his face. I could've slapped him when I saw it.

Instead I slammed him back with my hand.

"You're lying. You don't care at all. *Slimeball!*"

"What?"

"You don't know anything about what I'm going through. Keep away from me!"

I had really screamed those last words out and this is actually important. I don't think I have ever-ever-ever screamed like that, right into someone's face, and seen the effect it had. It felt fantastic. I ran out of the classroom and straight into Mrs. Carey and Mrs. Le Sauvage, who were standing, arms crossed, a little way down the corridor.

You can probably guess what happened next. No, I bet you can't. It was like one of those rubbish plays they put on at Beau Sejour, where everyone shouts and throws their hands about. I jumped on the mountainous Mrs. Le Sauvage, sobbing hysterically. She wobbled all of her chins at Mr. McCracken, who, of course, had come running into the corridor. She asked him what-on-God's-green-earth-was-happening, and he said he didn't know himself. That made my sobbing tidal. Looking back, I was crying for lots of reasons, but I blamed Mr. McCracken completely.

The Savage Mountain didn't know what to think and I let myself get lost in the moment/her bosom. From there I started stringing together my accusations. I said Mr. Mac had hugged and tried to kiss me. I called him a pervert. I started to hypervent, which made it all the more convincing. If I'd had to go on TV or tell my story to a national newspaper then I bet they would've paid me well. But that sort of thing only happens in England. In England they would've also called the police and carted Mr. McCracken off to prison. (I'm glad they didn't.)

Even so, all the shouty chest beating was just what I wanted. I was suddenly playing me in the film of my life and it wasn't some crappy play at Beau Sejour but a proper Hollywood blockbuster—the kind you'd never see in the cinema in Guernsey.* My audience was small but select. Mrs. Le Sauvage took me straight to Mrs. Perrot, who cancelled her Friday night Seroc class and sat me down with a box of scented tissues. Then Mum came rushing in from work to hold my hand and act like A Proper Mother for the first time in a long time. It all looked quite promising. And as Mr. McCracken got more and more flustered his voice went squeaky and irritated everyone.

"She's confused, she threw herself at me. What could I do? I've only ever tried to help her and be a support to her. But I never crossed the line! This is preposterous! It's insane!"

Mr. McCracken got so worked up. He said I'd come to him talking about problems at home. He looked at Mum accusingly and her perm went all static like a storm cloud.

"Is this true, Cathy?"

I shook my head so hard I thought it would fall off. I told Mum she was the best mum ever and that I loved her more than anything, which is why I hadn't told her about Mr. McCracken.

Mr. Mac then got very angry and went off to the staff room while Mrs. P. nodded sympathetically and watched me cling to Mum.

* Because it burned down.

"This is all such a shock," she kept saying. "We've never had a problem like this. I can't understand it."

Mr. Mac then resurfaced (stage right), brandishing a few of those nasty notes he'd been sent.

"Look at these!" He threw them down on the desk. "I've been getting them for a while, and I tried to ignore it but now I think it's clear who must've written them." He looked across at me. "She's fixated! It's a crush that's got out-of-hand, and these letters show she's angry and knows full well her feelings aren't reciprocated."

I blinked at the notes spread out in front of us, and wiped the tears from my cheeks.

"I never wrote those. I thought you were my friend. You were always giving me lifts home, and what about that Sunday afternoon when you took me to Island Wide?"

Mr. Mac's jaw tightened as I stood up to face him.

"We had such good chats when we met on the cliffs. You spent so much time with me and you know I never sent you those notes. I remember that time we found one on your windscreen."

Mr. Mac stared back at me. "Cathy, come on. This is all in your head!"

I looked again at the notes. Maybe it was all in my head, but just because it was in my head didn't make it any less real.

"I thought you genuinely cared for me. I wasn't the only one who thought so, either. The other girls tease me. You've always singled me out."

Confusion rained like cats and dogs. I promised Mrs. Perrot that I didn't know who wrote the notes, although there was something strangely familiar about the curve of the "S" and the crooked underlining. They were passed around and perusled. Our Reverend Headmistress then twitched her nose and asked Mr. McCracken why on earth he'd not brought them to her attention. I started crying again and suggested that some other "confused" pupil might have written them.

Mr. McCracken flapped his arms like a cartoon penguin.

"This is ridiculous! Are you all mad? Isn't it obvious this is some deranged form of attention seeking? Cathy, why are you doing this?"

"I'm not doing anything," I replied.

Mrs. Perrot carried on talking, but Mum stood up and walked over to the window. I watched her quietly out of the corner of my eye. She used to always stare out of the windows at home—especially at the weekends or when Dad was sailing on the boat. I wondered if she was watching for the little red hull to appear on the horizon. Dad would be out of reach somewhere and she'd sit close up to the glass, so close you could see her breath on it, like she was trapped and wanting out. I never knew why she did it until that night in Mrs. Perrot's office. It was then that I realised the window was a mirror. Mum was staring at her own reflection, at another impenetrable surface. I'll be honest with you, Mum was never much of a masterpiece oil painting—not even one by a Post-Impressionist—but she could arrange her face more carefully than the Mona Lisa.

"I didn't bring my daughter up to be a liar," she said quickly, turning back.

There wasn't even a flicker in the eyes to give the game away and I knew then that she was the most brilliant liar. The very best liars, after all, are the ones you never know about.

At least now I *do* know. Poor old Mr. McCracken. He didn't stand a chance against us. He was the only person left and look what I did to him. Why did I want everyone to suffer for my mistakes? It wasn't fair, but nothing was fair and I couldn't change that. I wanted to believe the lies I was spinning, and I needed to feel like an innocent victim—even if I wasn't. I can't explain why. I just did.

I suppose it was one of those lessons I had to learn myself.

[PRESS CUTTINGS FILE]

Guernsey Evening Press,

Tuesday, 21st December 1965

· PUBLIC NOTICES ·

DEATHS

Rozier, Charles André, died after a long illness at his home in Icart, robbed of his youth but not his dignity.

—*A bientôt, mon vier.*

"Judge not, that ye be not judged.

For with what judgement ye judge,

ye shall be judged: and

with what measure ye mete, it shall be

measured to you again."

MATTHEW 7:1–2

22nd December 1985, 2 a.m.

'm quite a fan of the Bible, which is very gripping, especially the Old Testament. Whenever I can't sleep I read about plagues of locusts or people being turned to salt. The New Testament is more predictable but plenty of bad stuff still goes on. It's amazing what people did to each other, and all in the name of Love.

I know a lot about this thanks to Grandma, who was a bit of a religious megalomaniac. She was forever spouting great chunks of the Bible. That's when she wasn't telling me about her Genius Son Emile, who won every prize in school, or the sea monster in the Little Roussel or the witches of Les Landes. She used to tuck me up in bed so tight I could hardly breathe, and make me promise not to run off anywhere in case I got lost and didn't come back. She asked that most nights because she was going senile. Dad told her to stop scaring me and when I was ten she had a stroke so he pretty much got what he wanted. We put her in the Câtel hospice and I r

259

emember she'd always be sitting up in bed, smelling of lavender talc, staring at the photographs on the dresser. There was one of my grandpa in profile, and another of that blond boy with crooked teeth holding up his baby brother. I was amazed to think that Dad had ever been so small.

Grandma died just before I turned twelve. Mum said Dad was very upset about it and I do remember him spending hours and hours alone on the boat. Then he decided to write Grandma's life story and went back into his study. I listened to the tap-tap-tap of his typewriter and wondered what I'd have to do to make him write my story. Of course, back then my story wasn't so riveting, whereas now he'd have plenty to get his teeth into, and he'd do a much better job than I am doing. He'd be good at skimming over the ugly stuff and he'd make me a much more sympathetic character. He'd make sure you knew that I was lonely and eager for approval, and he'd explain that I only made stupid jokes out of serious things because I was scared. He'd also call me naive and easily led, and I honestly wouldn't mind.

I made such a mess of things and, please note, I am truly sorry.

After my shameful accusations as per Mr. McCracken I had plenty of time to think about what I'd done. I had to stay off school while they sorted things out. I felt terrible but there was no way back, and I went a bit demented, pacing about the house and weeping into the fridge. By now Mum's patience was rice-cracker thin and she told me to pull myself together. She started to say that a lot, actually. She also decided we should re-paint Dad's study. She didn't announce this publicly, but I was woken up one morning by the sound of a loud bang. I came downstairs and found her dragging Dad's old desk out into the hall.

I (stupidly) asked her what she was doing.

"What I should've done ages ago," she replied without looking up. "I'm redecorating and you can help."

Of course I'd help. I didn't like the idea of Mum sorting out Dad's study on her own. I might have been through everything a zillion times already—I had so many of Dad's files under my bed they were pushing up through the mattress—but even so, I had to be there in case Mum found something that I'd missed.

The first thing we did was clear out his remaining books and take them down to Guille-Aillez Library. Then we went through the last files and piles of letters. Some of them were shifted to the cupboard under the stairs, others were dumped into bin bags. After that came the hard work of moving the furniture. I don't think we said a word to each other the whole time we were doing it, and I was sure Mum was angry at me. It was only when we were wrestling with Dad's old filing cabinet that she spoke, and that was because of the bottle. It rolled out in front of us and came to rest at her big toe, a bit like a hand grenade. We both stood still and stared at it. I thought I'd found and drunk and therefore got rid of most of Dad's whisky bottles, so I felt a bit guilty for missing this one, but I was also pleased Mum had to see it. She picked it up and turned it over in her hands.

"Look at the dust on this," she said matter-of-factly. "It looks like it's been stuck back there for years."

She turned away from me and took it into the kitchen, and a second later I heard running water as she rinsed it out. I don't know why she had to wash the bottle straightaway—perhaps it made her feel better, or perhaps she knew I'd want to drink it. I tried to shift the cabinet a bit further towards the door and that's when I noticed the leather folder resting against the skirting board. It must've been jammed behind the cabinet as well. I heard the back door slam and guessed Mum was tramping down the garden path to the bins. I opened the folder quickly, hoping I'd find something else she wouldn't like.

Grandma's death certificate fluttered out. Underneath it was a tiny black prayer book with gold-edged pages. The name "Hubert E. W. Rozier" was written inside. Grandpa had impossibly fancy handwriting, the way only old-fashioned people do, and I ran my fingers over its loops and curves. There were also some yellowed press cuttings folded up messily. Grandma had kept the notice in the press announcing Grandpa's death, and there were cuttings of other death notices from her side of the family. I was a bit surprised by this, since I'd never had her down as a sentimental person. There was also a long thin envelope with pale green stamps that didn't look as old. I remember thinking the stamps were worth keeping. But I was distracted by another discovery—seven A4 sheets folded up at the back, some in Dad's handwriting.

I scanned the first page and felt a horrible prickling at my temples. Poor Dad. He'd never stopped trying to finish Uncle Charlie's story, and he must've asked Grandma for help, because her name was scribbled in the margins. But there were so many crossings-out. Maybe Grandma was too old to remember by the time Dad got round to asking. Maybe that's why Dad got meaner. Or maybe he got meaner because Grandma died. Or maybe he got meaner after he started drinking.

And maybe I was mean to Mr. McCracken because Dad was mean to me. That's what happens, hate or anger is passed down from one person to another, and you never hit the right target because you always aim too late. Mum used to promise me that Dad did love us, she said he just didn't know how to *show* it. But he could have written it, couldn't he? Why didn't he write it?

I thought if I copied out Dad's notes then I'd understand them better, for myself. So I left Mum rinsing out the filing cabinet on the patio and cycled up to Island Wide. I wanted to buy a brand-new notebook and I needed some fresh air, and as I cycled along I didn't think about food, or Nic, or how much I hated myself. I didn't even think about Mr. McCracken. But I should've done. I was chaining up my bicycle when his car pulled into the garage forecourt opposite. Talk about Fate or Karma.

Only Fate or Karma was on my side because I was able to dive behind a newspaper stand before he saw me. I peered through copies of the *Guernsey Evening Press* and watched him go to the petrol pump. For the record, he was looking quite smart in a navy-blue Guernsey,* and had started shaving again. I was glad he'd made the effort. Then he pulled out a pump and tugged it to the side of his car. I wanted to go and talk to him, to tell him how sorry I was and ask if we could sort things out, but I didn't know how to and then I missed my chance. A white BMW pulled up and I realised it belonged to Therese. Of course, she only lived two streets away so I wasn't surprised to see her. She lifted herself out of the car and brushed down her blue jacket. It was the kind of blue you see in adverts for holidays (not in Guernsey) and Mr. McCracken obviously liked it, too, because when he turned and saw her he nearly dropped his pump. I thought he'd spill petrol everywhere and maybe start a fire—which would've been exciting. Therese very kindly went over to help him. I could see her face quite clearly and her expression was soft and dreamy, like she was looking at a cream cake she couldn't eat.

I also remember that her lipstick matched her nail varnish. She rested her hand on Mr. McCracken's arm and talked straight into his ear. When she finished saying whatever it was she was saying I thought she'd turn to go but he tried to keep her there. Big Mac's pump dripped petrol onto his shoes. They talked for only a few seconds more and I knew they weren't talking about me

---

* A "Guernsey" is a sweater, as well as an island (yes, like a "jersey"). It is made of indestructible wool, and it is heavy and warm, and has special patterns at the shoulders. Different Guernsey families had different patterns, so that when they pulled a bloated, drowned corpse from the Channel they could identify it and bury it in the right parish. (Nice.)

because Mr. Mac was smiling. Then he brushed the hair from Therese's face.

Obviously they were saying important, adult things to each other, things I was too young to understand. They stared into each other's eyes until I had to blink. I should've been Outraged-and-Appalled-of-St.-Peter-Port, but actually I was happy. It's nice to see two people in love and able to show it. I wasn't even surprised so maybe deep-down I already knew it. I ran inside and did my shopping quickly, then I cycled home and although it's uphill all the way I didn't notice.

I wasn't planning to tell Mum what I'd seen, but when I got home she was waiting for me in the hallway.

"I've been on the phone to Mrs. Perrot," she pronounced. "Mr. McCracken has resigned. He accepts he misjudged things and they've come to an agreement. I must say I'm surprised he backed down so quickly, but Mrs. Perrot gave me the impression that it didn't come out of nowhere."

I nodded.

"So, it's over and done with."

I nodded again.

Mum was obviously expecting me to say something. She peeled off her rubber gloves.

"You should be happy. You can go back to school."

I was thinking about what I'd just seen at Island Wide.

"You never believed me anyway."

Mum arched an eyebrow and I made a little shrug.

"You may as well admit it."

She pulled back her shoulders, obviously wondering what to say next.

"The thing is, Cathy," she began, "you do have a habit of exaggerating things, but . . . you're my daughter and I love you, so actually you are wrong. I *did* believe you."

She almost looked sincere. I almost wanted to hug her.

"Did you love Dad?"

"What?" She blinked. "Of course I did."

"Well," I said, "you believed what he told you, and he was lying."

She opened her eyes wide.

"There's a difference between lying to someone and not telling them the whole story. Your father kept a lot to himself. He thought it was better that way. That's just how he was."

I nodded. "So not telling someone the truth is OK?"

Mum sucked in her lips. The shutters were about to come down.

"When you love someone you want to protect them. You do what you think is best at the time. One day, Cathy, you'll see that."

And I do see that, I really do. People do terrible things for Love.

That night I watched Mum in the sitting room, quietly reading her book. When I told her I was going for a walk she barely even looked up. She probably knew I was going to La Petite Maison, to see the "For Sale" sign for myself. That's when I noticed Therese's white BMW parked a little way up the road. I didn't have to ask myself why it was there. I remembered how she'd looked at Mr. McCracken at the garage. It reminded me of how they'd looked at each other that time at Les Paradis.

I now understood why Mr. McCracken never told Nic off in class, and why he'd been driving around aimlessly one Sunday and jumped at the chance to run me to Les Paradis. I don't know when he first met Therese, but Mr. Prevost's nights at the Royal must've given them time to meet again. Therese and Mr. McCracken. What a lovely couple. She'll change her name and move to England and wear all those clothes she bought and kept in the spare room.

I stood in the darkness outside La Petite Maison and there was the sound of things clicking into place. It was like when I'd pulled apart my Rubik's Cube and put it back together with all the colours matching. I realised it was Nic who'd sent those nasty letters to Mr. McCracken. It wasn't just the curve of the "S" and the crooked under-lining, it was the fancy felt-tip pens that I'd seen her buy in Island Wide. She was always so snide about Mr. McCracken, she played up in class and he never did any-thing about it. How long had she known? It's probably the only reason she started coming to my house and pretending to be my friend. I was just a decoy. Wasn't that clever? Wasn't she clever?

I suppose I was relieved that Mr. McCracken wasn't so innocent, but I also felt pretty Stupid. It doesn't mat-ter how many times I come top of the class, when it comes to the stuff that's happening around me I'm a proper (Village) idiot. I don't understand the first thing about living human people—why they make the choices they make, why they keep secrets. I suppose I have to

The Charlie Rozier Story
Concluded:

"The Night and Fog Descend—
A Son and Brother Lost"

*[Special thanks Colin Turrell and Valerie Priaulx
for new information supplied, credit and
thanks also to Arlette Rozier]*

Charlie Rozier died in late December 1965. He therefore
left the story of his arrest and imprisonment during the
Occupation incomplete. It fell to me, his brother and
confidant, to continue alone the journey upon which we
had embarked together. I have done so as best I am able.

Charlie was rearrested by three Feldgendarmes on
the morning of 13th December 1942. It was reported in
the *Press* later that day that his father, Hubert Rozier,
had been shot "whilst attempting to escape." No further
details were given, although it is believed that an officer
on night patrol had seen Hubert walking onto the beach
at Belle Grève and, after shouting several warnings,
had opened fire and fatally wounded him. Hubert was
clearly planning to end his life, one way or another. He
had already provided the Occupying Authorities with
a detailed confession, wherein he accepted full respon-

sibility for the charges of "espionage" and "sabotage" that had been laid at his door. Thus and therefore, he knew he would be shot. As an ex-officer with the Royal Engineers who had seen active service during the First World War, and as a former POW and German speaker, he fitted the enemy profile of an underground agent, even though the majority of his fellow islanders would later dismiss the idea as preposterous.

Despite Hubert's fervent denials, the German interrogating officers remained convinced that father and son had been working as a team. The very night his father was shot, Charlie was rearrested and passed into the hands of Achim Burkhardt and Paul Heider, two officers of the Abwehr (Espionage, Counter Espionage, and Sabotage Service of the German High Command). Heider was rightly suspicious of Hubert's confession, and promptly concluded that his death was "an act of martyrdom."

However, it was only after Charlie's death that his mother would finally admit the lengths that Hubert went to in order to deflect all blame from his eldest son. According to Arlette, when Charlie's notebook was discovered by German soldiers on 9th December, Hubert immediately claimed it as his own, and said that his wife could support this. He then nodded to Arlette, who deliberately and erroneously identified the handwriting as that of her husband.

But with or without Hubert and Arlette's efforts Charlie did not escape trial and punishment. Hubert's tragic death did not save his son, and may even have made his predicament more perilous. The German authorities were thrown into disarray and became anxious about a possible scandal. There was irrefutable evidence of espionage activity, and the discovery of tracks on a slipway near Bordeaux confirmed that there had been an escape attempt.

Although determined to maintain the image of a "Model" Occupation, the Germans were also desirous to assert their control. There was no unanimity over what action should be taken and Charlie was kept in custody at the notorious Paradis prison. A week passed and there was much debate back and forth between Burkhardt and the Feldkommandant on the neighbouring island of Jersey. But because no one could make a decision an unfortunate fate befell Charlie. He was placed under the Nacht und Nebel Erlass (Night and Fog decree).* Thus it came to pass that my brother, then aged fifteen, summarily vanished from Guernsey soil.

Most people believed that he was dead, and even his own mother had given up hope of seeing him again. When he returned to the island after Liberation he was unrecognisable as the high-spirited teenager taken by the Nazis. He was but a shadow of his former self, his mind greatly altered by the trauma of his exile.

* The Night and Fog decree came into force in December 1941 and was designed to curb the rising tide of resistance activities in Occupied Europe. It stated that any offender who could not be brought to trial and sentenced within *eight days of capture* could be held incommunicado by the authorities, before being tried by Special Tribunals. This ensured the "efficient and enduring intimidation" of local populations by denying them any knowledge of the fate of the offender.

The bare facts of his captivity were only then divulged. Having spent a fortnight in the notorious German military prison of Fresnes, Charlie had been sent to Natzweiler-Struthof concentration camp, 31 miles south of Strasbourg, hidden in the Vosges mountains of Alsace. Natzweiler was the only concentration camp established on French soil and became the recipient of a great number of "NN" prisoners, many of whom were either exterminated in the gas chamber or died working in the large stone quarry.* Charlie worked a twelve-hour day and survived repeated beatings and constant deprivation. During that time, not a day passed when he didn't wonder about the fate of Ray Le Poidevoin, his onetime partner in crime.

Le Poidevoin (as it has now transpired) fared considerably better than young Charlie. He did indeed make it to Southampton, having been picked up by an English warship on the evening of 10th December. (*Sarnia Chérie* was then described by one eyewitness as a "floating wreck.") Although suffering from hypothermia Le Poidevoin was able to give British Military Intelligence a brief account of his escape. He had left Guernsey on the night of 9th December in great haste. A terrible storm blew up and he had been tossed to and fro in the heavy waters for many hours. With waves continually washing over the boat, he was unable to keep a steady course. At one point he considered turning back, but he realised it was too late. Convinced he wouldn't make it through the

---

* The camp records revealed the full extent of the systematic shootings, hangings, and gassings, medical "experiments," etc. Further research required.

night, he lay in the bottom of the boat and prayed, and it appears his prayers were answered in that the storm propelled him out to sea.

Le Poidevoin later wrote a heavily embroidered version of events in his book *Flight from Fortress Isle* (Channel Islands Publishing, 1969), which caused much excitement at the time of its publication. It remains a bitter paradox that, once the Occupation was over, the stories of successful escapees became celebrated whereas those whose escape plans had failed—and who were deported and imprisoned—received far less postwar recognition and were often criticised by their fellow islanders for putting the wider population in peril. Charlie was never seen as the innocent victim, but more as the "Prodigal Son" who had paid a heavy price for his own careless acts.

In his book, Ray Le Poidevoin claimed that he and the unfortunate J-P Duquemin were taken by surprise when they heard of the house search at the Rozier residence on the night of 9th December 1942. Colin Turrell of Les Moulins had met with them at La Folie Inn and reported that "the whole Rozier family" had been taken in by the Germans and were "most likely done for."* With *Sarnia Chérie* in imminent danger of being discovered, Ray and J-P went directly to the boatshed and agreed "to go it alone," knowing the dangers of their hasty and ill-prepared flight in highly unseasonal waters. "It was a risk but we had sworn an oath to each other and our-

---

* Turrell later corroborated this: he was the nephew of Blanche Gaudion and had heard the news directly from his aunt (see interview E.P.R. 12/2/68—Gaudion Family file).

selves," wrote Le Poidevoin. "I believed that Charlie could hold out against the Hun for a few hours and that might be all we had. Yes, we left Charlie behind but if we'd stayed we'd have been shot."

The boys were unable to set off from the intended slipway north of Bordeaux and instead dragged the boat down as far as Les Houmets. J-P went to fetch the last of the supplies, and promised Ray he'd be a matter of minutes. Ray heard a distant explosion approximately half an hour later. He waited as long as he felt able, then, assuming the worst, he launched the boat alone.

Le Poidevoin spent the rest of the War in Cornwall, where he lived with his aunt and three younger sisters (who had all been evacuated in 1940). He returned to Guernsey only briefly, with the British liberating forces, and is currently a resident of South Australia. There, he describes himself as a "manager of properties." Although disinclined to reply to my letters, he did finally respond to some of my questions via his youngest sister, Valerie Priaulx (née Le Poidevoin). He categorically denied acting as an informant for the Germans and reiterated that it was never his intention to desert his "friend," but he was left with no choice by the collision of circumstances.

It is unlikely that the events of December 1942 will ever be clarified. When Charlie returned to Guernsey he spoke out against Ray, but few people gave credence to his feverish accusations. Indeed, it did seem unlikely that Ray would have put his own plans in jeopardy by informing on Charlie. Why would he have acted so rashly? Le Poidevoin admitted to there being a history of animosity between himself and his young friend, but could boyish bravado warrant two dead bodies and three years in a concentration camp? Perhaps other persons wanted revenge on the Roziers for allowing the Germans to take control of their printing press. Many islanders who ended up in concentration camps began their journey because of an informer. We may never know all the names.

Charlie was always convinced of Ray's guilt and spoke out against him almost immediately upon his return to the island. From the moment of his liberation his fragile mind was set on retribution, but the British military authorities who were then in charge of hearing any grievances vis-à-vis collaborators, remained deeply sceptical of all claims made, declaring that ultimately they had too much basis in "suspicion and hearsay." The Channel Islanders were still not to be trusted!

Arlette never blamed Charlie for what happened but she did not look to place the blame elsewhere. Like many islanders, she strongly opposed all talk of retaliation, believing that it would cause further suffering and heartache. Out of respect for his mother Charlie kept silent for many years. Decades passed and he didn't mention Ray's name, but for months he would isolate himself from everyone, trapped by a crippling depression and unable to sleep or eat. Mother and son could not be reconciled and remained for the most part estranged, even until Charlie's death. Although they loved each other it was hard to be reminded of the suffering and the sacrifice, the great burden of loss.

[MIDDLE LANDING]

Once Dad's study was empty Mum said we had to put the past where it belonged. But nothing was or is that simple. I remember when she drove me back to school the day after Mr. McCracken had resigned. She told me everything would be fine and that my classmates wouldn't know anything.

"They might've heard he's resigned, but they won't connect it to you," she promised. "Mrs. Perrot wanted everything kept quiet."

As per ever she was wrong. Everywhere I went it was like the parting of the Red Sea (or was it the Dead Sea?). I was an outcast as per the Indians, or a leper from Africa. The Chinese whispering made it properly United Nations. I don't know who had started the rumours but apparently I'd been caught screaming my head off at Mr. McCracken and had totally exaggerated whatever had happened. One of the Sixth Formers brushed past me in the hallway and jumped back, screaming "Rape!"

Hilarious, *je* don't think.

NB: There were only two rapes reported in Guernsey during the whole of the German Occupation. That might be a sign that the Germans were incredibly well behaved. But it might also mean the female population were pushovers. Mud sticks, apparently.

"Some people think you made it up to get back at Mr. Mac for giving you bad grades."

That's what Vicky told me.

We were filing into Double English and I was asking her what I'd missed. I was actually referring to homework.

"I don't care what people are saying," I replied. "If Mr. McCracken's innocent then why did he resign? He must've done *something* wrong to just give up his job. Honestly, Vick, do the maths. Nobody's who you think they are."

She opened and shut her mouth, like a goldfish catching flies.

"So you mean you and him, *for real?*"

"Not a chance," said Lisa, pushing past me with her bony elbow. "I wouldn't trust her version of anything. All the stories she comes out with . . ."

I smiled my best fake smile. "At least my stories have a point to them."

The classroom was filling up and I caught sight of Nic standing behind Lisa. Her expression was still and serious, like one of the waxworks of German soldiers in the Occupation Museum (although in fact those waxworks look like their faces are melting). I was expecting her to say something bitchy and smirk, but she didn't. She just stared at me.

I can't pretend I didn't feel a weeny bit smug. There I was, a dark/Trojan horse, crammed full of dangerous secrets. I was seriously tempted to give everyone a news-flash update vis-à-vis Therese and Mr. McCracken. It was bound to come out sometime and I could've shut them up for good. But when I looked at Nic I realised what was at stake. It wasn't that I was scared of her. If anything, I felt sorry for her. I didn't want all my cretinous classmates knowing her business. Yes, Mr. Mac was a guilty sleaze, but maybe it was better to let them think he'd been a guilty sleaze with me. Not with Nic's own mother.

I hope this is proof that: (1) I'm not all bad and (2) I'm growing up.

Of course, growing up is not necessarily a good thing. The older you get, the more lies you tell. Just think about all the lies Therese must've told. People were shocked when Mr. McCracken stood beside her at Nic's funeral. She looked lovely, though. She'd had her roots done spe-cially, and she was as brown as a nut. That was probably what shocked everyone the most.

I hope they get married and stay together forever. I hope it wasn't just a silly affair. I've kept their secret for them all this time, so they'd better make it worth my effort.

But it's hard to know what secrets should stay secret, and here's another good example.

It was the most important day of Dad's life. We'd arrived an hour early at White Rock, and we were all dressed up like it was a party. It was a lovely spring day and I felt so proud. I stupidly imagined that I'd finally see Dad happy once he had the Memorial in place. I remember looking around at all these people and thinking they were clapping for him as he stepped up to the microphone. He was wearing a dark blue suit—I think it was the suit he'd married Mum in. I looked at her and smiled. That's when it all went wrong. Dad never normally read from notes but he pulled some crumpled papers from his jacket pocket. Then he started speaking, but he slurred and stumbled over his words and he was swaying like he'd fall right over. People started murmuring and I had to grip Mum's hand. When a man in the crowd told Dad to speak up he glared back. Suddenly he turned and lurched down from the platform. Everyone was talking and I wanted to go after him, but Mum held on to me. I don't remember her saying anything to anyone about blood sugar, but apparently she did, when people asked her what was wrong. Oh well. Maybe I heard it, maybe I didn't. That only came out later, after he was dead.

Dad was diabetic. Mum said it might've come on because of the Occupation, if he was undernourished as a baby. Her and Dr. Senner were the only ones who knew and at first it wasn't a problem, since Dad kept fit and super-healthy and ate his rabbit food. But over time things started to slip. Mum says she saw the changes after Grandma died—Dad complained of headaches and his moods went up and down. Eventually Dr. Senner persuaded him to have some tests. They said Dad needed insulin, which wasn't good. He hit the roof, and that's when he threw the TV out.

relief, after he'd cut his hand. I thought that sounded right. Until I found the other bottles. That made me worry more. So I went and asked Dr. Senner if Dad had been in terrible pain. Dr. Senner told me that diabetics don't necessarily feel pain because their nerve endings go numb. Dr. Senner said Dad didn't realise how serious his hand was, because it didn't even hurt.

It's hard to know who or what to trust, but I suppose I can trust what I saw. It was the night after White Rock. Dad was in his study with the door firmly closed, and I was on the stairs. I was sitting on the very spot where I'm sitting now, in fact. I like it here, because I can see halfway into the kitchen and all the way into the sitting room, and I can listen out for the study door. I used to sit here all the time when I was meant to be in bed, hoping to see Mum and Dad touch or hug or kiss like a married couple should. I never did, and I had to wonder what it was that kept them together but so far apart.

That night, Mum had already gone to bed. She'd hardly talked to Dad since the unveiling, and she didn't even bother to tell him "Good night." I was worried she was planning to leave him, and I honestly couldn't blame her. But I didn't like Dad sleeping in his study on that rough old sofa again. I imagined myself going in and telling him so. I planned to knock on his door and surprise him and then we'd have a proper chat about important, adult things. I probably would've also tried to hug him, even though he'd have been appalled.

Standing up quickly I padded downstairs, but once I got to his study door I waited for a minute. Then I bent down. I know I shouldn't have done it, and I promise you I never normally look through keyholes and spy on people.

Dad was sitting in his chair with a bottle on the desk in front of him. It was definitely whisky, and it was half drunk already. His hair was messed up and his eyes looked red and tired. He was staring down at a piece of paper and running his fingers over its edges. Then he picked up the bottle with his good hand and took a long slug. He wiped his mouth and looked back at the paper. I knew it was a letter because it had been folded neatly to fit in an envelope. I don't know what it said but it was bad news, for sure. At the time I imagined it was a letter from Mum saying so long and good-bye, you good-for-nothing husband. But later I decided it was a letter from Dr. Senner saying come into the surgery or you'll soon be dead.

It was only much-much later, when I found the letter tucked inside Grandma's leather folder, that I worked out what I'd actually seen. Then everything I thought I knew had to change again. It was annoying, because by then I'd gotten very attached to my version of the truth.

I suppose that's the thing about History, there are always several versions of that thing we call the truth.

A Mother's Story [Extract]

By E. P. Rozier, 12/4/81

hortly before my mother suffered her second and fatal stroke she provided me with fresh information regarding the imprisonment of her eldest son, Charles André Rozier, during the years of Occupation. Her statement, which was only offered on condition that it never be published, goes some way towards explaining her years of silence.

Shocking though this now seems, my mother believed that it was her husband, Hubert Rozier, who had alerted the German police to their eldest son's activities. Hubert had become anxious about Charlie's increasingly irresponsible behaviour. The Occupation gave young people ample opportunities to misbehave, and Charlie for one showed no respect for authority and was continually going out after curfew "looking for trouble." The sense of crisis and fracture between father and son deepened as the years wore on. Hubert had never recovered from his experiences of the First World War, and the Occupation brought back many bad memories. "It was as if an old wound was reopened, and it slowly bled him dry," said Arlette.

Hubert withdrew from family life, leaving his wife to run the household single-handedly, which she did as best she could, but by that time Charlie was spending large amounts of time outside the family home and there was little she could do to stop him. She often heard Hubert muttering about this. Hubert felt certain that some tragedy would befall his eldest son and warned Arlette that Charlie was mixing with "bad company."

Arlette was certain that Hubert informed on his own son in a desperate and misguided attempt to stop Charlie doing something foolhardy and life-threatening. He intended it as a warning to his teenage son, hoping to show Charlie that he was putting himself and his family in danger. Having found an unlikely friend in the form of Anton Vern, Hubert confided in him and the two men planned the house search.

Their plan might even have worked had it not been for Charlie's scrapbook, hidden under the floorboards of the spare room Hubert now occupied. Arlette was adamant that Hubert knew nothing of the scrapbook until it was discovered. Had he known of its contents or its whereabouts, he would surely never have allowed the search to take place. This would explain his readiness to claim it as his own.

Sadly, at this stage in her life La Duchesse was not the most reliable of sources. Although she was able to recall events from her early childhood with almost photographic accuracy, the years of the Occupation were marred by tragedy and heartbreak. Her voice would falter when asked to recall these troubling times:

"Hubert was becoming like a stranger to me. I'm not even sure if he trusted me. Working for the Germans was hard on all of us and Hubert locked himself up in a strange world where we were all against him. He could become agitated and suspicious for no reason.

"He'd often ask me where Charlie was, and if I shrugged and said I didn't know I could see the despair in his eyes. When the German soldiers came to search the house I felt sure it was because of something he'd said to Vern. He wasn't at all surprised. But then they found this scrapbook and I didn't know what to think. I was terrified we'd all be sent to France, and I could tell from Hubert's face he wasn't expecting it. Still, he knew what he had to do and in that moment I was reminded of the man I had married.

"None of what then followed surprised me. It was entirely in his character to lay down his life on a point of principle. I suppose that was his last show of strength, but it was all because of what? A stupid mistake? I wasn't ever angry with Charlie but I put him out of my head. I thought he was dead, which might make me sound heartless but by then my heart was broken. All I had was you. Don't think I didn't love your brother, but after the War he came back so full of bitterness and anger, and he still idolised his father. Hubert could do no wrong in Charlie's eyes. There were times I wanted to tell him the truth about the sorry mess of it. I wanted to remind him of what his father put us all through. Hubert had fallen

22nd December 1985, 6 p.m.

[In the box room,
pretending to look
for missing fairy lights]

Dad stayed in his study for two whole days after his Waterloo at White Rock, but I don't know that for sure because I was at school. Mum said she checked on him the morning he died, but she wasn't able to say when. She was frustrated with him, she admitted, and she was worried he'd not taken his insulin. But she didn't call Dr. Senner about it. All I remember is that she dropped me at school early and I spent the whole day dreading going home. In the end I went over to Vicky's for my tea.

When I got back at six Mum was in the hall, with her ear glued to the phone. She told me to go and sit in the garden, which is exactly what I did. Dr. Senner drove up, and then there was an ambulance. Dad's heart had already stopped, though. When Mum told me it was heart failure I thought that sounded right.

But it was a lot to take in at once and I don't think I processed all the facts. I usually have to write stuff down and repeat it over and over. Perhaps you can see why I've become a bit suspicious. It doesn't take a (Village) idiot to work out that there's no simple or single explanation for anything, there's just an OFFICIAL VERSION that tidies all the secrets away.

And here's the biggest secret so far: I wasn't ever very interested in the Bloody-Stupid German Occupation, but I thought I might find something in Dad's books and journals and letters to explain what Mum wouldn't. Shouldn't History explain everything?

But then, knowing everything doesn't necessarily mean you'll be happier/better off. Sometimes the more you know, the worse it is. I wish I hadn't known about Therese and her affair, for instance, or that I'd *told* Nic I knew. I wasn't trying to stir up trouble—I just wanted to show Nic that I could keep a secret. I wrote her a letter, explaining how I finally understood why she was being so horrible to me. I told her that it couldn't have been easy for her, living with lies. I said I was sick of it, too. I laid it on mega-deluxe thick but was still so deep-pile nice to her. I told her we were just the same. And do you know how she repaid me? You wouldn't believe it. Well, you probably would.

Every year on Bonfire Night there is a firework display at Saumarez Park. Saumarez Park is Guernsey's only proper park—you'd think there'd be lots of open, rolling fields and green space but, according to Miss Jones, Guernsey is more densely populated than most of Northern Europe. This is on account of the Posho Porsche-Driving English People and their Swiss-Wanker Bankers (who, of course, pay for the fireworks).

Perhaps it was odd that Vicky had asked me to go with her to the display, but I'd helped her collect dandelions for her New-Recipe Dandelion Wine and I'd even been her guinea pig. I thought that meant we were friends again. I was glad. It felt like things were getting back to normal. When we got to Saumarez Park I didn't smell a rat (i.e., her). I didn't want to look a gift horse (i.e., two-faced cow) in the mouth.

Mum was running the stand for the Christian Aid Tin Rattlers and offered to give us a lift. I almost got excited, since I hadn't been out forever. I did notice that Vicky went quiet in the car on the way there, but I just assumed it was because we'd been talking about her birthday at the end of the month. She was planning a big party and was worried re: inviting me.

But by the time we got to the park she was acting as shifty as a tax dodger. I kept suggesting stuff to do or eat, but she wasn't interested. All she did was stare off into the distance, and I wondered if she was looking out for girls from our class.

"Are you embarrassed to be seen with me?" I asked.

"Don't be daft!" she replied. "You're so paranoid."

I said sorry (of course), but then I lost her in the queue for the sparklers. The minute my back was turned she vanished. I wasn't surprised, really. I assumed she'd gone to find someone more exciting.

I'm not too fond of crowds and I didn't want to go on any of the rides by myself. I therefore focused on the food, of which there was a lot. I'd eaten two slices of ham and pineapple pizza and some Dolly Mixtures when the display started, and as pink stars exploded in the sky everyone was looking up and making "ooh-aaah" noises. But I wasn't in the mood to be all filled with wonder, what with everyone elbowing me.

I decided I'd had enough and walked all around the bonfire, still looking for Vicky. As I milled about, the people's faces, all lit up by the flames, began to look quite devilish. I had a strange feeling, and it wasn't indigestion. I walked past Mum's stand but she wasn't on it. Then I did a circuit of the beer tent. Everyone was chatting and laughing—families together, young couples, etc. Then I thought I saw Vicky walking off into the wooded bit of the park. I ran after her, calling out, past groups of people or couples snogging. I was heading towards the children's playground, away from the crowds, which was maybe not too clever. Then I felt someone tug at the hood of my anorak and I heard a clicking sound. It took me a minute to work out what was happening and by then I smelled burning. Nic stood back, holding a cigarette lighter with its little flame still flickering. She'd tried to set fire to the fur trim of my anorak. It was fake fur and had therefore melted, but the smell was disgusting.

She shoved me and I fell, and then I heard Lisa laugh. I remember blinking as liquid was poured onto me. It was White Spirit (I recognised the smell from art class) and I shook my head about. I also tried to stand back up but Lisa put her hands on my shoulders.

Nic flicked the lighter and held it up. "Scared now?"

I don't know for sure if they'd have done it, or if they were just trying to scare me.

Nic said, "You are a filthy little liar! Repeat after me: 'I'm a filthy little liar!'"

"No," I spluttered. "Why?"

Out of the darkness someone called, "Hey there!"

I vaguely focused on a fluorescent jacket and realised it was one of the safety-wardens-cum-parking-attendants.

"Bloody kids. What are you playing at? Get back to the fair or I'll take you to the police tent."

I stood up and brushed myself down. Of course everyone else had vanished. I said thank you to the man but he gave me a dirty look, like it was all my fault, and propelled me back towards the bonfire. The last thing I wanted to do was go back into the fair. I wondered where Vicky was. Had she been watching? Had she lured me into a trap? She must've really hated me, to do something so low. I checked the time on my Swatch. 9:15. Mum had arranged for me to get a lift back with Mrs. Senner at 10, which meant I still had 45 minutes. *Quel nightmare.* I made for the main part of the park, knowing Nic and Lisa were lurking somewhere, getting ready to come after me again. I thought about calling Mum but the nearest phone box was on the Cobo Road, and all my money had gone from my pockets. Had I spent all my money on pizzas or had someone stolen it? I spun round and stared hard into every dark corner, but with all the noise and commotion and crowds, I couldn't see much. I just knew I had to get out so I followed painted arrow signs to the car park. My heart was beating so fast I thought it would explode out of my chest. I kept checking over my shoulder to see if I was being followed. Then I imagined myself on fire as per a real-life human Catherine Wheel, and Nic laughing demonically while Lisa spun me round.

I was about 10 metres from the big "Way Out" sign when it happened. WHAM! I was facedown in the gravel. It was like I'd been knocked over by a car or lorry until I felt something hard between my shoulders. The heel of a shoe.

"Get off me!" I tried to push myself up but ended up on my side with Nic crouching over me.

"Look at me." She tried to turn my head. "Look at me!"

I closed my eyes tight. I felt a sharp pain along my spine (lower down this time). It was dark and wet and the gravel was digging in. I tried to cover my face with my hands.

"Only pigs roll around in shit," said Nic, pushing me down.

I told her to stop it.

"And how will you make me?"

Of course I couldn't. Then I felt someone kicking me so I tried to curl up like a hedgehog. Nic had grabbed a chunk of my hair and was trying to pull my head back.

"Get off me! Leave me alone!"

Then I heard a man's voice and everything stopped.

Nic was muttering, "We're only mucking about" and tugged roughly at my anorak.

"It didn't look to me like mucking about."

I blinked my eyes open. For a second I thought it was an angel and/or Dad.

He leaned down.

"Cathy, can you stand?"

I sat up and let Donnie hook me under the armpits to pull me to my feet.

"Come on, let's get you home."

I hadn't seen him since the summer so of course I was surprised, but I didn't say anything because I was too scared. He had his arm around me as he steered me away from Nic and Lisa, and then I saw Shelley standing right behind them. I thought my legs would give up before we reached his car.

"You can't take her home, you're not her dad." Nic tried to grab at him. "I'm going to call the pigs on you. You're sick."

"Ignore them." Donnie propelled me forwards.

I stumbled on something, twisting my ankle.

"I'm talking to you, *perv*." Nic was tugging at Donnie's cuff. "What are you going to do with her?"

I didn't see Donnie push her but he must've done, because she fell.

I heard someone tell him he shouldn't have done that.

He dived round one side of his car and started unlocking the door. I went round to the passenger side but Nic was up and pulling at me. I yanked myself free and by now Donnie was in the car and the inside light was on. I watched him climb over to open the door on my side. Then he reached out his hand and hauled me in.

I slammed my door shut. Donnie started the ignition and went into reverse. I really hoped we'd run someone over. I didn't care. But as we turned Lisa jumped out in front of us, looking a lot like an axe murderer thanks to the full-beam headlights.

She thumped her hand on the bonnet.

I was now very scared and Donnie didn't much help with his hysterical "Christ Alive"-ing. He revved his engine and the car lurched forward, like it might knock

Lisa down. She took the hint and got out of the way. We swung the car round and tore out of the exit.

We sped past the Post Office, heading for the coast road. Those pizza slices were doing star-jumps in my stomach, and my ribs and shoulder ached. Plus Donnie was bug-eyed and hyperventing.

"Donnie," I said, "thank you."

Donnie didn't take his eyes off the road. I could tell that he was shaken—his skin was shiny and he was driving well over the 35 mph speed limit. Then we started going faster and faster, and I thought we'd definitely crash off a cliff.

"Slow down."

He ignored me and gripped the steering wheel. He wasn't a very good driver, like most people on the island, so I was waiting for us to turn a corner and skid and do a somersault. But I preferred crashing with Donnie to being pulverised/set alight by Nic. Trees and hedges were flashing by, I held my breath and shut my eyes and maybe said a few prayers. Suddenly we hit a bump and the car lurched onto soft ground, coming to a stop on L'Ancresse golf course. All I heard then was our breathing.

Seconds passed. I reached out to try to touch Donnie's shoulder.

"Don't!"

I'd never seen Donnie angry but I'm glad to report it didn't last long. He breathed in and out a few more times, sat back and pressed his hands into his face, then closed them round his nose. A couple of rockets flew up into the sky and lit up the golf course. I could see a low bunker in the distance.

Donnie turned to look at me.

"You're all right? Good. Good." He sighed and swallowed. "What just happened back there. What just happened, *didn't* happen, do you understand?"

I didn't.

He wiped the sweat from his chins. "You won't tell anyone."

"O-K," I said slowly.

"You see why. Those girls could have me for assault. It'd be their word against mine and I wouldn't stand a chance."

"Don't be daft." I shifted in my seat and made the leather fart.

Donnie shook his head. "Didn't you *hear* them? What if anyone else heard?" His chest rose and fell. "They could pin whatever they liked on me and don't pretend your local police force wouldn't take their side. Teenage girls, I'm easy pickings for that lot, aren't I?"

I stared down at my muddy hands and remembered the last time I'd seen him.

"You know what Nicolette's like—she'll say anything to get a reaction."

I heard Donnie sigh. "It's about more than that. You and I both know it."

Another firework went off and I looked up into the sky, but Donnie was watching me.

"I've never made anyone do anything they don't want to. I'm not some dirty old man. I shouldn't have to explain myself. There's nothing to explain."

I glanced back at him and his eyes were glittery from the fireworks.

"You don't think what she thinks, do you? I'm not some *pervert*."

I remembered Mr. McCracken and all the things I'd called him, and then I pictured Donnie, with his shirt unbuttoned, sprawled on his sofa.

I shook my head. "You're not a pervert. You've only ever tried to be my friend. Whatever anyone says, I'll back you up."

He stared off into the distance. I watched him chew at the nail of his index finger and wondered what else to say. I wanted to tell him that I'd missed him.

He sighed again, this time like he was emptying his whole chest.

"I've tried to keep a low profile, since the summer. I'm sorry for what happened between us and if I overstepped the mark. I hoped things would blow over. I should know better, of course. It is what it is and it always turns out the same. I come somewhere new and think things will be different, people will be different. They never are." He glanced across at me. "Do you know what that's like?"

I wanted to say I did but I didn't, since I'd never been anywhere foreign except France on our boat (which doesn't count) and Tenerife (which is full of English people). Mum took me there after Dad's life insurance money came through and we stayed in a fancy hotel with two enormous swimming pools. It was my-first-proper-foreign holiday and it should've been the best-thing-ever, only Mum kept worrying about how much everything cost. I never understood why she worried, since nobody doubted her OFFICIAL VERSION of how Dad died, and they never once asked for the money back.

Mum worried too much—just like Donnie. He was convinced he'd get arrested and thrown into prison and nothing I could say would make a difference. That's the real reason he's packed up and left, by the way. I tried to convince him to stay. I honestly did. I reminded him that Guernsey wasn't like other places on account of its History, but he wasn't listening. If only he'd read Dad's books he'd have realised that in Guernsey guilty people never go to prison—that's why it's full of posho English people and their swish-Swiss bankers.

In Guernsey, guilty people always get a second chance.

Anton A. Vern
56 Bandestrasse
34015 Vienna
12.12.83

Dear Emile Rozier,

It has been some years since you last wrote to me, and I am sure you have long since given up hope of a reply. I thank you for the many pamphlets and journals that you have sent to me. It is clear to me that you have understood a great deal about your island's history. However, it is your own family history that still troubles you, as I can well understand. You wrote to me in the hope that I might shed some light on the matter and I regret very much that I can. You are the person to whom I must explain things, but this will be a great burden for you. Perhaps you of all people can appreciate that there are more than two sides to any story. The truth is like a prism through which the light shines, but the patterns it creates can distract and confuse.

I am 61 years old—which is perhaps not old, but I have cancer. I am too sick to write, therefore a friend is typing what I speak, and by the time this reaches you I trust I will be dead.

What I would like to say first is sorry. I remember you only as a small child, and since that time you have known much loss. Your late brother endured great hardships and I can well understand why he resisted talking of his experiences for so long. I have often thought of him over the years. I am sorry he did not have children. I have three sons and I am very proud of the men they have become. I will miss them.

I will say what I have to say and no more. I do not like my memories, and my emotions become troubled when I think of your island. It is still beautiful, I have no doubt, but it was never a place I would wish to return to. When I was posted to Guernsey I felt differently; we were very impressed by the beauty of the cliffs, and we felt comfortable and fortunate. I personally did not want to be sent to the Front because I was not convinced by Hitler or his War. I was pleased to be but an administrator, and did my utmost to smooth relations with the local population.

Despite my being many years his junior your father had to work for me. He did so with grace and dignity. Perhaps it helped him to know that I did not enjoy giving orders. I often felt myself to be as unhappy as a great many of the islanders. I was a long way from home and I had never been away from my loved ones before. Hubert was a quiet, devout man, greatly troubled by the War. Early on, before wireless sets were confiscated, we would listen to the BBC news together. I made the excuse it might help me with my English. I noticed he often held his Bible close to his chest and he once told me he believed that God was subjecting all of us to a most gruelling test. I sensed a deep spiritual turmoil beneath his surface, yet I could not have predicted how events would unravel.

I must now confess to my own terrible weakness. I was

a young man and very immature, inexperienced, and easily swayed by my passions. I regret very much that I found myself falling in love, but that is precisely what happened. It was the kind of love I had never before known, a love that was doubtless intensified by the unusual circumstances. It became my great obsession. This is a secret that I have carried with me these years.

When I first learned of your mother's death I was unable to write to you and tell you the truth of what happened because I did not want to tarnish the memories you have of her. She was an extraordinary woman. I was very much in love with her from the moment I first met her. She only once professed to feel the same and after all these years I cannot believe it was ever true. I am sure it pains you to learn of her infidelity, but please remember the confusion and uncertainty of the time, its humiliations and temptations weighed heavily on us all.

Quite what was between us is now so difficult to describe in words. I do not wish to cheapen it. I know now there were delusions on both sides: a false longing, a need for intimacy. Arlette was still a beautiful woman, some years younger than Hubert. She doted on you, her baby boy, but found herself increasingly alienated from both her husband and her teenage son. She once told me she had chosen the security of an early marriage out of fear that she might be "left on the shelf." As I understand it a great many Guernsey families had lost sons in the First World War. Arlette entertained the notion that the man she should have married had died in the trenches. She spoke of this on more than one occasion. I know that she was very young when she married Hubert and Charlie was born not long after. I am not trying to make excuses for my behaviour, but by the time I arrived on Guernsey husband and wife appeared to be ill at ease with one another. The pressure of the Occupation would only drive them further apart.

I found it difficult to hide my feelings for Arlette but I had no intention of making them known. She was a married woman and a mother. I therefore kept within my boundaries. I would bring extra rations of butter or sugar when I could, and I would like to think this went some way towards keeping you nourished. All I wanted was to make life easier for the family. I am not sure how things changed, even now. The "affair," when it finally began, was fleeting, and ended in the tragedy you are now so familiar with.

I must stress that it was not until 1942 that our friendship blossomed. This was a difficult year for everyone. The Führer's grand plan of making the island an impregnable fortress dominated all other considerations. The arrival of more and more slave workers and the endless building work led to extreme shortages of food and basic necessities, tighter security, and harsher punishments for "miscreants." It was difficult for soldier and civilian alike. Although in a position of authority I never felt powerful and I was worried that I would be dispatched to a fighting zone at any time. I confided my fears in Arlette and slowly she began to confide in me. Hubert by then was much changed. I sensed the Occupation had broken his spirit and he was often struck down by rheumatic fever. He soon admitted to me that he was too ill to continue working in the office and I accepted this, perhaps too readily. He thanked me for my patience and asked me to keep an eye on Charlie.

Charlie was supposed to work in the office alongside me,

but he did not care much for my company. Despite repeated reprimands from his mother his time-keeping was erratic and I became accustomed to his long absences. I can only assume that he had already befriended Ray Le Poidevoin. I was quite unaware of their activities, however, and paid little heed to Charlie's absences since it allowed Arlette and me to become closer. I finally had the opportunity to confess to her my feelings. She admitted she had known all along.

After that I wanted to spend as much time with her as I could, away from prying eyes. We hit upon the idea that she would wash and press German uniforms for extra money, and so she could come to my quarters during daylight hours and not arouse suspicion. It was the perfect subterfuge, although I soon learned that a number of other soldiers had concocted the same scheme. Perhaps you were not aware of this but "doing laundry" for the occupying forces became a code for other activities, from which mutual benefits might be drawn.

For a brief period the excitement and anticipation of our encounters afforded us an escape from daily life. Arlette was a passionate woman. I told her I would marry her when the War was over. She reminded me that she was already married. "What do you intend to do about that?" she asked. I had no answer for her.

It was during the spring that some papers entrusted to me went missing from the office. There is no mention of this in the previous letters you sent me—were you ever aware of it? It was a most serious matter and I was reprimanded by my senior officers. Arlette was convinced that Hubert was responsible and suggested that he had been spying on us. I found this hard to believe since Hubert was obviously unwell. Arlette told me not to be fooled. She also hinted to me that her husband's espionage activities went further and that he would eventually humiliate me. She had seen him making notes, she said, and she had found some kind of map. Hubert was an intelligent man and understood German. Although his physical health was poor, nothing escaped those watchful eyes. Arlette insisted that I confront him and demand the truth. I was too afraid. The guilt of our affair was a colossal burden. That was when she said she would go to my Commanding Officer. I took her threat very seriously and was filled with despair. I feared those in authority above me. I was under no illusions what would happen to me if it was known that I had let a "resistant" get the better of me.

I acted in haste and organised the search of your then family home in St. Sampson so that I could discover the truth once and for all. I assure you we had no information from Ray Le Poidevoin regarding either Charlie or Hubert Rozier. The search was entirely my doing and I expected to find nothing. I wanted to show Arlette the depth of my devotion and my commitment to her. We searched the upstairs rooms first. Hubert calmly watched on, at one point remarking, "If you could tell me what exactly you are looking for, then maybe I can help?" The map on the wall of the box room obviously intrigued us, although on closer inspection it appeared that Hubert had marked it up with information gathered from German-controlled newspapers. But the loose floorboard was soon discovered, and then this extraordinary notebook. Hubert remained calm. His life hung in the balance, but his confession came so swiftly we were taken aback.

"Those documents are mine," he said. "My wife will confirm that they are in my handwriting. There shouldn't be any secrets between a husband and wife but the War's changed all that, hasn't it?" He looked directly at Arlette but she did not meet his gaze. She glanced at the open notebook and nodded. "Yes, that is my husband's handwriting. Hubert—what have you done?" Hubert then levelled his eyes on me. "You have got what you wanted." His words chilled me to the bone and in that instant I felt sure that he knew of our affair, and had always known. I glanced back at Arlette and she was now staring at her husband. There was almost a look of defiance in her eyes. I was confused and greatly perplexed. It was then Charlie made his entrance and began his protestations.

I must reassure you at this stage that the only "rumours" regarding Hubert acting as a spy had come from his own wife. Charlie's boasts about his father's alleged spying never reached our ears and did not contribute to the case against them. Furthermore, it was never Hubert who informed on his own son. This last suggestion is preposterous and troubles me greatly. Whoever made such a claim is at best deluded and at worst vindictive. Why blacken Hubert's name?

To the best of my knowledge, Charlie was never regarded as a serious threat. He was very impudent, however, and I recall Major Wessel referring to him as an "undesirable." He noted that Charlie tried to take responsibility for the notebook and I remember him stating that father and son were evidently "working together." Arlette was arrested and brought in for questioning separately to Hubert and Charlie, but this was a formality. She corroborated Hubert's confession and was released. By then, of course, she knew her husband and eldest son were in serious trouble.

I wanted to console her but there was no time, events were spinning far beyond our control. Within hours an abandoned boat trailer had been discovered and the body of a young mechanic was recovered from a nearby minefield. It was clear there had been an escape attempt. I was under the confidence of Wessel and he told me that there was a secret army at work. He was a Gestapo man and very hardened. I realised Charlie and Hubert would be given more than a prison sentence. Their crime was serious enough to warrant death by firing squad. I went to Arlette immediately to break the terrible news. You were in the room, playing happily at her feet, quite unaware of the tragic events of the previous night. She kept leaning over to stroke and fuss with your hair. I reminded her that I had only been acting as she'd asked. She denied this and told me that I had completely misunderstood. I then asked if my suspicions were correct and that Hubert had discovered our affair. She replied: "He knew, all right. I was a good wife all these years but what does that count for now? He's the saint and I'm the sinner, it's as he wanted."

I was surprised by the bitterness of her tone and tried to comfort her, but she told me to leave and never come back. She wanted to forget everything that had gone on.

It seems clear to me that Arlette would have done any-thing rather than be confronted with her own shameful truth. She had spoken out against Hubert in the interest of self-preservation, for fear he would denounce us. I was meant to warn him off and no more. But I am certain she never imagined he might end up facing a death sentence. I have now had more experience with women and as far as I see they often act impetuously. In this respect, Arlette was true to her sex. She was worn down by the Occupation and lashed out indiscriminately.

Hubert's confession had already sealed his fate. Once he was in the grips of Wessel and his men it was merely a matter of time. He chose to walk out across Belle Grève Bay and die on his beloved island, rather than die in the camps or be shot by the firing squad.

I fully accept the part I played in this most appalling tragedy. No words suffice to tell you how I regret my involvement. I am quite prepared to accept any punishment I receive in the next life, but I would like you to know that I have prayed every day for forgiveness.

To complete the story, I asked to be transferred to the Russian Front immediately. My Kommandant was most sympathetic and wished for no scandal. I never spoke with or saw Arlette again but I know she was full of guilt for what we together had caused. She did write to me once, via the International Red Cross. It was a brief note telling me that Charlie had survived and returned to the island. She said there was little chance of them ever being reconciled, since she could not even look him in the eye. She reminded me of my promise never to speak of what she referred to as "a silly mistake."

I did note that she signed herself Arlette Prevost, which I remember to be her maiden name. I suspect that she was too ashamed to use the Rozier name thereafter.

I am in doubt whether my disclosure helps you any. I am sure that you must now hate me and your mother, but I believe we gain very little from hating the dead. As a father,

I believe parents rarely live up to the expectations of their children. We are human, flesh and blood. And please believe me when I assure you that, as long as I lived, I tried to be a better man.

Your obedient servant,
Anton Vern

[BEDROOM, PACKING]

Warning: shock and horror ahead. It's been almost a day since I last wrote this and you won't believe what's just happened. Vicky tried to kill herself. Yes, that's right. My so-called, onetime friend who abandoned me to potential incineration on Bonfire Night, has taken an overdose and ended up in hospital. Apparently she feels guilty and blames herself for what happened to Nic. Therefore she decided to end it all.

Fortunately Dr. Senner found her in time and rushed her to Casualty and she's currently having her stomach pumped, which actually sounds like fun. I feel a bit jealous of all the fuss and excitement. After all, I was the one who was meant to kill myself, that's what Nic said everyone wanted. I should've beaten Vicky to it, but instead I'm left here sorting through boxes of Town Church jumble while Mum rushes off to feed the Senners' cats.

I'd feel more sorry for Vicky if we hadn't had that massive row after Bonfire Night. I accused her of setting me up. She called me a Nutcase but I called her Worse, so she said I couldn't come to her birthday party (not that I was surprised). She then spent the next three weeks going on and on about disco lights and party invites and what to wear. The Little Cow.

Things only changed between us when I saw her at Nic's funeral. She looked awful. She was sobbing so much I thought we'd all drown. I don't want her to feel guilty and she doesn't deserve to die. That would be wrong, and also a bit pathetic. Plus, it's not like she was the one calling me up in the middle of the night or flushing my homework down the loo. That was all down to Nic. She just wouldn't leave me alone. Sometimes she was on her own and sometimes she was with Lisa. Either way, it went on right through November.

It was the Thursday before Vicky's party and I was looking for my gym kit in the toilets when Nic came in and cornered me.

"Are you OK? Only you're looking a little pale. Been on the booze again, like your dad?"

I told her I was fine. She flicked her hair and peered over the basin at her own reflection.

"You've only got yourself to blame for your problems, Cat. You've got no friends left."

I swallowed. "I should've known right from the start not to be friends with a scumbag Prevost, you're all the same, the lowest of the low."

Nic pulled a stupid face and pretended to look insulted. "Oooh! That really hurts! Like I care what you think. You with your shabby little house and your cheap, nasty calendars. Don't talk to me about my family—look at yours! I felt sorry for you. I couldn't understand how you could come top of the class but still be such a *loser*."

I stared at the flecks of mascara on her eyelashes. "Why didn't you just leave me alone?"

"I don't know." She shrugged. "It was just a bit of fun, really, but now my mum and dad are splitting up because of you. If you hadn't told those lies about Mr. McCracken he'd never have resigned, and Mum would've lost interest soon enough."

It was a relief she had finally admitted it.

"But you started this," I said. "I just did what I thought you wanted me to do."

In a split-nano-second she grabbed me and pushed me back against the wall. A few inches to the left and I would've cracked my head on the towel dispenser. I was surprised by the massive force of it. She was holding on to my collar and glaring at me.

"I did nothing!" she hissed through her teeth. "*You're* the one who fucked up and I want you to pay."

"OK. OK." I stretched out my hands. "How?"

She narrowed her eyes and pushed me away. "I'll think of something."

And she did. The next day I found two packets of Paracetamol on my desk, with a little note that read: "Dare You."

It's shocking, isn't it? But not as shocking as this next bit. I'm off to meet Michael at Donnie's.

[BEDROOM FLOOR,
HUGGING PILLOW]

Things never turn out quite the way you think they will. Michael wasn't at the White House like he promised, which was most annoying. I stood in the pouring rain for 45 minutes and then went round to his house.

Mr. and Mrs. Priaulx live in one of the two matching bungalows at the far end of the Village. I've only ever been there once before, for a barbecue when I was seven. This was humiliating because I accidentally squirted tomato ketchup on my new lilac Clothkits dungarees, which Michael called an improvement. (The Priaulx kitchen is the colour of baby sick, so he's hardly one to talk.)

Michael was surprised to see me because he'd completely forgotten about our secret rendezvous. I told him he was useless but he didn't look useless. He was wearing a ripped-T-shirt-and-jeans combo and had had his head shaved like a convict. All in all, I thought he looked *très* manly, especially since he was drinking Pony Ale* out of the can.

"Thought you'd be up at the hospital," he said. "Didn't you hear about little Vicky Senner? My epidemic idea is catching on."

I followed him into the hallway and wiped the wet hair from my eyes. "What do you mean?"

He tipped up the can and emptied the last of the Pony Ale into his mouth. "You know, it's like with sheep, follow the flock, eh? If one does it, they all do it."

I nodded without understanding and he swung his delicious upper body towards me. "Who'll be next?" Then he staggered backwards, pinching the bridge of his nose like he was seeing things and/or had a headache.

"Are you OK?"

He smiled again. "Get your coat off. You're dripping on the carpet."

We went to his bedroom (!!!!). It's at the back of the house in a badly made extension and it smells of burnt leaves and is painted black and red and purple (but you can't see the purple because of all the posters of soldiers/ skulls/mutilated bodies). I have to confess I thought his room would be a whole lot nicer, but then, he is a boy. He sat next to me on his bed, which wasn't really a bed but more a mattress on the floor. And it was a single mattress so we sat very close. We had a long and meaningful chat about death and Vicky.

* Brewed in St. Peter Port since 1868, Pony Ale is so-named because it smells of horses and is best used to clean stables. It is also very effective at getting the rust off pots and pans (Mum says).

"Too right she should feel guilty. That mind-bending homebrew was probably what made Nicolette jump and I told her so, eh. I told her she should let us all know how bad she feels."

I stared at Michael in rocky-horror. "What? You saw Vicky? When?"

He lolled his head seductively. "I was down at the Batterie yesterday evening. D'you know I managed to force the lock on the tunnel entrance? It *fuuuu-cking* stinks down there, but I was poking about when I heard someone. I snuck and took a look outside and realised it was little Vicky with a bunch of flowers. She was obviously going to throw the flowers off the cliff . . . very poetic. I just thought I could have a bit of fun."

I was mentally running to catch up.

"So you talked to her?"

Michael nodded and sniggered. "I told her flowers wouldn't do much for Nic and why didn't she do something more serious. The face on her! I suppose I was the last person she expected to see jumping out of that doorway. It was like she'd seen a ghost. I asked her if she felt guilty and all that."

I couldn't help but feel a bit sorry for Vicky—Michael doesn't know about her deep fear of Nazi Zombies hiding in tunnels. I asked him if he knew what she'd overdosed on, and he made some comment about Dr. Senner's medicine cabinet being like a Pick 'n' Mix, then he reached across me and produced a packet of pills off his bedside table. He said they were antidepressants. I was shocked and then not shocked, and then a little jealous. I asked him if they worked. He opened another can.

"Try them if you want."

He offered me some beer and I took a long gulp. I then explained how there was no depression during the War because no one had the time or energy to be depressed.

He lay back on the mattress and I admired his thick, long lashes for all of a minute.

"Yeah, but that's because they didn't know what was *really* going on, eh?" He rested his hands under his head and showed off his manly armpits. "No one knew about the concentration camps and the hundreds of thousands of people being gassed and killed, they were told what the government wanted. They were fed *propaganda*."

I thought that was a stroke-of-genius point and I told him he was cleverer than he looked. Then I said looks weren't important. I was jiggling my knee without even knowing it—I do that sometimes when I'm nervous.

He reached out and pressed my thigh.

"Relax. Lie down next to me if that'll stop you fidgeting."

I lay down beside him and breathed in Eau de B.O.

"Must've been a fucking good party that I missed. Did you enjoy yourself?"

My eyes blinked open. "Oh, I wasn't invited."

Michael turned his head and his chin pressed against my ear. "She didn't invite you? But you two are mates."

I quickly explained that Vicky and I had had a big row because she'd sided with Nic on everything and was indeed a sheep following the flock, perhaps also in a ship of fools that was also full of rats and sinking. I explained how I was the only one who saw through Nic and for that reason I wanted nothing to do with Vicky's birthday party and was very glad not to be invited. (So there.)

Michael nodded. "You must've been the only one on the island who didn't go. How come so many people turned up?"

"Nic invited them."

I then explained that it wasn't really Vicky's fault things got out of hand, since Nic did most of the organising, and she was the one telling everyone to come. I also pointed out that Dr. Senner shouldn't have been so stupid and gullible, since no properly developed adult would've gone out and left a bunch of teenagers alone with his year's supply of booze. Dr. S. should've known what would happen, just like he should have known better than to allow Vicky near his stock of medicine. As I see it, if a person is feeling depressed and/or vulnerable they should never be left in charge of any medication, even if that medication is for them.

I must've gone on for quite a while because Michael yawned.

"I get it, I get it. Don't worry. I'm not going to do anything stupid."

I remembered his pills. "Oh, I didn't mean *you*!"

He rested his hand over mine. "Shhhh."

We lay very still. Our breathing was totally synchronised. Our clothes touched.

It was incredible.

We were like that for ages, in fact, and I thought I heard him snoring. Then he rolled onto his side towards me. His eyes were still closed. I felt his fingers touch my arm so I turned to look at him. I stared at every bit of his face and tried to memorise it. He has nine large-ish freckles on his right cheek and one on the left which is more like a mole. He has a single vertical crease between his eyebrows and a little diagonal scar just above the right one. His lower lip is a third thicker than his upper lip. He has blackheads on his nose but so does everyone. I imagined myself squeezing them when he suddenly opened his eyes.

"If you had a choice, how would *you* die?"

I wanted to tell him I'd be happy to die right there and then with him, but instead I said I'd like to die in my sleep.

"B.O.R.I.N.G.!"

"OK." I held my breath. "We-ell . . . I think the way Nic died is cool. I mean, you think she jumped but everyone else thinks she fell, and she *might've* been pushed."

Michael sat up a little. "You think she could've been pushed?"

I didn't know how to reply to that. I hadn't intended to confess to killing Nic there and then but I was quite keen to shock Michael, so he might think of me differently and therefore maybe fancy me. Only I got so flustered! Michael always does this to me. When I used to see him in Town I was always too embarrassed to say hi so I'd pretend to rummage in my bag and then drop every-thing and all the time I'd be thinking about what I'd say if he came over and I'd be wondering if he'd noticed me. Of course, by the time I turned back around he'd gone.

"It's easy enough to kill someone and make it look like suicide."

Michael nodded. "Go on."

"It's like what I said about the Germans pushing slave workers off the cliffs. I bet people do that all the time. Wives kill husbands or vice-versa because they wished they'd never married them, and divorces can cost so much. But then, a lot of people cover up a suicide and prefer to call it an accident because they believe suicide is wrong or shameful and they don't want to admit that any friend or relation was that unhinged or depressed . . . or . . ."

Michael was staring at me in his bestest psycho-killer way.

"*Or?*" he said.

"Or they want the money."

He was gripped. "What money?"

"Well"—I smiled—"if your life's insured for lots of money but you kill yourself, then the insurance people won't pay up. You have to make your death look *acciden-tal*, or, at least, natural. Then your loved ones would be able to pay off your horrendous debts and even take a foreign holiday."

Michael leaned back, nodding slowly.

I took another swig of beer. It was so exciting to have his full attention I forgot how bad Pony Ale tasted.

"Of course," I said, "most people who kill themselves leave a note, which is a giveaway."

"But Nic didn't, and neither did I. I didn't even plan it—it just happened, like there was this other force inside of me or outside of me."

We looked into each other's eyes and it was like we almost understood each other. Michael relaxed, propping his head under his hands.

"Heavy-duty, eh?"

I tried to nestle into his armpit and pretend we were a couple.

"I read your dad's book—the one about the tunnels."

I had to sit up again. "Seriously?"

"Yeah. If what he says is right they run for miles right under us and they're as good as a mass grave. No wonder bad shit keeps happening. There's probably weird gases leaking out of the Batterie and nobody even knows it."

I stared at Michael in shock-awe-lust. Talk about a proper connection! As I have already said, *Guernsey Gas Chambers and Other Myths* is a really excellent read and tells you all about the German tunnels and "Underground Hospital,"* and how it was never meant to be a hospital at all. Michael grabbed it off his cardboard box and as he did so I saw the papers underneath. He had a copy of the timetable for Sealink ferries to Portsmouth

---

* The German Underground Hospital was built by slave workers, many of whom died/were buried in it. Even so, it's now a museum and café, and because it is very successful as a museum and café no one questions why the Nazis needed a hospital *underground* and miles from the fighting zones. We all know the Germans only built hospitals because they were going to do horrible experiments.

and Southampton and Calais.

My stomach did a back-flip. "Are you going somewhere?"

He looked at me, then his dark eyes danced over to the wardrobe. There was a beaten-up barrel bag beside it, with clothes hanging out of it. He'd been packing!

"You can't tell anyone."

My stomach was now in my mouth and my heart was being ripped out somewhere else. "You can't go! You can't! You've only just got back and you're not better. You're *crazy*."

Michael smiled his cockeyed smile. "Think we've already established that."

I stared and stared and stared (at him). "Don't leave me."

"Oh come on, you'll be OK. You're clever, you can go to university and do whatever you want. Me? I've not got much and I know if I stay here then . . . I don't know what I'll do."

It was truly impossible to resist him when he said that. I sat up on the bed, hands clenched into fists.

"Take me with you."

He blinked. "What?"

I didn't stop to think about what I was saying. "If you're going then I'm going. I've got to get away, as well. You don't know what I've done but I can't stay here any more than you can."

Michael looked me up and down and inside out. "What have you done?"

I had to give in. I had to.

"Can't you guess?"

Michael looked melt-in-the-mouth gorgeous.

"What?"

There was another pin-drop moment.

"I'll only tell you if you agree to take me with you."

He hesitated. "You got any money? There's a ferry at 9.30 tomorrow night. Last one before Christmas."

"I'll meet you at the entrance to Fort George at 8. We'll take the cliff path down to Town."

Michael was staring intently. "Why the cliff path?"

"We should stay off the main road," I said, standing up, "and if you want me to tell you what I've done I may as well show you while I'm at it."

I don't know if he understood, but the way he looked at me made me turn to jelly so I had to leg it out of there. And now I'm just so excited. I feel amazing. I'll take him to where I killed Nic and tell him the truth, and then I'll never have to tell anyone ever-ever again. It's going to be my big confession for one night only. I'll have to write it down, just so I don't miss anything out. Yes, that's it. I'll prepare a speech.

HANDWRITTEN NOTES, PRESUMABLY INTENDED
FOR E.P.R.'S SPEECH AT OCCUPATION MEMORIAL
UNVEILING CEREMONY

*[Transcribed by
Catherine Rozier, 20/11/85]*

Ladies and Gentlemen, Bailiff,

My name is Emile Rozier and I have a confession. I have built up something of a reputation as an expert on our German Occupation, but today, standing before you, I am a man who knows nothing.

I was only a child during the War, so I personally remember very little about it, yet I have spent my life trying to compensate for that fact. I, like many of you here today, have been told every kind of Occupation story, stories that show the resilience of islanders in the face of the enemy, stories that tell of heartbreak and hardship, and still other stories that tell of betrayal, wrongful accusations, and even death. We hear so many different stories that it is hard to believe they were once based on single, simple fact.

The German Occupation was not marked by bloody

conflict, but its History has been quite another matter. For many years there was silence, when people preferred not to share their troubled memories of that time. More recently our States Tourist Board has done an excellent job of packaging it into a kind of light entertainment for outsiders.

My hope has always been that the names on this memorial will prove more solid and immovable than popular opinion and marketing campaigns.

These names listed here are our names. They should ground us and remind us that we have nothing to be ashamed of. My father, Hubert Rozier, is included. He was shot by German soldiers in 1942. He was only guilty of continuing the work that he loved. My brother, Charles Rozier, was arrested for collecting information about the German fortifications. He was deported and imprisoned. The loss and suffering within my own family only made me more determined to set the record straight. But the desire to uncover deception can be self-deceiving.

For many years my brother thought he was betrayed by a person in his confidence. In fact, that is the fate that befell *me*. The past has foretold the future in a way even I could not have expected.

Ladies and Gentlemen, Bailiff,

I'm deeply moved to stand here today and see this memorial unveiled. It is proof of the trials and tribulations of some very brave individuals who stood up to the Nazi occupier. Not everyone was so brave, however, and there are some who resorted to a lifetime of lies. Despite their denials we cannot deny them, and so their lies define us. There is one name listed here which should not be.

Ladies and Gentlemen, Bailiff,

I have fought a long battle for a true and complete account of the German Occupation. I thought the truth would mean an end to any doubts and uncertainties, but the lies are all that's certain now.

Ladies and Gentlemen, Bailiff . . .

[IN PRISON (*KIDDING*)]

know it's not enough to say something, and if I say it over and over it won't make it better. But. I never planned or meant to kill Nic. I didn't even want her to die, and even after it happened I didn't believe she was really D.E.A.D. I thought I was imagining it, that maybe it was a dream, so I went to bed and tried to wake up. Perhaps it was a bit like that for Mum. She probably saw Dad lying there and assumed he was sleeping off a hangover. Did she think his breathing sounded strange? Did she check he'd taken his insulin? Did she check *how much*?

I suppose it only occurred to her afterwards, when it was too late. We'll never know how much he took.

Remember what Michael said: accidents don't just happen, people make them happen. Dad decided his fate and I decided Nic's. That's the real reason I can't go back to school—I can't face Vicky or Lisa or in fact any of the girls in my class. They'll see straight through me. They knew Nic and I were fighting. They must wonder about it. I suppose they never saw me at the party so they can't imagine how I could be involved.

I should've told the truth from the start, but the truth is slippery, like soap in the bath. Everybody would want to know why I was out on the cliffs after dark, and then they'd think it was too much of a coincidence that Nic turned up as well.

Beaucoup de Bollocks. Why did I have to go out that night? Why couldn't I stay in and watch bad telly as per usual? Why did I have to sneak over to Vicky's house and spy on that stupid bloody party? Of course that was what Nic wanted, but why did I play into her hands? Well, there *is* (at last) a single, simple answer—I went because of Michael.

It was after six on the night of the party and Mum was out in the garden, weeding or pruning or some-thing. There was a knock at the door and without even thinking I went to answer it. Like I said before, we never lock our doors in Guernsey so Nic was already in the hallway. I walked slowly down the stairs, hoping and praying Mum would come in any minute.

"What do you want?"

"Oh, you know"—Nic smiled—"I wanted to ask if you were coming to Vicky's. Everyone'll be there. We'll have a laugh."

I held on tight to the banister. "Of course I'm not coming!"

"That's a shame," Nic carried on, smiling, "Michael will be there. Oh well, I'll be able to fill him in on what you've been up to. I'll tell him all about your lies and poor Mr. McCracken. What fun that'll be!"

The news that Michael was back hit me like a train. I didn't know if it was true, but it definitely could have been.

"You're bluffing!"

Nic shrugged. "Suit yourself. I must say I'm *really* looking forward to seeing him. You know there was always that spark, and I'd like to see if it's still there. Maybe I'll take him out onto the cliffs with me and show him a good time."

I heard Mum come in from the garden. She was wiping her feet on the doormat in the kitchen.

"Hello Nicolette," she called. "Haven't seen you for a while. How are you?"

"I'm fine thanks, Mrs. Rozier. I'm just trying to persuade Cat to come to Vicky's party tonight."

"Oh? I'd forgotten." Mum pulled off her gardening gloves. "Aren't you going to go, Cathy? You hadn't said anything."

"That's because I'm not going. I'm not feeling great and, well, I'm not in the mood."

Mum looked puzzled. "Well, if you're sure."

"Boooo-ring!" Nic cocked her head to one side and tried to look saccharine-sweet. "Oh well, if you change your mind I'm going over there now to help Vicky get ready."

Mum nodded. "I'll try and persuade her."

But she didn't. We didn't say another word about it. Instead we had dinner on our laps in the sitting room. I watched *Doctor Who* while Mum read a library book, and I got the feeling she was glad to have me there. She told me things were "getting back to normal" (and she'd bought Arctic Roll for dessert so I knew she meant it). Trouble is, I only pretended to have an early night just like she did, then I was up and out the back door, and crouched in a rhododendron bush by approximately 10 p.m.

I'd already been past Vue du Lac five times and found no sign of Michael, so I was 99.99% sure he wasn't back, but I had to go to Vicky's house to check. The Senners' house is at the end of Becquet Road. There's a wide row of bushes facing their driveway so it was dead easy to hide.

There was such a lot of people, sitting out on the front lawn and crowding around the porch. I craned my neck to look for Michael but it was hard to see anything. Poor Vicky—her house was full to bursting. Inside, I could see right into the chaos in the kitchen, and all the lights were on upstairs. Nic was easy to spot in a sparkly mini-dress. She hung around the porch and nibbled at a plastic cup while flirting with Paul Kelley. Paul Kelley is two years above us at the Grammar and has spiky blond hair and these excellent trousers mostly made of zips. I wondered what Pete thought of him, but Pete was now with Nikki Guillemette. Everyone knew that.

The music was blaring out so I'm not surprised Mr. Le Lacheur next door complained. Pete and Jason told him to get lost. Then some bikers turned up and there was a commotion. At this point I completely lost track of Nic and got cramp in my left toes. It was cold in that rhododendron bush. The next thing I knew, Dr. and Mrs. Senner had pulled up in their Volvo estate. A girl with half her head shaved was vomiting in their flowerbed. Mrs. S. swore loudly. She then ran inside but Dr. Senner couldn't. His hand was frozen fast to the car door handle and he stared up at his house like it was an alien spaceship, and with all the house lights blazing it did look pretty alien. Greasy Caz Mitchell staggered up to him, drinking from a bottle of his homebrew. That's when he exploded. Within a minute he was inside and shouting at everyone to "Get the Hell out!" The lights upstairs flickered and there was banging and thumping and the sound of smashing glass. People started spilling out into the front garden. I saw Isabelle and Shelley. Shelley had her hair back-combed and looked unbelievably stupid. They huddled together like convicts and I didn't watch too closely where they went. I was still looking for Nic and Michael. But I only saw Vicky in the porch, crying.

I was a good way off from everyone and therefore thought I was safe, but then a group of lads including Jason and Pete came over. They were trying to get some distance from Dr. Senner's rabid ranting.

"What'll we do now?" asked one of them.

"Where you parked?" asked another.

"Up by the Military Cemetery."

Then I heard Nic's voice: "Did you see his face! *Fucking loser!* Fuck him if he thinks he can tell us what to do."

"Come on, let's go."

"What about the *woooods*." Nic giggled. "Come *on*!"

"You off your head?" snarled Pete.

"Like you've got any better ideas!"

There was now a little crowd forming but I was too scared to look at their faces. I heard a girl say something about being cold, and then Pagey (I'm sure it was Pagey) slimed up to her and said he'd keep her warm. (Yuck.) There was the sound of clanking bottles and someone told Nic to shut up. She was obviously being bitchy, since she was always bitchy when drinking. There were a few more minutes of idle chat when I held my breath and didn't dare look, then everyone moved off towards the cemetery. I peered out. They were just about to disappear round the corner when Nic turned back.

"My jacket!"

I froze and waited as she came back up the lane. She ducked around the side of the house—she was going to sneak in the back door.

I waited a few minutes and she didn't reappear. I now know that she was having a row with Vicky. Nic had a row with everyone that night. Slowly, I backed out of my bush and looked up and down the lane. There were still a few people vomiting/waiting for lifts home, and there was a boy and girl having a snogathon. I hadn't seen Michael. Had I missed him in the crowds? I hurried down the road after Pete and Jason, but keeping a good-ish distance.

I followed them off the road and onto the footpath past Bluebell Woods. Vicky and I used to have a lot of fun building dens down there. Jason and Pete had been joined by Pagey and Lisa, Paul Kelley, Isabelle and Shelley, André Duquemin, Caz Mitchell and Nikki Guillemette (the one who'd been sick in front of Mrs. Senner). The wind carried their voices back so I knew they weren't far off, but I wondered where Nic was. I kept checking over my shoulder, just in case. Then I reached the entrance to the car park, which is also the entrance to the woods. I headed down to the woods, because I didn't want to get stuck in between Nic coming back from the Senners', and Jason and Pete and their mob.

Like I think I've mentioned, there is a main footpath

running all the way through Bluebell Woods which eventually forks—you can go right towards Fermain or left towards Clarence Batterie and Town. I was a little way into the Woods when I heard voices above me and coming closer. I was scared and ran on ahead, climbing off the path the minute I could. Then I waited in a dampish hollow. The mix of voices got nearer and nearer. I heard Nic bickering with someone about Becca Le Messurier (who is or is not a "slag"). There were screams and laughter. Then I saw Lisa stumble. Pagey helped her up. Jason was easy to make out because he's so tall, and he was running around howling like a werewolf. The boys were trying to scare the girls, who were shrieking and throwing damp leaves at them. (Very funny, I'm sure.)

Then I heard Nic's voice. "You should've been there—she blamed me for everything!"

"It's not her fault."

"It is!"

"Where are we going?" asked Lisa (I could see her skinny outline). "I'm cold, this is stupid."

Nic was still drinking—the boys had stolen bottles of homebrew and she swung one around and skipped between the trees. Was it just me, or did she stare into the trees like she was imagining an audience?

I told myself that there were enough people mucking about and making noise that I'd never get noticed, and I was also a good way off, but I was also terrified that Jason would do one of his demented sprints in my direction. I was almost relieved when it started to rain. Paul suggested they all go back to the car park and a lot of the boys agreed. Pete and Nikki headed off first, but Nic

was being stroppy and calling someone "booo-rrrring."
I wasn't going to stick around. I pulled up my hood and
climbed out of the ditch, and practically crawled my
way through mud and soggy leaves to the wall that runs
beside the White House.* Then I used it to guide me
down towards the cliff paths. I could go left and head for
the Clarence Batterie, or I could go right and end up at
the Moorings or Fermain.

I'm not going to pretend that I stopped to think about
it. I headed for Town because it was quicker, downhill,
and the path's less overgrown. The rain was getting
heavier, but I didn't run because I didn't want to slip in
the mud, and I had to be careful of the nasty tree roots
trying to trip me up. At one point I imagined they were
human hands pulling me down.

(I'm good at scaring myself silly.)

I never normally go out on the cliffs at night, it's
really just too creepy, and I got so freaked out that I
pulled down my hood just to make sure I could see and
hear better. And even though I didn't hear anything I
was worried there was someone behind me. My heart
was going clappety-clap and I lumbered along as fast
as I could. I thought about climbing off the path and
into the bushes but I worried what was in the bushes.
The wind was whipping through the trees and making
funny shadows. I kept slipping in the mud and nearly
fell twice, and then, I promise you, I heard someone call
out. I'm sure I did.

---

* Cf. earlier note re: Guernsey being small, i.e., Bluebell Woods is, in
fact, the size of a paddock.

I was thinking the Nazi Zombies were going to come and eat me alive, or the lost souls of poor slave workers were going to chase me off the cliff. But on I went, through the cold and the wet, looking straight ahead. Thank God it wasn't much further to the Batterie. I saw the big white sign with the red exclamation mark that warned visitors about the cliffs. Then the undergrowth thinned out—there were no more spooky trees or mud slides, and everything was flat and familiar. I stopped, breathed, and tried to calm down. Then I stood up straight and looked around at the benches and the bunkers, and out at the big, wide open sea.

'd never been down to the Batterie at night before and it was almost romantic. I could just make out the lights on Herm and the floodlit ramparts of Castle Cornet down in Town. I want to take Michael there to show him how beautiful it looks. I was probably even thinking about him as I leaned against the middle bench. I felt so much better, despite the rain, and I forgot everything for a second. Then I turned back around, looking for some shelter.

She came straight at me out of the darkness. I saw the bottle first, then her face. I don't know why I was surprised. Of course it was Nic.

"You going to jump?"

She hit me first in the stomach but I lifted my arm to protect myself, then I reversed around the bench so that it blocked her.

"You followed me."

"I thought *you* were following *me*. I saw you in the bushes. Ha! I knew you couldn't resist!"

I glared at her. I was terrified.

"Why are you doing this?"

She came round the bench and lunged at me. I remember reaching out for the bottle but she was grabbing my wrist and twisting it back.

"Why not?"

If I'd managed to get away I might've run but Nic wasn't letting go, and she could run faster anyway. We tussled back and forth and I hit my elbow on the edge of the bench. Nic dropped the bottle to get a better hold on me, and I swung about, hoping to shake her off. I was thinking that Jason and Pete would turn up at any minute and I'd be done for. I could hear the sea way down below us.

"Please!" I said. "Stop!"

I was feeling so helpless, but I pushed her as hard as I could. She fell back and nearly sat down on the bench. That's when I got my bearings and saw the bottle on the ground. I reached down to grab at it. I remember thinking I should smash it against something hard and then use the jagged bottleneck with proper Deadly Intent. But before I got anywhere near it Nic was up and at me, and we were back to all the shoving and spinning stuff again.

I wasn't sure what we were fighting for. At one point I know she had her arms wrapped tightly around me and she obviously wanted to knock me off my feet. How I kept myself upright I don't know. I also don't know where she got her energy. I was gasping and spluttering.

The wind was getting stronger and I had to blink away the rain. I was on a mental cliff edge, but I couldn't see the real cliff edge. She wanted to throw me off it (I'm sure) so I kept trying to drag us both away and back towards the path.

"Stop it! You'll kill us both!" I told her.

"I hate you!" was all she replied.

Neither of us was giving up.

What's the last thing I remember? I can't be sure. Maybe it was Nic calling me a "Stupid Fucking Bitch." She was behind me with one arm around my neck. I shut my eyes and wondered what to do. I wasn't strong enough to keep on fighting. I couldn't breathe and I couldn't turn around. There was really only one thing left to do, which was the one thing Nic didn't expect. I pulled my elbows in and dug deep into her sides, throwing my whole body into reverse, ramming us both backwards. You have to understand I just wanted to get free. I don't think I realised we were so close to the edge and by then I didn't care.

I heard myself shriek from the effort, and that's it. Suddenly Nic wasn't holding on to me anymore and I was spinning round and falling onto grass. I was soaked through and gasping for breath, but alone. Completely alone. As I sat up I realised how close I was to the cliff edge. I quickly pulled myself back a few inches. The lights on Herm had disappeared. I stared out at the blackness and reminded myself to breathe. Then I looked to my left and to my right. Nic had gone, but where had she gone? I didn't understand at first, and then, when I realised, I was just too scared to look. The cliff was there, right in front of me. A sheer, dead drop. I checked all around, saw the shape of the benches behind me, and slowly I leaned forward, digging my fingers into the soggy earth. I called Nic's name. Nothing came back. There were flashes of white foam rising up out of the darkness, then vanishing as quickly.

I couldn't stand up so I crawled towards the nearest bench and pulled myself onto it. My teeth started chattering like those wind-up toys you get in Christmas crackers. I hugged myself and waited. It was too unbelievable. Had Nic gone over the cliff? She must've done. But I couldn't understand why we hadn't fallen together. She'd been holding me so tightly.

Then I decided Nic wasn't dead at all. I looked over my shoulder to check she wasn't about to jump out at me. I called for her to stop mucking about. I even laughed. After about ten minutes I went and rattled the padlocks on the tunnel entrance.

"Come on!" I screamed. "I've had enough!"

You can't blame me for thinking it was all some stupid stunt. I half imagined Jason and Pete or even Pagey would come out of the bushes, going "Ha-ha, Fatso!" Nic could've faked all of it, she could've done! So I told myself it was a joke. I sat, huddled next to the tunnel entrance, and I waited for someone to deliver the punch line.

I waited and waited. I didn't know what to do so I didn't do anything. The world went blank. I was numb with cold and shock. The only thing I remember was thinking about Mum and Dad and how easy it was to die. I was crying, most definitely, when I finally headed back along the path. I still didn't understand how it had happened, so how could I explain it to anyone else? People would think I'd hurt Nic on purpose because she'd bullied me—no one would believe it was self-defence. I wasn't even sure if it had been. What had I done? Had I done it? I was probably hysterical. I was terrified. I went home.

I did think about waking up Mum when I got in, but it was long past midnight and I couldn't think what to tell her. She'd said things were getting back to normal and look what I'd gone and done? I sat on the landing and listened to the rain, and the longer I waited the worse I felt. I thought I was going to be sick. Then I tried to pretend nothing had happened. Perhaps I'd got things muddled and dreamed it all. I wondered if I was going demented like Grandma.

It was early morning when I crept into the bathroom. That's when I saw that I'd gashed my elbow badly, plus there were marks on my ribs and my tummy. I knew I'd be bruised because I bruise so easily, and those bruises were the proof. I *had* fought Nic. I *had* been there. But when I looked at my face it was no different. I had the same small eyes and podgy face. No scratches or cuts. I could cover up my elbow as easily as Dad had covered up his hand. No one need know.

I looked at my face in the mirror for a long time that night and I managed to convince myself that everything would be OK. I went into my bedroom and got undressed. As I pulled on my nightie I pretended it was any other winter's night, with the wind howling outside and me all warm and cosy. I lay back on the pillows and stared at the ceiling. It *was* self-defence. I'd never wanted a fight and I'd begged Nic to stop. She'd thrown herself at me. There was nothing else I could've done.

There didn't seem much point in telling people after that. They didn't need to know the whole grisly truth, which would surely just cause a lot more pain. It's the worst thing in the world to watch someone die in front of you, knowing you can't help them. It's the sort of thing you want to deny for as long as possible, maybe forever. Right, Mum?

Therese and Mr. Prevost didn't even worry when Nic stayed out all of Saturday night—it was only on Sunday evening that they called around Nic's friends, although they can't have been that desperate because they never called me. When Nic didn't show up at school on Monday morning Mrs. Perrot made A Special Announcement. Everyone thought Nic had run away.

"If any of you know anything," she said, "will you please come and tell me?"

Lisa was looking worried and Vick was looking sick. There was an electric buzz of chatter at lunchtime, but I steered clear of it. Then I saw the police car outside the staff offices and some of the girls from Vicky's party were called in by Mrs. Perrot.

Nic's body was washed off the rocks and a fisherman had picked her up with his lobster pots that very afternoon. They couldn't work out what had happened, but everyone said Nic was drunk and then a blood test proved how much. Fortunately alcohol hangs around in the blood for ages, unlike insulin, which is absorbed by the body after only eight hours. (Yes. I've done my research.)

There are plenty of things I can never be sure of, but I do know Nic was drunk when she attacked me, and she was a mean drunk and therefore capable of murder. Maybe she'd have fallen anyway, on account of her reckless nature. Maybe it was *Karma*. Donnie had always talked about Karma—i.e., you reap what you sow. Dad thought Karma was rubbish and that you couldn't choose your Fate because History had already dictated it. Either way, I never wanted Nic to die and sometimes I wish I'd died with her, and I still don't know why I didn't.

Maybe *that* was Karma. But if it was, doesn't that mean something bad will need to happen to me? Isn't that inevitable? Isn't that my Fate?

24TH DECEMBER 1985, 7 P.M.

[DAD'S STUDY]

So now you know everything. This is it. The End. You probably think I'm mad or really horrible, but the truth is I'm neither. I'm ordinary. I'm not pretty or special or good at sports and I'm not even clever, I just work very hard. Nic and I should never have been friends. What I did was very wrong, I know. But do you remember what Michael said about that other force around or outside of him? I swear it was like that. I did what I did because there was no other way.

And now it's my turn to say good-bye and the funny thing is, I've never felt more alive. I'm excited and I'm scared, but I'm also very calm. So calm, in fact, I went and made my peace with Vicky. I knew it wasn't right to leave things as they were—with her feeling guilty for what happened to Nic. I wanted to bury the hatchet (and no, not in her head).

She got back from hospital after lunch and I went

round the minute I heard. I must say the Senners' house was looking very Jingle Bells. For a second I wanted to stay another day. They've got a huge Christmas tree propped up with presents and spray-on snow around every window. Vicky was sitting on the sofa, wrapped up in her duvet and looking so snug, and Mrs. Senner plied me with sugary tea and excellent shop-bought mince pies. Then Dr. S. appeared and was freakishly nice to me. He went on about starting a youth club and "making-sure-Young-People-know-they-matter." He sat next to Vicky and gave her a cuddle and said he was counting his blessings. I tell you, it was cheesier than quiche.

I had to wait for ages before Vicky and I were alone, then I asked if she was really all right. She fingered the poppers on her Garfield duvet.

"It's all my fault."

I told her that was rubbish and a watched a big tear plop onto Garfield's droopy eyelid.

"It *is*. Michael Priaulx said so. He gave me such a hard time, Cat. He said I was to blame for what happened to Nic, he said I should be dead instead of her."

I sighed and fidgeted and felt guilty as per ever.

"Yes. I know, he told me, but I also know he didn't mean it and he's very sorry."

Vicky looked up. "Really?"

"Don't worry about Michael. As of tonight you won't ever have to see him again."

Vicky asked me what I meant and my mind raced ahead of my mouth and fell over.

"Me and Michael, we're running away together," I said.

Vicky looked impressively morbidified. "You what?"

"We're going to England first and then we'll work our way round the world and hopefully, eventually, end up in Australia. He's got an uncle there I want to meet."

Vick shook her head. "You've lost it. You are totally off your head."

"No," I replied. "You're the one who's off her head if you think you're to blame for what happened to Nic. You have to put it behind you. She got what she deserved. I'm going tonight and I don't like to think that you'll be left sitting here feeling guilty plus miserable over something you can't change. I'm sorry I was a bad friend and I went off with Nic and I'm sorry I got stuff wrong. I hope you can forgive me. Blame me if you have to blame anyone."

Vicky wiped her nose. "Why should I blame you?"

I would have maybe answered but Mrs. S. came in with a big box of jumble.

"It's for your darling mother." She smiled. "She asked me to have a clear-out and we seem to have an awful lot of rather useless things. Be an angel and take it back with you."

I smiled politely and said something very deep about how you can't hold on to the past for ever.

When I looked across at Vicky I knew she wanted to ask me more, but I said I had to go.

I've got no idea what Vicky's going to do. She might tell her mum and dad what I've got planned, and then they'll ring Mum in a panic. Is that what I secretly want? But then it's just as likely that Vicky will keep quiet.

She knows I tend to exaggerate and she probably thinks I'm bluffing. I'm not, though. I might not make it as far as Australia but I swear I'll get on that boat and I won't look back. I'll ignore the nagging feeling that is telling me to wait. It's stupid! I hate this miserable rock, so why do I suddenly not want to leave? It's what I *should* do. Actually, I'm in a bit of a hurry so I'd better just get a move on. I'm all packed up and ready—I've packed spare socks and trousers, my sleeping bag and two cans of Impulse Vitality. There's no room for any books, in fact, not even ones by Dad. And maybe that's a good thing. I won't need them where I'm going, and I think I've told you what you need to know.

So. Mum, now you have the full History I know you'll be upset. It can't be nice—to find out that your daughter's killed someone. The fact that I killed a Prevost might make it seem less awful. I don't especially like the name Prevost now I know what it means. That's not a good enough reason to do what I did, though. I'm probably crazy to think if I get away from here it'll finally make everything right, but at least now I'm sure about Michael, and I want us to leave together. We'll be in Southampton for Christmas. How cool is that?

Mum, I'll miss you and I'm sorry for putting you in this horrible situation. Now you know what I've done you'll want to do the right thing and tell Constable Priaulx. As a good Christian you should have me stopped and arrested, so that I can face a proper punishment. If it's not murder, it's manslaughter—right? Taking away any life is wrong as per the Bible and I must be punished. Justice must be served.

But if you *are* going to the police then you'd better be careful what you tell them, and you certainly won't want to show them this. You should come and talk to me first. I'm sure you must realise that there are quite a few secrets that I've kept for you. It's here in black-and-white if you read between the lines. Dad's heart stopped working for a very particular reason and I know that you lied. Did he leave a note? Did you get rid of it? How long did you have to wait before calling Dr. Senner? Did you lie for the money or was there another reason? I've read every book in this house, every letter, every file, and every scrap of paper left, but there are still some questions I can't answer. I think it's time you answered them, otherwise I'll imagine all sorts. And, Mum, I do imagine all sorts.

It's easy to kill someone and make it look like a suicide, and it's easy to make a suicide look like something else. I now understand why people prefer lies. The truth isn't easy. Still, here it is: Nic's dead and I'm to blame. I might not have meant to kill her but I saw it happen and I didn't stop it. Does that sound familiar? If you turn a blind eye to something, if you sit back and watch, you are still guilty. You're as guilty as anyone else.

I'm sorry, Mum, I'm *très* mega sorry, but I hope I've finally got your attention. Now it's just you and me and what we know, and you have to decide the next step. Are you going to keep my secret and let me get away from here, or are we going to face our lies together? I used to think that I was so much smarter than everyone else but

I'm still a kid and I'm asking you, my mother, to show me what to do. I can't make these decisions on my own. I'm in your hands. If you come now, to Clarence Batterie, you might just catch me. I promise I'll listen to what you've got to say. One of us might still get on that boat, but at least we'd both be free.

Oh Mum, look what I've done. Look at me and look at this. You always had your nose in a book, so I went and wrote one just for you. I hope it has been more than entertaining. In fact, this should be just about the best book you've ever read, what with its gripping conclusion. It's got all the things you like best.

It even has a proper twist at the end.

The twist is that you get to choose it.

Acknowledgments

There are many people I'd like to thank, and top of the list is Georgia Byng, who gave me such good advice just when I needed it. Thank you also to my brilliant agent, Natasha Fairweather, for her unstinting support and critical insights, and to Marie Darrieussecq, for her love and constant encouragement. Writing is a lonely business, but I count myself extremely fortunate to have had the support of Devorah Baum, Claire Bishop, Susie Boyt, Sarah Ghai, Anouchka Grose, Vicken Parsons and Louise Wilson, who reminded me why I wanted to do this, as did Vincent Dachy. I'm also very grateful to Patricia Whitford, for reading various drafts and never taking offence.

The title of this book is deceptive—there is plenty of fact within the fiction. I owe a great deal to the parents and grandparents of my school friends who first shared their memories of the Occupation with me and fired my interest in the subject. I am also indebted to the islanders who recorded and published their own remark-able accounts. *Silent War* by Frank Falla, *Isolated Island* by V. V. Cortreviend, and *Never To Be Forgotten* by Joe Mière are all extraordinary memoirs. Histories of the German Occupation are considerable in number, rang-ing from *Islands in Danger*, by Mary and Alan Woods, first published in 1955, and the important and contro-versial *Model Occupation* by Madeleine Bunting. More recently Paul Sanders has produced *The British Channel Islands Under Occupation 1940–1945*, the most compre-hensive, detailed, and objective study to date.

I read widely, but it was the personal narratives that stayed in my head. Books such as Miriam Mahy's *There Is an Occupation* remain on my bedside table, and it was Miriam and her cousin Cynthia Lenormand who helped me with the Guernsey patois translations. Their pa-tience and good humour were greatly appreciated. I'm also very grateful to Gregory Stevens-Cox, an inspiring teacher, whose many publications on Guernsey history have always been enjoyed and appreciated by my family, and whose recent book on Victor Hugo in the Channel Islands makes fascinating reading. A special thank-you also to the real-life Kez Le Pelley and André Duquemin, for letting me use their names in this fictional context, and to Victoria Kinnersly for her wonderful map.

When I first started writing *The Book of Lies* I never imagined anyone else would read it, but I'm so glad the right peopled *did* read it. Thank you to Jamie Byng for believing in the book, and to Andrea Joyce, Norah Per-kins, Anya Serota, and everyone at Canongate for their patience, support, and enthusiasm. But above all, a massive thank-you to Ailah Ahmed, an excellent editor who reigned in my crazier ramblings and guided me so carefully to this point. She was the perfect other person to talk to besides the characters in my head.

About the author

About the book

Read on

Insights,
Interviews
& More . . .

A Note from Mary Horlock

I STUDIED HISTORY OF ART at university and worked first at Christies, and then as a curator at the Tate in London. This meant I was used to writing about art for exhibition catalogues and journals. It was a long time before I had the confidence to start writing stories. I don't know quite how it began, but very quickly I was writing during my lunch hours or in the evenings, or very early in the morning before anyone else was awake. This new kind of writing became my guilty secret, and from that came the idea behind *The Book of Lies*. I thought I should write a story where someone confesses to their own guilty secret, writing frantically and furtively at odd times of the day and night.

I based the story in Guernsey because it's a place I know intimately from my childhood, and whenever I sat down to write I imagined myself back in my old bedroom, looking out over the cliffs above Fermain Bay. Although I had lived in London for years I always felt that Guernsey was my home, and not just because I still had family there. When I was away I missed the sea, the cliffs, and the quiet. Of course, during my teenage years I was desperate to get away from the island, and this was all I ever talked about with my friends. It was only much later that I became nostalgic for the past, perhaps after the births of my own children.

It was on one of my regular trips

home that I found my battered adolescent diaries and the idea for Catherine Rozier emerged from those messy, inky pages. I was embarrassed to rediscover my tragi-comic teenage ramblings. I'd always known that I was not very successful as a teenager—I'd found it hard to keep a best friend, I'd had crushes on all the wrong boys, I'd worn terrible clothes, and suffered hideous perms. In my diaries I was constantly cracking jokes and trying to make light of my terrible eating habits and lack of social skills, but it was so obvious what was really going on.

Then I found one diary that seemed different from the rest. It was dated from when I was fifteen, and I realised it was written during the summer after my father had died. What surprised me was that there was no mention of him at all, and instead I had filled page after page with obsessive rantings about a boy I was madly in love with and a girl who refused to be my best friend, and what a devastating tragedy this was. I was confused and upset, until I started to read between the lines. I had been unable to accept my father's death so I had tried to ignore it. I had focused my emotional life entirely on school friends and boyfriends to stop me thinking about anything else. Of course, what happened was things spiralled out of control and I became quite self-destructive. Fortunately I didn't kill anyone! ∾

Behind *The Book of Lies*

THE BOOK OF LIES is about history and how every story changes with its telling. It's also about coming to terms with a death. At the very beginning of the book Catherine introduces herself as a murderer, announcing that she has just killed her best friend Nicolette by pushing her off one of Guernsey's cliffs. Catherine feels guilty for what she's done, but she's also rather annoyed that no one suspects her. Then, almost in the same breath, she mentions her father (who has also recently died) and her mother (who doesn't seem to care). She suggests that a lot of other people on the island should feel guilty apart from her. Perhaps the crime she means isn't the one she's supposed to have committed.

There are more questions than explanations, right from the start, and Catherine's unreliable narrative is swiftly interrupted by another voice— that of her uncle Charlie. Charlie Rozier's chapters take the form of transcribed tape recordings, edited and annotated by his younger brother Emile (Catherine's late father). Emile Rozier was quite the expert on island history, we soon learn, and his particular obsession was the German Occupation of the Channel Islands. Emile had published many books on the subject, but the one book he never finished was the one that mattered most—this story about what happened to his brother. When Catherine discovers the typewritten sheets, she believes Charlie's story will provide clues to how and why her father died, and it might even explain why she has killed Nicolette.

History holds the answers to everything, apparently, and so the past continually interrupts and bears down on the present. Just as Catherine begins explaining how she became friends with Nicolette, Charlie tells of the older boy who first pulled him off the boat leaving for England in the summer of 1940. Ray Le Poidevoin is the perfect foil to the young and skinny Charlie, just as Nicolette is Catherine's polar opposite in looks and character.

These unequal, unstable friendships are what drive the two plots along. However, the crucial difference is that Charlie and Ray are teenagers during the Second World War, at a time when Guernsey was under German rule. During this time young people were the ones most likely to get into trouble with the Germans—idealistic teenagers who were more inclined to rebel than their elders, and who thought they had nothing to lose. A lot of schoolchildren were evacuated from the island, but for the ones left behind, the isolation and frustration was unbearable. Catherine and Nicolette are not as isolated as Charlie and Ray, but they are cut off from their parents and they quickly become as frustrated, as disillusioned, and as angry. ∾

Have You Read?

I HAVE ALWAYS BEEN INTERESTED in history, and by that I don't just mean the grand narrative of nations and empires. I prefer the personal and the local. My first history teacher, Gregory Stevens-Cox, was an extremely clever and colourful man who wrote and published his own books on Guernsey's history and folklore. I used to read everything he produced (including, *The Giant Cabbage of the Channel Islands*, which Catherine mentions in her footnotes). I became interested in local history thanks to him, but also because in Guernsey the history is imprinted on the landscape. The coastline is dotted with concrete towers and bunkers—you simply cannot ignore them. As a teenager I was drawn to them, and I wasn't the only one. Gangs of us would race around the coast road on our mopeds, smoke and drink cheap booze on the cliffs, and then stare moodily out to sea and wonder what life was like "out there." Those empty, neglected bunkers and towers seemed to echo our own sentiments.

I grew up with the bunkers, just as I grew up hearing stories about what went on in them. The German Occupation is almost as potent as folklore—in the eighties, when I was a teenager, I would hear all kinds of things from my friends' grandparents, and from my mother, who always had an ear for a good yarn. What amazed me were the constant contradictions:

some people were bitter, others glossed over events, others made it sound quite exciting. No one really forgot, though, and I remember vividly being told how a certain local man never got planning permission to extend his bungalow because of what he'd done in the war. There was plenty of gossip like this, and an uneasiness about what other people were thinking or saying behind closed doors. Of course, that's what you'd expect to find in a small community, and I think because of this it became difficult to agree on or "settle" the true history of what happened. Islanders still get very angry and defensive about anyone from the outside accusing them of collaboration.

Collaboration takes many forms, as does an occupation. The situation in the Channel Islands was quite unlike anywhere else in Europe and I hope I made that clear in the book. A small minority of people did cooperate with the Germans for personal gain, but the Occupation lasted five long years and exhausted civilians and soldiers alike. Most islanders ultimately had no choice but to cooperate with the Germans in some way if they wanted to feed their children, keep their homes, and survive. Organised resistance, like organised escape attempts, were virtually impossible considering the concentration of troops within such a small space. Few people managed it.

Paul Sanders wrote an excellent book called *The Ultimate Sacrifice*, which gives details of the Night and Fog prisoners who were deported from Jersey during ▶

the Occupation. Many of them were teenagers who never made it back to their island. There was also *Prison Without Bars* by Frank Keiller, which offered a brilliant insight into the impact of the German Occupation on the younger generation. Keiller was only thirteen when the Germans occupied the Channel Islands. He was court-martialled twice, imprisoned and then escaped, spending the last years of the war in hiding. *Silent War* by Frank Falla and *Isolated Island* by V. V. Cortreviend were two memoirs published not long after the Occupation and both gave a fascinating glimpse of life in Guernsey during the war. Falla was a newspaper journalist and was arrested for publishing an underground news service (GUNS). After the war he devoted much time campaigning for compensation for islanders who had been imprisoned and deported. *Never To Be Forgotten* is another book worthy of mention: a very moving memoir written by Joe Mière, who fell foul of the Germans several times in Jersey but survived and later became the curator of the Jersey Occupation Museum.

There are also innumerable official and unofficial histories of the Occupation and some are better than others. One of the first, *Islands in Danger* by Mary and Alan Woods, is still incredibly relevant and captures the relative unease that many people felt in the decade following the Occupation. More recently, *Model Occupation* by

Madeleine Bunting caused widespread outrage among islanders. It was widely felt that Bunting sensationalised events, and that instances of collaboration were given undue emphasis to make the story more "newsworthy." Nonetheless, it is an important book and contained some interesting new testimonies. It also raised questions about the fate of the Jews in the Channel Islands. In the aftermath came further research, which was undoubtedly a good thing. Paul Sanders has recently completed *The British Channel Islands Under Occupation 1940–1945*, the most comprehensive, detailed, and objective study to date.

But a balanced account of the Occupation has been a long time coming, and in the 1980s, when *The Book of Lies* is set, there was still much debate and disagreement. With that in mind, I knew I couldn't turn the German Occupation into some sort of easy-to-read romance, with the more difficult truths tidied up and trimmed. I wanted it to be difficult. I think that was one of the reasons I used local patois. This was very important to me, since as a language it is dying out, with fewer and fewer people able to speak it, let alone understand it. I have clear memories of spending time with the grandmother of a school friend who would happily talk over our heads to her daughter, complaining about our bad table manners, knowing we couldn't understand a word of what she said. ▶

Have You Read? *(continued)*

Patois was a secret code dividing the young and old, and during the Occupation the islanders used it because the Germans couldn't understand it. And so, the past mirrors the present still.

I hope it's clear that although my book is called *The Book of Lies*, the facts about the Occupation are—to the very best of my knowledge—true. Guernsey is still coming to terms with its history, and it's only now, in 2011, that an Occupation Memorial is being planned and dedicated to the people who resisted the Germans. I think this proves that you need an awful lot of distance on the past before you can really try to understand it. ∾

Don't miss the next book by your favorite author. Sign up now for AuthorTracker by visiting www.AuthorTracker.com.